ROCCO AND THE NIGHTINGALE

ROCCO AND THE NIGHTINGALE

Adrian Magson

THE
DOME
PRESS

Published by The Dome Press, 2017

A CIP catalogue record for this book is available from the British Library

ISBN 978-0-9957510-1-9
[eBook ISBN 978-0-9957510-2-6]

The Dome Press
23 Cecil Court
London WC2N 4EZ

www.thedomepress.com

Printed and bound in Great Britain by Clays., St. Ives PLC
Typeset in Garamond by Elaine Sharples

To Ann, who always saw Rocco as a slow burner,
and never let me give up.

One

1964 – Picardie, France.

JoJo Vieira didn't know what to make of back-country roads. A Paris-born *voyou* and proud of it, anywhere outside the familiar streets of the city's north-western *banlieues* was an alien world. He especially didn't care for any location where food, drink, entertainment or a chance to make an easy few francs weren't immediately available. And this remote spot, deep among the fields of northern France, had none of those.

He swore in frustration, his smoker's rasp startling a few birds and a solitary cow nearby. The battered moped he'd been riding until a couple of minutes ago was deader than yesterday's cold mutton, and his efforts to propel the machine forward had proved futile. He'd tried working the pedals, but his legs weren't up to it, weakened by a lifetime of bad habits and little exercise. He took the cap off the petrol tank and shook the handles, hearing only a faint movement of liquid inside. Barely half a kilometre from where he was now standing, the engine had begun to cough intermittently, before giving a death-rattle and drifting to a complete stop.

The moped was already a step down from the motorbike he'd

1

borrowed from his brother-in-law, Nico; but that had developed a flat tyre yesterday and he'd been forced to abandon it on the outskirts of Beauvais. Even if he'd possessed a repair kit he wouldn't have known how to use it, yet another of life's skills that had eluded him. Short of cash and desperate to avoid public transport, he'd stolen the moped from outside a café. It was a poor choice, as he'd just discovered; it had held barely sufficient fuel to get him even this far.

Now he was on a narrow, deserted patch of rough tarmac in the middle of nowhere, the surface dotted with cowpats old and new, shining wet from a recent fall of early morning summer rain. To cap his misery, his shoes, made of finest Italian leather according to the market stall owner in Clichy, had turned out to be cheap Moroccan fakes and were now little more than damp cardboard. His once sharp suit, of which he'd been proud, now hung like a rag around his skinny shoulders, the fabric dotted with fragments of straw from a cold and uncomfortable night in a filthy, rat-infested cowshed back down the road.

He hurled the petrol cap away in impotent fury. It glittered briefly in the sunlight before falling into the ditch a few metres away. He'd have to walk, there was no other choice. Worldly-wise JoJo wasn't, but he had instincts enough to know that he couldn't stand around waiting for good fortune to come along, because it so rarely did.

He had to reach Amiens. Then he'd be safe.

JoJo had followed a deliberately meandering route north out of Paris to this point, avoiding major roads and shying away from contact with other travellers apart from the forced diversion into Beauvais, wary of seeing a known face that would only mean disaster.

The face he wanted to see instead was that of a man who might save his life. A cop, to be sure, one of the hated breed for a career criminal with JoJo's background. But it belonged to the one man he'd decided might guarantee his safety... in exchange for the right information.

Information that might save the cop's life as well as his own.

He unstrapped a leather bag from the rack on the back of the moped before kicking the machine over on to its side. It crashed to the ground and the small residue of petrol left in the tank gurgled out as if mocking him, forming a multi-coloured patch that shimmered in the light. He was debating giving the machine a vengeful kick when he thought he heard an engine somewhere in the distance. He glanced back along the road, but saw nothing save for rolling fields, a few straggly trees and a crow feasting on a piece of roadkill.

A tractor, he guessed, too far off to be of any use. He had only the vaguest notion that the bird might be a crow, and even less knowledge about what the mess of fur and blood might once have been. You didn't get much roadkill in the city; and what there was usually wore clothes and was drunk.

He shivered and scoured his pockets for a smoke, finally dragging out a dog-end from last night. He straightened it out with care before taking out a cheap metal lighter and flicking the wheel. The flame caught, puttering faintly in the breeze as it sucked fuel out of the wick. The first mouthful of smoke was sharp and bitter, part pleasure, part pain as it scorched his throat. He took it deep into his lungs before coughing harshly, bending with the effort and wincing at a familiar stabbing sensation in his chest. He spat to clear his mouth, and stood up, watery eyes blurring the landscape around him. If he could find anywhere in this wilderness that boasted anything like a shop or café, he'd get some more smokes, along with a couple of stiff drinks to repel the cold that was penetrating his bones in spite of the sun.

As he straightened up, he caught a movement from the corner of his eye and saw a grey Citroën van bumping along the road towards him. As common as a new day's dawn, it was the kind used by market traders, bakers and delivery men all over France, and he relaxed. Where he came from the sound was a constant you learned to ignore, a background feature in a city that rarely slept. But out here it was a stroke of luck not to be passed up: the chance of a lift to civilisation. And safety.

The van pulled to a stop and the driver leaned out, a sun-bronzed arm hanging over the sill. He was young, wearing a blue shirt, sunglasses, and a beret pulled down over his forehead. A second person was sitting in the passenger seat alongside him but JoJo couldn't see him clearly.

'You look like your horse just died,' the driver said with a sympathetic smile. 'Want a lift?'

JoJo tossed the cigarette end away. The reference to a horse eluded him but he didn't care; if these people could get him to where he was going they could say whatever they wanted. 'I surely do, my friend. God bless you.'

'I doubt that'll happen, but a man can hope, right? Where do you want to go?'

He hesitated. 'Amiens. I need to get to Amiens.' It was close enough now; there was no need to make any more detours. He'd be there in no time and he could get a load off his mind.

'Lucky you. That's where we're going, too.' The driver stuck out a hand. 'I'm Romain.'

JoJo took it and said, 'JoJo.' He looked past the driver but the passenger appeared to have gone. 'Funny, I thought you had someone with you.'

'I do. She's called Lilou.' The driver got out of the van and tossed his beret and sunglasses through the window onto the seat. He stretched, showing an impressive spread of broad shoulders.

'Hello, JoJo.' It was a woman's voice, soft and almost musical, and came from behind him. JoJo turned, surprised by her reappearance, and caught a glimpse of blonde hair and an open smile. Nice looking chick. But before the thought could materialise further, the driver grabbed his arm and slammed him into the side of the vehicle.

'Hey, what–!' He tried to pull away but couldn't; the driver had an iron grip. Then he shifted his weight and JoJo felt a sharp blow to the side of his neck. A flash of unbelievable agony ran to the very top of his head and down his body. His legs felt weak and he tried to stop himself falling, but there was no grip on the smooth metal of the van.

As he began to slide, JoJo turned his head and had a moment of pure clarity. That face... wait a second... he'd seen it just a few days ago. There was a name, too, if only he could remember. But his thoughts were mashed together by shock and pain. Then it came flooding back; it wasn't a name... more like a title.

His legs finally gave way and he sat down heavily, the cool wetness of a puddle soaking through his trousers in a final chilling indignity. He realised that any ideas of seeing the cop he'd come all this way for had just faded. He'd been followed after all. He tried to ask how. But the word came out as an unformed rattle, thickened by a flush of blood gathering in the back of his throat.

'You left a trail, JoJo,' the man explained. 'First mistake, you told your idiot brother-in-law where you were going. All we had to do was ask him. He was surprisingly helpful, was Nico. Well, people

5

usually are when you apply the right motivation. Here, let me help you.'

JoJo felt a hand grasp his elbow and pull him to his feet. His vision clouded for a moment, then he felt himself being pulled away from the van to face the side of the road and the open fields beyond. A hand was pulling at his pockets, and he felt the meagre contents being lifted out. He wanted to protest, but any words were swept away on a wave of tiredness. If only he could lie down and rest… maybe back at the cowshed with the soft hay to lie on. Then he felt a push in the small of his back, shuffling him forward on shaky legs, feet stumbling on the grass verge. Two steps… three… four–

There was nothing beneath his next step: no tarmac or grass, no hand holding him upright. He felt himself falling as if in slow motion. As he entered the cold embrace of the ditch, his final thoughts were of his sister, Miriam, and the name of the man he'd failed to reach in time. The man who might have saved him, but now could not.

Lucas Rocco.

Two

'He has a what?' Rocco pushed aside a stack of paperwork that was fast threatening to overwhelm his desk and checked the clock on the wall of the Amiens *commissariat de police*. Three o'clock in the afternoon already and another lunch break gone without warning. This wasn't the way an investigator's day was supposed to go, he told himself.

'A hole. In his neck. He's been…' The voice faded on a bad line and Rocco winced as a ragged burst of static assaulted his ear. He put the phone down and waited for the caller to try again, which he did moments later.

'Where are you, René?' he asked, before he lost contact again. Dead bodies with holes in them were not that common in these parts and were therefore treated with urgency. And by the minute fragment of information he'd picked up so far, Detective René Desmoulins had discovered one.

'It was down some rat-arsed road outside Danvillers, about six kilometres from Poissons,' Desmoulins shouted, his voice suddenly clear. 'My car radio's useless and I had to come to a local café to use their phone. The line's a bit unreliable.'

'I get that. What have you found?'

7

'A farmer named Matthieu called from here earlier, said he'd spotted a body in a ditch. I had a quick look and he was right. It's a man and looks like he got stabbed in the side of the neck.'

Wet or dry, thought Rocco pragmatically, we get them all. Either drowned or – as in this case – with one or more holes in them. The news that this one wasn't far from the village of Poissons-les-Marais, where he was renting a house, was less of a surprise than it would have been when he first arrived in the region. Back then, he'd been resentful at being posted to the town of Amiens as part of an initiative to 'spread crime prevention and investigation procedures' as one Interior Ministry suit had explained in the national press. As a long-time city cop, Rocco had made the mistake of assuming that nothing unusual ever happened in rural backwaters save for poaching, drink-fuelled hunters shooting each other by accident and the occasional incident of assault and battery.

He couldn't have been more wrong.

This part of northern France, he'd quickly learned, had more than its fair share of violence and criminality lurking beneath its innocent, bucolic surface. Look beyond the rolling fields, gloomy marshlands and tiny, scattered villages making up the patchwork of life just a few hours from Paris, and you'd find just as much greed, venality and plain old-fashioned blood-lust as anywhere in the country. If Rocco had once missed the excitement of his previous job of gang-busting, which he'd pursued in Paris and other parts of France, Picardie had more than made up for it.

'I'll get Rizzotti and some men out there,' he told Desmoulins. 'Seal off the area and I'll be out shortly.'

'Got it. Don't worry about the men – they're on their way. You'll need your funeral coat, though; it's been raining out here.'

Desmoulins signed off, leaving Rocco to pick up his coat and car keys and head for the rear exit of the station, passing Doctor Bernard Rizzotti's office on the way. Rizzotti, the local stand-in expert on the unexplained dead, was ploughing through a late lunch of baguette and cheese at his desk, and looked round guiltily at the intrusion. Visitors to his small workroom were few and usually wheeled in on trolleys, not always in a presentable condition. The advantage to Rizzotti was that it kept the healthier occupants of the building away.

'We've got a dead one,' Rocco announced, leaning in the doorway. 'You want a lift?'

'Not likely,' Rizzotti grunted, the light reflecting off his spectacles. 'I've been in that black heap you call a car quite enough, thanks. I'll follow you.' He stood up, clamping the baguette between his teeth and reaching for his car keys. 'Where are we going?' he mumbled.

Rocco gave him the directions and the two men headed for the car park. Rizzotti clambered into the safety of his Renault while Rocco headed for his black Citroën Traction. With the sweeping design of a bygone age and a reliability unmatched by more modern cars, he refused to part with it for something 'more in keeping with a modern police force', even if colleagues like Rizzotti claimed both car and driver possessed a death wish. Rocco had been forced by senior orders to watch as a technician had brutalised the inside by installing a radio, a modern function he would approve of if it was reliable and clear. As it was, it gave him the feeling of being constantly under scrutiny, and in a regular act of rebellion he left it switched off whenever he could.

Thirty minutes later he was standing above a ditch at the side of a narrow country lane while Rizzotti clambered down the slope and

9

began a careful examination of the body. The rain Desmoulins had mentioned had moved on, leaving behind a welcome smell of wet grass and clean, fresh country air.

The deceased was a male, in a suit, shirt and stringy tie. He lay at the bottom of the V-shaped gulley, his body twisted at an angle unintended by nature. A leather bag lay by his side. Rocco judged him to be in his late forties, with the narrow features of a man accustomed to a hard life, like most men around here, he decided, although the suit looked out of place. In this area suits were reserved for funerals, weddings and suspects trying to make a good impression on a magistrate.

'Go on, surprise me,' he murmured after a couple of minutes. 'Drowned, punctured or broken?' It had to be one of the three.

'Don't rush me,' muttered Rizzotti, his voice distorted in the hollow. He scratched his head, disturbing a wispy frame of hair that gave him the appearance of a mad scientist. Although not a professional pathologist, unlike others Rocco had worked with, Rizzotti had quickly established his authority when working a crime scene. His rules were applied equally to senior and junior personnel: stay back, give him time and don't intrude on the scene until he said it was safe to do so.

Rocco was happy to let him do things his way. The Ministry of the Interior constantly promised to release funds and authority for a full-time pathologist, but as they hadn't come even close in the five years that Rocco was aware of, he wasn't about to hold his breath. In any case Rizzotti, who'd been a local doctor, was no slouch when it came to analysing causes of sudden and violent death, and Rocco doubted if a so-called professional would do much better. In his experience, all they did was dress up their reports with fancy language and technical detail, leaving him and other investigators none the wiser until provided with a translation.

Finally Rizzotti grunted and pulled himself up the side of the ditch, grabbing Rocco's hand to reach the top.

'Thank you. As far as a preliminary examination shows,' he puffed, eyeing the dead man, 'I'd say he died less than twelve hours ago. He was stabbed in the side of the throat with some sort of sharp instrument.'

'Not a knife?'

'Not like one I've ever seen. Too narrow and rounded in profile – a spike, perhaps, maybe a pitchfork, although there's no sign of anything like that by the body.' He nodded towards a group of uniformed officers scouring the road and the fields on either side. 'Maybe they'll find something out there.'

'A spike?' Rocco shivered involuntarily as a rush of cool air whipped across the fields and brushed his face. They were in the middle of summer and it seemed as if autumn was already on its way. He was glad of the coat he'd picked up on the way out. Long and dark, and described by Desmoulins as giving him the appearance of a funeral director or an avenging angel, depending on one's viewpoint, this one was a summer-weight version, his one concession to the time of year.

'I'd say so. Over a centimetre across at a guess, although the flesh around the wound is swollen, which tells us quite a bit.'

'How so?'

'Well, I don't think he died immediately, and he probably wouldn't have been able to pull out the weapon by himself. He'd have been in shock and probably bled out into the throat and choked. Not a nice way to go.'

'So the assailant must have pulled it out.'

'They must have done. I'll know more when I get him on my table for a closer look.'

'Any identification on him?'

'Not yet. I checked his pockets but found nothing. And I mean nothing.' The look he gave Rocco carried a wealth of meaning. As they both knew, even in hard times most people had something of value on them, especially a form of identity. Those who didn't had been carefully stripped to hide their origins for some purpose.

'What about the bag?'

'I haven't checked it yet. It was already open but I didn't want to risk losing anything of importance in the ditch.'

Rocco nodded. An opened bag beside a dead body didn't sound promising. If there had been anything of value to be had, it was already gone. He stifled his impatience and turned to survey the open countryside: the fields dotted with the white chalk scars of shell craters from the First World War, bordered by gullies and ditches like this one, and with an occasional clump of trees. Save for one old barn in danger of falling over in a strong wind, there were no houses or farms visible close by, so no obvious witnesses to whatever had happened here.

Desmoulins came across and nodded a greeting. Stocky and muscular, the younger man was growing in confidence since Rocco had begun to push more responsibility his way. 'Lucas, this is going to take a while. There's no sign of a weapon. If the killer carried it off with him, he could have disposed of it anywhere.'

'Any footprints?' Rocco was looking at the soil on the far side of the ditch, which looked loamy and soft and liable to carry traces of anyone passing that way.

'Not so far. I reckon whoever did this might have brought the victim here. There's no way he could have got here otherwise without walking, and it's a long way off the main roads.'

He pointed at the grass verge, which showed the imprint of heavy tractor tyres. 'The farmer who found him is at least eighty-five and built like a chicken, so I doubt it was him, and he stopped his tractor right here when he saw the body, so any traces that might have been useful have been obliterated.'

Rocco gave a thin smile. It was often the way with crime scenes; people being helpful often wiped out any evidence without realising it. 'You think eighty-five-year-old chickens can't kill?'

'Well, I suppose.' Desmoulins grinned. 'But not this one, as you'll see. I asked him to come with me and show me what he'd found, but he wouldn't budge. He was clearly in a state of shock. The café owner said he's harmless and wouldn't hurt a fly.'

'Where you phoned from?'

'Yes. He's probably still there if you want to talk to him. His name's Olivier Matthieu and the café's opposite the farming co-operative depot in Faumont. You can't miss it.'

Rocco nodded. He didn't doubt Desmoulins' instincts for spotting guilty men for a second, but he'd known more than one old man who'd committed murder. As with ambition, greed, power or even sex, advanced age didn't automatically mean everything ceased.

He left Rizzotti and Desmoulins to their tasks and made his way to the hamlet of Faumont two kilometres away. No more than a fly-speck on the map, it comprised four small houses, a long, low industrial building with two large hoppers belonging to a farmers' co-operative and a roadside café with an ancient Energic tractor parked outside, its trailer leaking strands of hay. Both tractor and trailer looked to have led a hard life, with soft, balding tyres and not much original body paint. Second- or third-hand, Rocco guessed, but better than some farmers locally who still used horses and their own muscle-power to do their work.

Two young boys were sitting nearby, sharing a stubby bottle of lemonade. They watched as he climbed out of the Citroën, then moved away as soon as they heard a burst of chatter from his radio, and disappeared behind the café. Bunking off from school, he decided, but right now that wasn't his problem.

He pushed open the café door and walked into a murmur of voices and the chink of glasses. If there had been anybody working in the depot, they were now crammed inside the café, no doubt taking the opportunity for a quick drink while they heard the old man out and counting this as a welcome excitement in an otherwise uneventful day.

Rocco eased through the crush. Most of the customers wore work clothes and heavy boots, the air around them thick with the smell of cigarette smoke and damp clothing. But it was easy to spot the centre of attention: he was near bald and nut-brown, with tufts of white hair sprouting from his ears, dressed in heavy rubber boots and the traditional *bleus* – the working jacket and trousers common to most men in the area. He was clearly enjoying his role as the spreader of shocking news.

Three

Less than half a kilometre away from the murder site, a man and woman sat side by side on a distant ridge, taking turns to watch events through a pair of high-powered binoculars.

'They're like a bunch of ants.' The man was the first to speak, his voice tinged with contempt. 'Helpless ants.' He turned from watching the uniformed men scouring the area around the ditch, to follow the progress of the black Citroën Traction as it disappeared along the road. 'And there goes the biggest ant of all.' He held out the binoculars and gave his companion a lazy smile which emphasised his youthfulness and carried hints of Mediterranean origins.

'Ants sting, did you know that?' the woman replied, studying the scene. The Citroën had gone, leaving behind a couple of men in plain clothes directing the uniforms.

'They can try, Lilou.' Romain lay back and looked up at the sky. 'They can try.'

Lilou smile and leaned over to kiss his cheek. Her blonde hair was cropped short in the new *gamine* style, and she possessed a steady gaze that occasionally had a disconcerting habit of wondering off-course as if it had lost interest. 'What shall we do now?' she said. 'I don't know about you, but I could do with something to eat.'

Romain nodded. 'Good idea. Let's go to Amiens. We'll find somewhere decent to celebrate, with a glass of wine.'

'One more down?'

He nodded. 'And one to go.' He stood and led the way off the ridge, feet scuffing through long grass. They scrambled down a grassy slope and arrived at a grey van parked down a narrow track. As they climbed in, Lilou sniffed and looked over her shoulder into the back. 'That thing stinks of cow muck and petrol. We should get rid of it the first chance we get.'

'We can dump it in the pond we passed earlier. It looked deep enough.' Romain chuckled. 'It's going to drive those idiots crazy not knowing how Vieira got there.'

'Or where he came from.' Lilou looked at him and touched his shoulder. 'And I thought I was the one who liked playing with the cops' heads. You're getting worse than me.'

'Well, credit where credit is due. I do my best.' He started the engine and drove down the track until they arrived alongside a small pond set in a gulley below the road. He got out and opened the back of the van, then pulled out the moped, bumping it down onto the ground. With a quick glance round to see he wasn't being observed, he wheeled the machine over to the edge of the track and heaved it down the slope. It bounced twice before hitting the scummy water with a splash and disappearing in an explosion of bubbles.

He walked back to the driver's side and climbed in, leaning across to take a kiss from Lilou.

'My hero,' she said, patting his chest. 'I love it when you go all manly, and that blue shirt really suits you, did I tell you that?'

'Flattery will get you everywhere, and yes, you did. I never thought I'd say it, but I like the colour, too. Ironic, don't you think?'

Four

Olivier Matthieu looked up at Rocco and blinked in surprise. He recovered quickly enough, though, and held up an empty glass, no doubt seeing a newcomer who might be persuaded to part with a few francs for a refill and a repeat of his story. The people around him weren't so sure; they took one look at Rocco and dispersed like a tide washing away from the shore. Country people they may have been but, as Rocco had soon discovered, they possessed an uncanny knack for spotting a cop when they saw one.

'I think you've had enough, *pépère*,' he said gently, and waved his ID in front of the old man's eyes. 'We need to talk about what you found.' He signalled to the café owner for two coffees, then drew up a chair and gave a couple of reluctant leavers a look which had them retreat to the bar out of earshot.

'Of course,' said Matthieu warily, his eyes struggling to focus. 'You're the fancy city *flic* from Poissons, looking for an easy suspect, am I right? I must say, it didn't take you long to get here.' He smiled and cocked his head at a song being played in the background. It was a woman's voice singing about not knowing anymore. 'Ah, the beautiful Dalida. Got a voice like warm chocolate, that one. Nice bodywork, too.' He gave a slow wink and laughed, showing stumpy teeth and a lot of gum. 'Found out who killed him yet?'

Rocco shook his head. Up close the old man gave off a strong whiff of body odour and what city folk would have called 'country'. And Desmoulins was probably right; he was too old to have killed someone and left them in a ditch... unless he'd run them down with his tractor, which wasn't the case.

'Not yet, *M'sieur* Matthieu. Even we fancy city cops like to ask a few questions before we accuse someone. It's part of our training. Now, can you tell me what you saw?'

He sat back as the owner brought two heavy brown cups and placed them on the table alongside a box of sugar cubes. The coffee was densely black and barely moved in the cup, like liquid tar in a barrel. Rocco reached automatically for the sugar, gathering several lumps and stirring them in. Strong coffee was fine, but this stuff looked as if it had been brewed from coal dust and molasses.

Matthieu viewed the cups with horror, but when Rocco pushed one towards him, he gave a sigh and took a reluctant sip.

'I was driving back after dropping off a load of hay for my animals,' he began, 'and saw a couple of crows hovering over a ditch. I slowed down, thought maybe a rabbit had died and needed a decent burial.' He gave Rocco a knowing look. 'There's nothing like a bit of fresh meat for dinner if you know what I mean. Better than all that fancy stuff you're used to in Paris, I bet.'

'You've been to Paris, have you?' The idea of Matthieu loose on the city streets seemed a stretch, but that was the thing about people: you never could tell. Maybe this crusty old man had history beyond being a farmer in Picardie.

'I haven't. No desire to go, either. But I can read, and you hear stuff.'

'Fine. But let's forget about Paris, shall we? What did you see when you stopped?'

The old man looked offended. 'All right, keep your hair on. Just having a bit of banter.' He cleared his throat and drank more coffee. 'When I got close I could see this shape in the bottom of the ditch. Wasn't a rabbit, I could see that. Too big for a start, so I thought it might be a boar. Then I realised it was a man.' He winced. 'Gave me quite a shock, I can tell you. Not that I haven't seen dead bodies before. Saw too many in the last conflict – and the one before that. But that was wartime. Not the same down a peaceful country lane, is it?'

'I suppose not. Did you go down into the ditch for a look?'

He gave a bark of a laugh. 'Not with my knees; I'd still be down there, otherwise. I suppose I should have taken a closer look, but I didn't need to. I could see he was dead, his body all twisted like it was.'

'How could you tell?'

'Because I knew.' Matthieu blinked and rubbed his face, producing a sound like sandpaper on wood. 'Like I said, I know a dead body when I see one.'

'What about the bag alongside it? You weren't tempted to take a look inside?'

'I didn't see no bag. But there was blood on his neck and I could see what looked like a hole just under the ear. I bet he was shot, wasn't he?'

'No. Have you ever seen the man before?'

'Me? No. He wasn't from around here.'

'What makes you say that?'

'He looked too pasty to be a local. Most people here work out in the open, like this lot.' He jerked a calloused thumb at the few customers

19

remaining at the bar, all of whom were worn and tanned by the elements. 'His suit looked too fancy for locals, anyway.' He looked Rocco up and down and gave a smirk. 'Unless you're a cop, of course. Nice coat you've got there. Pays good money being a cop, does it?'

Rocco ignored the dig. 'Did you see anything unusual lying around?'

'Like what?'

'Like a weapon of some sort?'

'No. I mean, there might have been, but once I spotted the body I didn't notice much else.'

'And nobody in the area, say, on your way here?'

'Like I said–' He stopped and thought. 'No.'

'You don't sound very sure.'

Matthieu scowled as if he'd been caught out in a lie. 'It was nothing. Just that I thought… I *thought* I saw a kid way off in the distance, on the brow of the hill. But I was most likely imagining things. I mean, kids are in school this time of day, aren't they? And it's too far out for them to play. I probably need my eyes testing.'

'Maybe.' Rocco wasn't so sure. He thought about the two boys he'd seen outside. In his experience the local kids roamed as far and wide as they liked and took no account of distance or school times and regulations in their search for something to amuse themselves. 'What did you do then?'

'I came straight here to call your lot.' Matthieu smacked his lips and said, 'Look, do you think I could get a drink before I head for home – a real one? This has been a bit of a shock and I'm not as young as I was. And this coffee's rubbish.' The last was said in a voice loud enough to carry over the other conversations in the room, earning a scathing look from the bar owner.

'Where's home?'

'My farm's just down the road. Why?' He stirred. 'Here, you don't think I did it, do you?'

Rocco ignored him and caught the owner's eye, making a signal for a small drink. The man filled a brandy glass and brought it across, placing it down with a scowl at the insult to his coffee. Rocco had his doubts about putting more alcohol in the old man's veins, but Matthieu probably had some sort of credit here, and if he wanted another drink he'd get one whether Rocco approved or not.

He stood up and nodded at Matthieu. 'Thanks for your help, *M'sieur*. I'll be in touch if I need more information.' He dropped some money on the table, making sure the owner noticed, then placed his card alongside it. 'If you think of anything else, please call me.'

'Thank you, Inspector.' Matthieu took a generous sip of his brandy and winked as he raised his glass. 'You're not as bad as they say you are. For a cop.'

'You'd better be sure you've told me everything,' Rocco warned him quietly, 'or you'll find out the opposite.'

On the way out he impressed on the café owner not to let Matthieu drive, and asked him about the two boys he'd seen outside earlier. They'd looked about twelve years old and as fit as most country kids. He didn't doubt they could have walked the couple of kilometres from the hill above the murder scene without much effort.

The barman pushed out his lower lip, allowing himself to pluck free the remains of a soggy cigarette, and said, 'They probably belong to one of the men from the depot, I should think. But don't expect any of them to own up because they won't. Sorry.' He replaced the cigarette on his lip and moved away down the bar.

Five

Rocco drove home to Poissons. It was too late to go back to the office, where he'd quickly find himself wrapped up in fresh cases and old gossip to no good effect. His mind was buzzing with questions about the as-yet unidentified dead man, and how he'd come to end his life in the ditch. How, for example, had he got to such an isolated spot? Maybe Desmoulins was right and whoever had killed him had brought him to the area. Had they argued and fought, and the killer used some kind of tool to stab him in a fit of anger, then panicked and pushed him into the ditch in an attempt to hide the body? If so, why strip the body of any possessions first, unless it was to confuse or delay identification?

He wondered if that pointed to someone local, although the victim's clothing suggested otherwise. There were several large towns in the region where a man in a suit might have come from: Amiens, Beauvais, Abbeville – even Arras. But short of stumbling on a missing person's report, trawling those towns would require a lot of legwork.

He arrived at his rented house and spotted Mme Denis, his next-door neighbour, kneeling in her garden. Of medium height and compact, she had white hair and thick glasses, and was dressed as always in a blue apron over a grey dress. A triangle headscarf was pinned neatly over her head. She looked up at the sound of his car and waved, then got to her feet with difficulty and walked slowly to meet him.

'What's this?' she murmured, rubbing her back. 'Back early? Have you solved all the crimes in the area this week?' She took three large spring onions from the pocket of her apron and handed them over, brushing some dirt off them. 'Here, make yourself a nice salad for a change; the freshness will do you good.'

'Thank you,' Rocco said, and took the vegetables. As he'd learned long ago, a refusal would offend and offering food had been her way of welcoming him to the village. She had continued the habit ever since, mostly with eggs, often leaving them on his doorstep if he was out. In her own way this gentle old lady had been largely responsible for making him acceptable here, in spite of the local antipathy and suspicion towards all forms of authority. He looked at her carefully and thought she looked unusually pale. 'Have you got a problem with your back?'

She waved a dismissive hand. 'Oh, nothing really. Old age pains, I expect. You'll get them yourself one day, believe me.'

'Have you seen a doctor?' Rocco didn't know her real age, but he guessed she was in her seventies. Like most country people, she was tough and obstinate when it came to ailments and brushed off any questions about her health. A little like his own mother had done years before.

'Actually, I'm going into town tomorrow,' she said, surprising him. 'A good friend in the village told me about a specialist who's holding a surgery at the hospital. The pain has been keeping me awake so I decided to see what can be done about it. There. Satisfied?'

'When tomorrow?'

She gave him a sharp look. 'Why – are you checking up on me?'

'Not at all. I've got some time off and I know the bus through here doesn't always turn up on time. And you won't be able to get back easily. So I'll take you.' He smiled. 'Who knows, if you behave yourself I might even bring you back.'

She scowled and began to protest but he raised a hand to forestall her. 'You can argue all you like, but I insist. Anyway, what will I do for eggs, vegetables and gossip if you're not well?'

She prodded his chest with a gentle finger. 'I've never asked you for anything and I never would. Understood?'

'I know that. But I'm offering – which is not the same thing.'

'Good point. As long as we're clear on that. My appointment is at four in the afternoon.' She smiled with gratitude. 'Can I make you some coffee? You look like you could do with it. While the water boils you can tell me all about your latest case.'

'How do you know I've got one?'

'Because you have that look about you; the one that tells me your brain is working overtime trying to tease out a puzzle. Am I right?'

He raised a hand in resignation. She was as sharp as a razor and didn't miss a thing, and he was still getting used to the fact that news travelled fast here, often much faster than in cities, even without the benefit of telephones.

'A coffee would be good,' he admitted, thinking that anything would be better after the black poison he'd had at the café. And any time spent with Mme Denis was a great counter to his daily work, even if she did like hearing about every detail.

'And a chat?'

'A chat, too. But strictly between us.'

She smiled impishly and led the way into her cottage. 'That goes without saying. Don't you know the best part of being a gossip is knowing something that nobody else does?'

Rocco followed her into her kitchen and sat down at the table. It was spotlessly clean, with the air of a room regularly scrubbed whether it needed it or not. She waved away his offers of help and busied herself heating water and filling an ancient aluminium cafetière topped by a glass lid. She poured two cups and placed them on the table with a box of sugar cubes and a small canister of milk. Rocco usually drank his coffee black, but he'd learned quickly that the old lady expected him to take milk with his, believing that too much black coffee was bad for the digestion. He wondered what she would say if she saw the stuff being served at the café in Faumont.

'So,' she said, taking a chair across from him, 'how's that young lady of yours? I haven't seen her for a while. Jacqueline, I think you said, wasn't it?'

Rocco smiled. He was pretty sure he hadn't said any such thing, but Mme Denis had her ways of extracting information from complete strangers within moments of meeting them.

'It's a long story,' he said, and made to drink his coffee.

'The best ones usually are,' she said pragmatically, giving him a look of total innocence. 'But we have time. Go ahead, humour an old lady.'

He sighed and gave in. He wasn't going to be able to leave this house without giving her a proper answer, so he might as well save himself the trouble of attempting to. 'I've faced tougher grillings from the Ministry of the Interior,' he complained, 'and I never tell them half of what they want to know. Why do I always tell you everything?'

'Because deep down, you need to talk. Most strong men do – they just don't like to admit it. My husband was the same, bless his memory. Now, drink your coffee – it'll help you unload.'

'Jacqueline's gone to Washington,' he explained. 'There's talk of setting up an embassy there in addition to the consulate general in New York. An advance team has been sent out to help with trade talks and other matters and she was selected to go with them.'

'You should have married her when you had the chance,' Mme Denis said with characteristic bluntness. 'I think I told you that at the time.'

'Really? I don't think you did.'

'Well, if I didn't, I certainly should have. What happened, anyway? I thought you liked her. She was very pretty.' She reached for the cafetière and refreshed his cup, her way of keeping him in his seat for a few more minutes. 'She'd have kept you warm at night, too.'

Rocco felt himself flush, and sank more coffee. 'I did like her – I do. But she's entitled to make her way in the world. She was offered the job, and has the skills, so it seemed a good chance to get on.' What he didn't mention was his suspicion that the job offer hadn't been quite so innocent as it might have seemed. Nominally at least, Jacqueline worked for the Interior Ministry. But as he'd discovered later, she seemed also to hold a floating position in the DST – the Directorate of Territorial Surveillance – the domestic intelligence service. And having been trained by a branch of the intelligence service, her skills would prove very useful when coming into contact with foreign diplomats and envoys.

The old lady wasn't having it, however. 'What you mean is, her father didn't want his daughter marrying a cop. It's usually the fathers in my experience.'

'That, too, probably,' he said wryly. Jacqueline was the daughter of a career diplomat. He'd never met her father, but François Roget was rumoured to be very protective of his daughter, driving away undesirables before they could get their feet under the family table. Jacqueline had denied any interference on his part in her selection for a post overseas, but Rocco had no doubts that the timing was more than just a little coincidental. The irony was, he'd recognised and liked her ambitious nature, and had suggested that the Washington position was too good an opportunity to miss. Whether that was a good move on his part he couldn't judge but, not long after, Jacqueline had called to say goodbye. It was mildly encouraging that she was tearful at the prospect of leaving him, but he wasn't sure how long that would last in the new and exciting surroundings of Washington.

Mme Denis reached out and placed a hand over his. 'Sorry – it's not my place to interfere. But I like to see a man happy. And she seemed a very pleasant young woman.'

'She was – is,' he affirmed, and finished his drink. 'Just not my young woman. Thank you for the coffee. It was nice.' He held up the spring onions. 'Now, if you'll excuse me, I think I'll make that salad you were suggesting.'

'But you haven't told me about your latest case yet.'

'I will, I promise,' he said. 'Tomorrow, in the car. I won't be able to escape then.'

He walked round to the house and dropped the spring onions by the sink. A couple of eggs, some ham and chopped vegetables might be a good idea. First, though, time for a bath. As he walked into the bathroom he heard a familiar scurrying sound overhead, and smiled. The fruit rats had their own little community up there, and had been resident since before he took over the house. Rocco didn't mind their presence. He'd quickly got used to their comings and goings, even welcoming the sounds of other living beings in the house when they played with dried walnuts left up there by a previous tenant, rolling them around the floor in a bizarre game of night-time football.

The phone rang, stilling the noises from the attic for a moment. He sighed. Forget the bath, he thought. Duty calls.

'Lucas?' It was Captain Michel Santer, his old boss and friend from the Clichy district in Paris. Amazing, Rocco considered fleetingly, how bad news could be heralded by the tone of a single word.

'Michel. What's up?'

'I hope you're sitting down, my friend.'

Six

'Sorry I can't dress it up better than this,' Santer continued, 'but I figured you wouldn't want me to, anyway. I've just heard there's a marker out on you.'

A marker, the alternative name for a contract or a hit. Most cops picked up at least one during their career, more if they really became a thorn in the side of someone who took being sent down personally. Most threats came from low-level criminals they'd put away, trying to make up for their own failings with verbal displays of bravado. Not even their criminal colleagues took them seriously, and the threats rarely came to anything. But some were real and had to be taken as they were meant. Rocco, like others, had helped put away many a low-life and a few of the bigger fish in his time. Not all of them bore a grudge, or were open about it if they did, some even accepting the pitfalls of their profession. But he could name maybe three men off the top of his head who had issued threats he'd taken seriously, any one of whom might follow them through one day.

'Who?'

'You remember Samir Farek?'

Rocco experienced a moment of surprise. Farek. Algerian, head of a gang based in Oran and now dead, shot by an unknown sniper.

Known as Sami by his friends, it was a far more genial sounding name than he'd ever deserved. He'd come to France on the hunt for his wife, who'd run away with their young son, and had sworn to kill Rocco for helping her. Rocco had barely known the woman or even whom she was married to, only that if Farek, a vicious criminal with many contacts and a long, vindictive memory, ever caught up with her, she would be in trouble. Fortunately, the man hadn't lived much longer.

'I remember. So?'

'After his death, his brother Lakhdar went away for a spell for theft and fraud. By the time he got out he was ready to take over Samir's operations, as we expected. He's been looking after the business ever since, cleaning out some of brother Sami's old mates and bringing in new blood. Anyway, just lately he's let it be known that he's coming after you for Samir's death. You know what these thugs are like: all muscle and no brains. It's an honour thing, intended to show him in a good light with his horrible family and his growing band of morons.'

'Growing?'

'He's staging a comeback. The word is he's recently taken over a couple of the gangs operating between Paris and Marseille by quietly displacing their leaders.'

'Seriously?'

'At least five known *chefs* have disappeared in the last few weeks: three from Paris, two further south. There's not a trace of them anywhere, so I'll leave you to join up the dots.'

Rocco wasn't surprised. Once a gang chief always a gang chief. There was no walking away and retiring to a quiet life in the country, even if you wanted to. Sooner or later somebody would decide you were better off out of the picture. Permanently. As to the honour thing, it was a smokescreen. The Fareks and their kind were big on the word, a twisted version of the real thing and more correctly filed under the title of revenge.

And that was what Farek wanted: revenge for his brother, who'd been shot by an unknown sniper during a confrontation with Rocco. Although the killing had undoubtedly been at the hands of powerful criminal enemies who didn't want to run the risk of Farek talking to the police, his family and criminal entourage preferred to look on Rocco as the root cause.

'How real is this threat? He must know he'll get pulled in if he tries anything.'

'He should do, but who said any of his kind deal in logic?'

'It doesn't really sound like him, though.' From what little Rocco knew of Lakhdar, he was more into business dealings and paperwork than ordering or carrying out a killing.

'Lakhdar's changed. He's grown out of Sami's shadow. Seeing his brother losing face like he did, it seems to have affected him. But he's got to prove he has the balls to those around him and this could be his way of doing it.'

'By settling old scores.'

'Correct. And you're one of them.'

'Who else?'

'The gang chiefs I mentioned, a couple who were thought to have had a hand in Samir's murder. But getting rid of them was considered small fry, as well as being strategic.'

'Whereas knocking off a cop will show what a big, bad man he is.'

'Exactly. You're not just any cop, though, are you? You've got a profile. A bit like big-game hunters who want to bag a lion.'

'Fine. Thanks for the comparison, boss. I'll keep my eyes open.'

31

Boss. He hadn't called Santer that in a while, but it had a habit of sneaking back in.

'Lucas, he won't come at you head on. Like I said, he's no longer in thrall to anybody, which includes any of the other gangs now, and with this honour thing driving him, he won't stop – he can't.'

'What are you saying?'

'Farek's no hero; he won't come calling with a gun in his fist. He'll get someone in to do it and sit proud and loud in his office so he's got an alibi. We're pretty sure he did that with another former cop recently.'

'Anybody I know?'

'I don't think so. He was a captain in Cambrai, name of Raballe. He used to work the northern smuggling routes into Paris until he retired last year. He crossed Lakhdar a couple of times and shut down an operation we think must have cost Lakhdar dear because he swore he'd get even with him. We thought it was the usual bullshit at the time, Lakhdar talking big to impress his friends, the way they do. But Raballe took it seriously. My guess is he knew Lakhdar well enough to think he wasn't just blowing hot air.'

Rocco sensed what was coming. 'What happened?'

'As soon as Raballe handed in his papers he moved to a village outside Dieppe, to his brother's place. I heard it's a middle-of-nowhere kind of place that you won't find on any map. He settled into a quiet life, probably thinking he was safe. But he was found dead two days ago while walking his dog. He'd been shot in the neck. The locals think it was some idiot with a rifle blasting off in the woods but I'm not so sure. It seems too coincidental. We can't tie it to Farek because he's got himself a watertight alibi for his movements, but he's the one who did all the shouting, so we can't ignore it.'

'If Raballe was so well hidden, how did Farek find him? It's a big country.' Especially, thought Rocco, if an ex-cop like Raballe had taken the threat seriously enough to duck below the radar. Working the drug gangs would have made him more than capable of making sure he could never be found if he didn't want to be.

'It certainly is… unless you've got someone on the inside who can keep track of a former cop's movements.' Santer sounded sick at the notion. Criminals having a contact within the police wasn't unusual, except that it usually involved the flow of information going in, not going out. 'He'd left his new address on file for pension purposes, and so we could get in touch if anything cropped up from one of his old cases.'

'Do you know who gave it out?'

'We think so. There's an officer rumoured to have got himself into debt with some serious people. He's close to retirement and working as a supervisor here. He suddenly came into a nice legacy and began splashing money around. Not that it'll do him any good; the roof's going to drop on his head any day now.'

Rocco thanked him for the warning and disconnected, then took a stroll around the garden and thought about the likelihood of Lakhdar Farek carrying out his threat. In the over-heated atmosphere of the criminal underworld, threats were almost a currency of their own, issued to gain position, to warn off competition and even to curry favour among followers who wanted a strong man in the lead. Not going through with a promise to take down a named cop wasn't like a politician breaking his word, which was par for the course in the shifting world of political power-plays. In Farek's world it would seriously call into question his courage and willingness to take risks. And that made a man vulnerable.

He wondered if he should tell Massin of this development. Having a viable threat made against a police officer was a serious problem, especially if it affected that officer's performance and that of his colleagues. Many senior officers would expect to be told, if they hadn't already heard. On the other hand, what was Massin going to do about it? He could hardly put Rocco on temporary leave or assign him a bodyguard; nor could he make a move against Farek himself. Making threats against officers was nothing new, and proving there was genuine intent would be impossible.

He went back inside and took his handgun from a drawer in the bedroom, the MAB D snug in its webbing holster, and checked the load. He didn't carry it with him every day, although he was supposed to. Unlike some colleagues, he'd never formed an unbreakable attachment to guns, perhaps a hangover from his army service. From now on, though, he'd better make sure he had it with him at all times.

Seven

The following morning Rocco drove to the station. As he entered, he was greeted by a young officer on guard duty. Rocco had heard he was a recent transfer-in from somewhere down south. With so many changes going on in police forces at the moment, he had a job keeping track of new personnel. The man seemed efficient enough, from the little he'd seen of him, if a little over-familiar towards senior officers for a newly-arrived *gardien*.

'There was a person asking after you earlier, Inspector,' the man announced, a knowing smile edging across his face.

'Really? Who?'

'She wouldn't say. Just asked if you were in. I said you were out on a call and she said she'd come back later.'

'Someone local?' Rocco didn't often get people asking for him by name, and almost never women. The people most likely to confide information to the police, accurate or otherwise, were usually male and shifty, while normal residents preferred to keep a respectful distance and only call on the law in times of need.

'I don't think so. She was too *soignée*, if you get my meaning. Well dressed, in a masculine kind of way.'

'Masculine?'

'Trousers and sturdy shoes, and short hair. Pretty face, though. Lucky you – I reckon you've got an admirer. Pretty unusual in our line of work, huh?'

Rocco wasn't amused. 'What's your name again?'

'Jouanne, sir.'

'Well, Officer Jouanne,' Rocco muttered coolly, 'next time I get lucky, get me a name. I don't like guessing games.'

He left the guard and his quickly-fading smile and walked into the main office. It was scattered with desks and filing cabinets, and the colour scheme always managed to depress him. He was convinced the Ministry of the Interior had a fixed list of colour tones for their offices, an unflattering variety of dull greens and creams. As he walked towards his desk he was greeted by muted nods from his colleagues but none of the usual raucous comments and chatter. In fact most of the officers were keeping their heads down.

Then he saw why. Commissaire François Massin was staring up at a large bulletin board pinned to the far wall. He looked no different from normal, which meant tall, aloof, unsmiling and dressed in an immaculately-pressed uniform, but it was unusual to see him down among the troops; he usually preferred to stay upstairs in his office. He gave Rocco a slight nod of greeting before flicking an impatient finger for him to follow.

A stranger was standing in Massin's office, studying a large map of the Picardie region. Smartly dressed, freshly shaven and in his forties, the visitor wore the pose and austere expression of somebody important. Or maybe he just thought he was, Rocco decided. He nodded a greeting as the man turned towards the door.

'Inspector Lucas Rocco, Gerard Monteo of the Interior Ministry,' said Massin briefly.

Rocco shook hands. Monteo's grip was a cursory attempt at politeness, accompanied by a murmur of something Rocco couldn't catch, as if the words were too valuable to waste. He gave the detective a fleeting once-over, then turned away.

I'm really going to get on with you, thought Rocco, and wondered what this was all about. Had someone in authority finally decided they wanted to reel him in for some past jurisdictional transgression?

'Mr Monteo has a special task he would like us to perform,' Massin explained, sitting behind his desk. 'Something I'm sure you'll manage effortlessly. Gerard?' He made a gesture for the visitor to continue.

Rocco's heart sank as Monteo visibly gathered his thoughts, eyes on the floor as if a handy script was down there waiting to be used. A visit from the Interior Ministry was rarely a precursor to good news, and 'special tasks' invariably meant somebody was going to end up disappointed. And he doubted it would be this man.

'We have an important overseas visitor recently arrived to this area, Inspector Rocco,' Monteo began, adjusting his already nut-sized tie and lifting his eyes to stare out of the window like a general about to declare war. 'We want somebody... reliable, to look after him, and Commissaire Massin has obliged by putting forward your name. I gather you have experience in these duties.' He finally turned to look at Rocco for confirmation. 'Is that so?'

'That depends what duties you mean.'

'Quite simple: the Ministry would like you to look after him while he's a guest here and to ensure his safety. His name is Antoine Bouanga and he's a former government minister in Gabon. As you can appreciate, he's a man of some standing and it would be... unfortunate if anything were to happen to him.'

Rocco shot a look towards Massin, who neatly avoided catching his eye. 'What – so some fool in the Ministry thinks I'm a bodyguard for foreign politicians? They already have a team of experts for that. I know because I've worked with some of them.'

Monteo gave a thin smile. 'What we in the Ministry think really doesn't concern you, Rocco. We have a job to do, your name was put forward based on your availability here and your past record, and I'm assigning you to it. Is that a problem?' He glanced at Massin for support. 'François?'

'No, it's not,' Massin interposed firmly, glaring at Rocco. 'He's being modest. You'd better give him the written instructions. That might convince him.' There was something in his expression which told Rocco that he wasn't happy at having one of his men poached for other duties, but that he had no choice in the matter and Rocco had better buckle under or else.

Monteo produced a folded sheet of paper and passed it across. Rocco opened it and read quickly. It was a letter of instruction and authority, informing anybody who asked, from Commissaire Massin on down, that officer (name left blank) was required for special duties, namely to ensure the safety until further notice of one Bouanga, Antoine, currently the Development Minister *in absentia* for the Gabon Republic in central Africa. There was a paragraph expressing how important Bouanga was, but Rocco glossed over it. If it was an instruction from the Ministry, Massin for one would make sure Rocco complied whether he liked it or not. The senior officer was not noted for telling the Ministry to take a running jump if he felt they were being too demanding. The importance or otherwise of the individual in question was a matter of detail. The address where the man was staying, Rocco noted with surprise, was not far from Poissons-les-Marais. A farm called Les Sables.

'Bouanga has only just arrived in the country,' Monteo continued, 'so we will have maybe two days at most before word of his presence in the area gets out. But I suggest you get acquainted with his location and its surroundings as quickly as possible.'

'What about my current caseload?'

'Share it out among the other investigators,' said Massin. 'That includes the suspicious death which occurred yesterday. This assignment is too important to go wrong. You've said before that Desmoulins can take a step up if needed, so I think this might be an ideal opportunity for him to do so. Agreed?'

'Yes, of course.' Rocco looked at Monteo. 'So what exactly do I have to do for this person of great importance?'

'Make sure he's safe and in no immediate danger. The house where he's staying has been checked, but I suggest you do it again to make it absolutely secure. I'm sure you've dealt with the concept of a "safe house" before?'

'I have. Is he under any immediate threat?'

Monteo pulled a face. 'Almost certainly, according to our contacts in Gabon. He is an experienced politician and therefore regarded as a threat to those now in power but also to others wishing to take over.'

'That sounds like a lot of enemies.'

'Perhaps. We flew him out of the country under cover, but his whereabouts will not remain a secret for very long.'

'And then?'

'Then we will have to see. As you might be aware, Gabon was a French territory until 1960, when they achieved independence. Since then there have been a number of changes at the top and Bouanga is one of the most recent ones displaced, shall we say, by a rival in the government.' He gave a sour smile with not a trace of humour. 'Not uncommon in that part of the world, sad to say. Unfortunately, as I said, Bouanga's not short of enemies and they have long memories.'

'Why, what did he do?'

'That isn't important, and in any case is mostly unconfirmed rumour. All you need to know is that serious threats have been made against his life and he was forced to leave the country at short notice and come to France.'

Rocco was immediately sceptical. When foreign politicians deserted their country and went into hiding, it usually meant that they had serious charges against them. 'Displaced, you said.' Rocco grunted at the euphemism. 'You mean he's on the run.'

Massin cleared his throat as a warning, but Monteo waved away the blunt assessment. 'No, Rocco. He's here while the… situation in his home country is resolved and normal relations can be resumed to everyone's satisfaction. The French government has seen fit to accord him refuge until such time as he can return home and resume his post. He's an important guest, not a fugitive and you are to treat him as such. Understood?' He reached out and took the letter from Rocco, and scribbled something on it with a silver pen. When he handed the letter back, Rocco saw his own name was now in the blank space.

'Got it.' Rocco folded the paper and put it in his pocket. 'Do I get any additional resources for this?'

'Resources? I don't follow.'

'Providing protection for a man with enemies is not just a matter of standing around and hoping to frighten them off. It takes time and manpower. You need a team with regular shifts and rest periods. I think I've been past this place. If it's the one I'm thinking of, it's in the middle of open country. If somebody is serious about assassinating this man, all they need to do is sit up in a tree and shoot him from a distance.'

Monteo looked sceptical. 'And how would extra manpower stop that happening?'

'It probably wouldn't, if they're serious. But having a visible police presence around the place might make them think twice about trying.'

'Well, I'm sure you're right about that, Inspector, but I have no extra budget for such a thing.'

'Can't you ask for an extension?'

'I don't have to.' Monteo lifted his chin with an air of self-importance. 'The Ministry has seen fit to grant me complete authority on this issue. Any decisions on budget and spending are mine alone, and I intend bringing this matter to a conclusion without any unnecessary calls on finances.' He looked directly at Rocco and added, 'I trust that clarifies my position to your satisfaction?'

Rocco wondered if there was something in the water at the Ministry that gave men like Monteo their overblown sense of position. He kept his cool and said, 'A couple of extra men is hardly going to break the bank.'

Monteo looked at the commissioner. 'Perhaps you can help there, François?'

Massin looked as if he were about to object, but seemed to think better of it and went for a reasoned argument instead. 'I have no spare officers, I'm afraid,' he replied. 'As you know we have the Tour de France coming through the area shortly, and all available hands will be focussed on keeping order, closing roads and safeguarding the route. Unless you feel Bouanga is more important than the Tour, of course?' He looked pleased at having lobbed the ball back to Monteo in the form of a suggested threat to France's biggest sporting event. But the Ministry man parried it with ease.

'I'm not sure I'd go that far. Surely you can spare one person, can't you? I think you'll find the Ministry would appreciate such... cooperation.'

The silky counter bluff worked. Massin chewed it over, then turned to Rocco. 'You can have that ruffian of a *garde champêtre* you've worked with before. What's his name – Lamont?'

'Lamotte. Claude Lamotte. But–'

'Good. Problem solved. Get him to wave his infernal shotgun about and I'm sure things will be fine. Carry on, Inspector.' Massin sat back with a satisfied smile, a signal that the meeting was over. Monteo said nothing.

Rocco left without shaking hands.

Eight

Rocco returned to his desk and spent some time sorting through his current case ready for Desmoulins to take over. He'd have to brief him on the order of priorities, but he had no doubts that the younger detective could manage perfectly well.

While he was doing that the office door opened and someone cleared his throat. It was Rizzotti, on a rare sortie from his den in the rear of the building. It meant he'd got something important to show Rocco.

The doctor slid into a chair opposite him. 'Sorry to interrupt, Lucas, but there's something I found about the deceased in the ditch that might interest you. I searched the leather bag, but there was nothing of any real consequence in it apart from this.' He passed a slip of crumpled paper across the desk.

It was a bill dated one month ago for a man's leather blouson-style jacket. The header, although difficult to read, was for a clothes shop named 'L'Homme' in the Rue Victor Méric in Clichy, Ile-de-France.

'Interesting.' Clichy and the surrounding districts were part of Rocco's old stomping grounds. Victor Méric was a side street off Boulevard Victor Hugo in the north-west of the city. He couldn't place the shop specifically, but anywhere off the Boulevard was generally more up-market than not, serving residents who preferred living outside the confines of Paris proper. It meant the victim had money... or at least had been in possession of some when the jacket was bought.

And there was a name just about legible in the body of the bill: J. Vieira.

He felt a buzz of excitement and nodded at Rizzotti. It might mean nothing but it was worth following up. 'Great work, Doc. This might narrow things down considerably.' He waved the bill. 'Did you find a jacket?'

'I'm afraid not. Maybe he left it at home. I hope it helps.'

'It might. I know where this shop is, and if the name belongs to the dead man, I know someone who might be able to identify your body.'

'Actually, it's your body now, not mine.' Rizzotti smiled modestly. 'I've done all I can – and none of it was what I'd call highly scientific. The paper was damp and scrunched into a small ball, but I managed to dry it out slowly enough to preserve the integrity. Other than that, there was nothing of much consequence save for scraps of hay and straw attached to the clothing.'

'From the ditch?'

'No. I checked that. I think he must have slept the night in a barn somewhere. Find the barn and you might pick up a useful clue. His suit was cheap with no maker's label, and his underclothes are available all over France. But there was no leather jacket. There was a washbag, also unhelpful. Typically the kind of stuff somebody might pack to go away for a couple of nights.' He reached into his pocket and produced two black and white photographs. 'You might need these for showing around – especially the one with the tattoo. I looked it up, by the way; it's the symbol for good luck.'

One photo was a close-up head and shoulders shot of the dead man. The second was a shot of the man's back. It was this one that Rocco studied carefully. It showed a tattoo of a Chinese character high on the left shoulder. He had no idea what it meant but he was prepared to take Rizzotti's word for it. A pity it hadn't worked in the dead man's favour.

'Thanks for these, Doc. I'll pass them on.'

Rizzotti went back to his chemicals and bodies, leaving Rocco trawling through his brain for the name Vieira. It rang a vague bell, but the precise details eluded him. Either he'd run into the name in the course of his previous work in Paris, or it was simply one of hundreds that passed across the bulletin board during the course of a year, either wanted by the police, the victim of a crime or a missing person. Sometimes they stuck for no other reason than possessing a sympathetic rhythm, lodging in the brain like a seed between the teeth.

He picked up the phone and dialled Michel Santer's number in Clichy.

'J. Vieira,' he said. 'Does that mean anything to you?'

Santer grunted. 'If it's the same J. Vieira I'm thinking of, it might. Don't tell me you've arrested him? No, of course you haven't. He wouldn't be able to find your neck of the woods unless he was taken there in handcuffs.'

'Not quite true, I'm afraid. If it's the same man, he's dead. Stabbed not far from here by persons unknown, his body stripped of identification.'

'Ouch.' Santer sounded only vaguely surprised, the news clearly not unexpected to a cop with long experience of death and misfortune. 'I'm not going to ask if you're sure about this; it's just that the J. Vieira I'm thinking of wouldn't venture out of the city unless his arse was on fire or somebody he'd cheated or robbed was after him with a pickaxe.'

Rocco smiled. If the two Vieiras were the same person, the comment said a lot about the deceased and his place in the scheme of things in north-west Paris. Santer wasn't usually given to overstatements, but he did have his finger on the pulse. If he said Vieira was a criminal, it was a declaration Rocco could take to the bank. 'That's good enough for me. We needed verification so I thought I'd start with you. He was carrying a bag, and our forensics expert found a bill inside for a leather jacket. I thought the name sounded familiar but I couldn't place him. The bill comes from a clothes shop in Victor Méric.'

'In that case I'd be surprised if it's the same man. The one I know is strictly a bottom-feeder; he wouldn't know style if it jumped up and bit him.' He paused. 'Wait. Oh, my God, hang on – I just remembered something.' The phone clunked onto the desk and Rocco heard Santer calling to somebody in the background. There was rapid exchange of voices before he came back. He sounded sombre. 'My apologies, Lucas – we probably are talking about the same person. I only had a brief glimpse of the details, but let me read the file.' There was a rasp of paper being turned. 'Right. Joseph Pierre Vieira, known as JoJo, one of the many city rats who lives off the misfortune of others: petty thief, wife beater and general nasty who'd sell his own sister for a drink. Spent time in prison, mostly for low-level crimes, but he's been known to mix with some unpleasant types who used him for anything from transporting messages or arms to selling drugs.'

'So why would he end up out here? It's hardly his kind of territory.'

'I was coming to that. Vieira walked into the station of his own volition a few days ago. He said he had evidence against three men involved in serious crimes, including murder.'

'Good for him. What did he want in return?'

Santer chuckled. 'You know the type too well. He wanted a deal. He was facing a three-year term for theft in another arrondissement and couldn't face it, so he was angling for a trade-off and protection.'

'Protection. Against anyone specific?' The moment a criminal turned informer was usually the start of a very short life expectancy, in Rocco's experience nobody liked a *mouchard* – an informer. Sooner or later the news would get back to their former colleagues and there was only ever one end in store for them.

'One of the men he was accusing: Lakhdar Farek.'

That name again. Rocco felt a familiar drumming in his ears. Hearing it twice in short order was bad news. First as a direct threat... and now in connection with a dead petty crook.

'It sounds like Farek didn't waste much time.'

'He or one of his people. Vieira would have known he'd be on a hit list from the moment he walked into the station. Once in the prison system he'd have been an easy target for a revenge hit. And that wasn't the only reason he'd have been scared; it would have come out in court in his defence that Vieira had been a paid informant for the last six months and that he's been earning cash for information all that time. I don't know all the gory details but I reckon he's been responsible for convictions against nearly a dozen members of organised gangs here and further south. There would have been a lot of men inside queuing up to get even with him for that, and it wouldn't have been pretty.'

'That would explain where the money for the jacket came from.'

'Exactly. My guys say JoJo liked to dress sharp, if cheap, and act the big man around town. But whatever money he had usually slipped through his fingers, mostly on drink.'

'Maybe this time he decided to buy something other than alcohol.'

'Maybe. Anyway, I hear he dropped out of sight three days ago and hasn't been answering calls. Now we know why.'

'He was on the run. But why out this way?'

'Beats me. Maybe he developed a taste for turnips. I'll get my guys to ask around, see what they come up with.'

'Thanks, Michel.'

Rocco put the phone down, deep in thought. Paid informants rarely lasted long before they were dealt with, usually because they couldn't keep their sudden and unexplained bouts of wealth to themselves. They drank, they talked, they flashed their newfound cash around, and if they were known petty operators like Vieira, customarily living hand-to-mouth, sudden signs of money were like a red light to their associates and enemies. It didn't take long before somebody began to wonder, especially if the cops showed signs of overlooking any transgressions. Putting all those things together signalled money coming from somewhere – and the most likely source was the police.

And now Farek was in the picture, and likely to be the instigator of Vieira's demise. It meant that if Farek was going to live up to his threats, Rocco should expect a visit any time soon. The thought didn't worry him unduly because he couldn't live like that. The job brought its dangers, but it was something he'd become accustomed to a long time ago. Even so, it wouldn't do any harm to take precautions.

Right now, though, he needed to find out more about Farek's

current movements and associates. Protection against an upcoming threat was only as good as the information available, especially about the men most likely to carry it out. And there was one person Rocco could think of who knew more about Lakhdar Farek than anyone else.

He picked up the phone and dialled a Paris number.

Nine

Marc Casparon, known as Caspar, had once been a top undercover cop with the *Sud-Méditerranée* Task Force and the Paris anti-drug group, targeting organised gangs involved in drug imports and bank heists. He had lived out of the mainstream, first in the south, then moving to Paris to follow the targets he knew well, working the streets and back-alleys, always on the periphery but rarely noticed. His record for gaining inside information had been unsurpassed, and he had never been rumbled. But the pressures of living such a stressful and lengthy lie had been enormous, and had eventually taken their toll. He'd been forced to retire, with considerable persuasion from Santer and his close colleagues, who'd seen what it was doing to him.

When Rocco had last spoken to him, he'd been working as a security expert and missing the excitement of his old life. But Rocco wasn't about to ask him to step back into the gutters; that would have been cruel. Instead, he was after Caspar's inside knowledge of the Paris gang community and in particular, Lakhdar Farek.

'Lucas.' Caspar sounded pleased to hear from him. 'You were lucky to get me. I was on my way out.'

'Work?'

The other man chuckled. 'Yeah, but not the old kind. I'm reviewing security for an electrical factory up near Orly. The pay's good and I can choose my hours. Anyway, how are you? It's been a while.'

They traded information for a while, until Caspar said, 'What can I do for you? You know I'm not in the job anymore, right?'

'I know. But I was guessing you might still have your ear to the ground. I need information on someone you might know.'

'Go on.'

'Lakhdar Farek.'

There was a brief silence, and Rocco could picture Caspar trawling through his memory, the name rolling through files and slotting into position like a juke-box selector. Eventually Caspar said, 'What did you want to know? You know he's not like Sami, right? He's worse.'

'So I gather.' He relayed what Santer had told him about Farek's threat, and added the latest information on the death of the supposed JoJo Vieira.

He heard Caspar take a deep breath. 'Yeah, I heard Farek was going after a cop, but I didn't realise it was you. And I'm a bit surprised about JoJo being on the take as an informant. I knew him from way back and he was strictly fifth grade, mostly surviving on what he could steal, which wasn't much. I never thought he'd risk being a snitch; he wasn't any kind of a hero. He might have seen it as an opportunity to get a regular handout for whatever he could slip past the cops as information, but he must have also been pretty desperate. Are we sure it's the same man?'

'Not totally. But if it helps, this one's got the Chinese symbol for good luck on his left shoulder.'

'There are plenty of those, but it might narrow it down. I'll see what I can dig up.'

'The other thing I'd like to know is, who does Farek use for his dirty work?'

'He's got a couple of guys, both from down south and clean – at least, on the surface.'

'Suspected but nothing proven?'

'Not yet. The most obvious is a Corsican named Borelli. Jean-Michel Borelli. He's dark, with short cropped hair, aged thirty-five and looks like a boxer. Imagine Aznavour only bigger and uglier. I heard he had to leave the town of Bastia when he got into a fight over a woman with the son of a local clan chief – one of the 'old men' who control things down there. Borelli beat the kid up but stopped short of killing him. The father gave him two hours to disappear and he came to Paris via Marseilles. The other man is younger, an Algerian, like Farek. His name is Mokhtar Abdhoun. He looks like a teenager but don't be fooled – he's vicious and very quick-tempered. He comes with a bit of a reputation back in Algiers.'

'Are there any photos?'

'Not sure. Like I said, they're clean as far as I've heard, so unless you can get something from official travel records, no. But I'll see what I can find. It might cost you a few drinks, though.'

'I'll cover whatever it takes. But I don't want you getting close to Farek or his people. It's too risky.'

'Nor do I. I have an old contact who probably knows more about Farek than most people and owes me a favour. Anyway, I just got engaged, so I've got good reasons to stay safe.'

Rocco was pleased to hear the news. 'Congratulations. Who's the lucky girl?'

'Her name's Lucile. She's a former cop so she knows the game. We're getting married next year and probably moving out of the city. You'll have to come.'

'I'd like that. Just make sure you don't get spotted with this Farek thing. I prefer weddings to hospital visits.'

'Me too. Anything else?'

Rocco remembered the receipt for the jacket. He read out the number at the top and Vieira's name. 'If you could follow that up for me, it would help a lot. Anything you can get. I'm stuck here on a protection job, so I can't get away. I'll make good any expenses.'

'Don't worry about it. I'm glad to help, to be honest. Gets the old blood moving again. I think I know this shop so it shouldn't take long.' With a promise to call as soon as he had anything, Caspar rang off.

Ten

The house assigned to Bouanga went under the name of Les Sables, which was a misnomer; if there was a grain of sand anywhere within kilometres, outside of a construction site, he'd be amazed. Maybe the original owner had been a secret beach lover, consigned by circumstance to a life far from the sea.

He climbed out of his car and studied the building. Hidden behind a spread of trees at the end of a long track, and secured by twin wooden gates, it was quite an impressive sight for this region. A traditional French farmhouse originally, it had been given an almost colonial look, complete with columns at the front door and small balconies at the upper windows. The garden had once been neat and carefully styled, he noted, but was now a shadow of its former glory. Whoever had lived here last hadn't wasted any time on keeping up appearances, and clumps of weeds and coarse grass ran rampant everywhere.

A number of outhouses and a small barn lay to one side and to the rear of the property, and in the distance a couple of rusting farm implements were sinking into the soil. A plough he recognised, but the others, all angles and brutal lumps of brown metal, were a mystery.

He looked beyond the house towards where he calculated Poissons-les-Marais lay, some half-dozen kilometres away. Unlike the marshlands around Poissons, the countryside here was wide open, with a few trees dotted about in an almost random fashion and an occasional ditch or embankment to mark the edge of one field and the beginning of a neighbouring plot. Any optimism he might have harboured about this task was dwindling fast. The basic start-point in keeping someone safe was at least to have them in a secure environment. And this place was like a giant bar-billiard table.

He lifted the heavy metal knocker in the shape of a horse's head and let it drop, producing a loud echo from inside the house. The door was sturdy, a plus point, as were the metal shutters over the windows. Preventing access to a safe house was a must, but rarely achieved one hundred per cent.

The door was opened surprisingly quickly, which indicated that his arrival had been noted, and he saw a small figure standing in the shadow of the interior.

'Can I help you?' The voice was pitched high, and little more than a whisper. It took a moment for Rocco to realise that he wasn't being greeted by a child, but a very thin and small but perfectly-proportioned man. He had deep button eyes set in coffee-coloured skin, and was dressed in a crisp, white shirt and a neat suit over shiny shoes. He was holding one hand behind his back and looked up at Rocco without expression, waiting for an answer.

Rocco introduced himself and handed over the letter of authority from Monteo. 'Are you Mr Bouanga?'

The man shook his head. 'Bouanga? No.' He studied the letter for a moment, his lips moving slowly, then said, 'Wait one moment, please.' He closed the door in Rocco's face and his footsteps faded into the background, leaving Rocco with what he was certain had been a glimpse of a pistol in the man's other hand.

Two minutes later the footsteps returned and the door swung open again. This time the little man had both hands free. He beckoned Rocco inside and led him down a darkened hallway towards the rear of the house. The air smelled stale, evidence of a building unoccupied for a long time and showing its age, but it seemed clean enough. The ceilings were high, with moulded edges and a web of hairline cracks in the yellowed plaster, and the floor of the hallway was tiled and cool. Rocco's footsteps echoed loudly in the silence of the building, whereas the other man appeared to drift along with barely a sound.

They arrived in a space ablaze with light, a stark contrast after the hallway, and Rocco was surprised to see he was in a glass conservatory dotted with large pot plants in decorative urns. A couch occupied one wall, with two armchairs and a coffee table. The air here smelled fragrant, the atmosphere warm and welcoming.

A man was seated on the couch flicking through a thick folder of papers. Dressed in an immaculate suit and a white shirt, he was heavily-built and bespectacled, his head shaved and glossy under the light. The letter of authority from the Interior Ministry lay beside him on the couch.

'Bouanga,' said the little man, and stepped back.

The man on the couch looked up. 'Inspector Rocco?'

'That's correct. I'm here to check the property and see how we can make you more secure during your stay.' It made Rocco feel as if he were a hotel flunkey checking that the pillows were soft enough and the carpet was of the right depth, but he couldn't think of any other way to describe his reason for being here. Bodyguard seemed altogether too dramatic a description. 'You're very exposed in here,' he suggested. 'It might be safer if you could work in one of the other rooms.'

'I will take that advice into consideration,' said Bouanga. 'Anything else?'

Rocco noticed a bow and a quiver of arrows lying in one corner. It seemed out of context in this pleasant room, like a theatrical prop someone had left behind in error.

'Yours?' he asked. The bow looked in good condition and something told him it was no museum piece. Partly wrapped in tooled leather, it was decorated with various motifs and looked well-used, like the quiver alongside it.

'It belongs to Delicat,' said Bouanga. 'I was dismayed to learn that he is not permitted to carry a gun in your country. The bow, however, is allowed. I'm sure your ministry will confirm that they have no objections should you feel the need to ask.'

'I'll be sure to check it out,' he murmured politely, and wondered who Delicat was. Monteo had made a brief mention of a housekeeper and a servant accompanying Bouanga, but so far he'd seen only the small man who had remained silent and was now standing nearby. In the meantime, however, there was a problem with the gun he'd seen in the little man's hand.

Before he could speak, Bouanga indicated the small man, 'Delicat is my bodyguard. It was he who let you in.'

Rocco turned his head and met Delicat's blank stare. 'If he has a bow, why does he carry a gun?'

'Does he?' Bouanga feigned innocence but didn't look at Delicat. 'I can't think where he got it. I'll have a word with him. He speaks very limited French, I'm afraid – barely the basics, in fact.' He smiled, as if that were the end of the matter. 'Leave it with me.'

'Why do you need weapons, anyway? Have you received any direct threats since arriving in France?'

'So far, no, Inspector. I'm hoping that very few people know that I left the country. But that situation cannot last long, I fear. There are eyes and ears everywhere.'

Rocco said nothing, and Bouanga sighed and took it as a sign to continue. 'I cannot return to my country due to a… a change in the political situation there. As you may have been informed, I was forced to leave in a hurry after receiving death threats and having my house attacked by an angry mob stirred up by opposition malcontents. I have many enemies at home who would be happy to see me dead, wherever I am. So yes, I feel there is an element of danger for me.'

'Even here.'

'Especially here. There are members of existing opposition groups expelled from my country in the past couple of years who have taken up residence here while they plot against the democratic government. Certain individuals, myself included, have been receiving threats of assassination for a long time now. These groups will not hesitate to take advantage of the… turbulent situation I am in to make a move against me if they think it will help their plans. I have explained the situation to your ministry and they have accepted my need for caution, for which I am most grateful.' He looked around with a frown. 'Tell me, where are your other men?'

'He's on his way here. He won't be long.'

'He? One man?' Bouanga looked astonished. 'I was told there would be more. This is not acceptable, Inspector! I am a guest in your country and require more protection. I must insist on more personnel.'

Rocco took care in formulating his response. He wasn't sure how important Bouanga was in the grand scheme of things and in his limited experience ministry officials in Paris had a habit of saying much but not always delivering. No doubt that was even more the case in the tricky area of international politics. 'Sorry. All you have is me and one other. But don't worry – he's an excellent shot.' Just then the sound of a car engine intruded on the silence. Rocco stepped across to the end of the conservatory where he could see the approach from the main road. Claude's ancient 2CV was bouncing along the track, dragging a cloud of dust in its wake like a long, floating scarf. 'In fact, here he is.'

With a warning sign for Bouanga to stay where he was, Delicat disappeared like a wraith, leaving his boss looking disgruntled. Rocco ignored him and studied the fields to the rear of the house. If he couldn't get Bouanga to move somewhere more secure, he'd be wasting his time, no matter how many guards were posted. Minutes later Delicat returned with Claude Lamotte in tow. The *garde champêtre* looked huge next to the bodyguard and was dressed in his usual all-weather clothing. With him came a distinctly earthy smell of the great outdoors, and Rocco guessed he'd been out on his patrols.

'Morning all,' Claude said cheerfully, and held out his hand to the minister, who looked at it with reluctance before touching it with the tips of his fingers. 'Nice place you have here.' He nodded at Rocco and said with unaccustomed formality, 'Reporting for duty, Inspector. Where do we start?'

Eleven

Bouanga looked puzzled. 'I thought the extra man you mentioned would be a police officer, Inspector. This man is a civilian, is he not?'

'Officer Lamotte is a policeman, Mr Bouanga,' Rocco confirmed, thinking that Lamotte just didn't have a hope in hell of looking like one. 'He will be on duty patrolling the grounds.'

The minister didn't look happy. 'So, far from not giving me adequate protection, which I had been assured would be provided by your own interior ministry, instead I am being watched over by one policeman and... someone else.' He was staring at Claude's clothes with obvious scepticism.

'He looks this way so he can blend in.' Rocco batted the argument right back in a reasonable voice. It was easier than trying to explain that Claude's normal duties, which included policing the marshes, lakes and riversides of the area, made wearing a serge uniform every day impractical. In fact Claude was the most reluctant wearer of the blue shirt and trousers that Rocco had ever met. 'He's also a professional hunter and an expert shot.'

That seemed to be an acceptable explanation to Bouanga, who stood up and moved towards the door. 'Very well. I suppose that will have to do. I will leave you to carry out your work, gentlemen. You will find Excelsiore, Delicat's wife, in the kitchen, but don't expect to get a lot from her – she doesn't talk much with anyone, save her husband.'

'Will any of your family members be joining you here?'

'No. My wife has been taken across the border to a safe address in Cameroon. While I'm here her brother will look after her. He's the local chief of police there.' He gave a dry smile. 'If I have to move again, it will be easier if it is just the three of us.'

'I understand. And will you be leaving the property at any time?'

'I'm not sure. Why do you ask?'

'Because if anyone does intend making an attempt on your life, they might wait for you to go out. The roads around here are narrow, and setting up a roadblock would be easy. If I'm to protect you properly, I'll need your assurance that you won't leave without letting us know first.'

Bouanga inclined his head in agreement, but said nothing. With a flick of his head for Delicat to follow, he disappeared along the hallway.

Claude watched them go before saying, 'Not the easiest to get on with, is he?'

'Not really.' Rocco scowled at Claude. 'Did you really say reporting for duty? You've never reported for duty in your life.'

Claude grinned. 'Well, you said he was a VIP so I thought I'd better play the part of the willing and obedient servant.' He indicated his clothes. 'Sorry – I thought if I was going to be spending time here *and* blending in, as you cleverly pointed out, I might as well be comfortable. Who's the little fella, by the way?'

'His name's Delicat. He's Bouanga's bodyguard and I suggest you don't refer to his size in front of him. I get the feeling he might take offence.'

Claude kept a straight face. '*Eh bien*. I hope he's up to the job. This place is like an open field. I thought the Ministry wanted to keep this man safe.'

'They do. All we can do is make sure the house is tight and keep our eyes open and ready to repel uninvited strangers.'

They set about checking the house from top to bottom. He could only guess at the original use of several rooms. Most were devoid of furnishings and had clearly been empty for many years, with the heavy smell of damp lingering in the air and layers of dust on every surface. Rocco led the way, inspecting the shutters and windows, especially to the rear of the house overlooking the fields where he felt any attack might originate. Fortunately, the structure was in good condition, and it took a matter of minutes to confirm that, save for the conservatory, intruders were unlikely to gain access very easily without the use of a battering ram.

They finally came to the kitchen, where a lady sporting a beautiful, multi-coloured head-cloth was tending a cooker and surrounded by steam. Excelsiore was considerably taller than her husband. She gave a shy half-smile, but offered no greeting. Rocco smiled back and checked the door to the gardens was secure before returning to the front hallway, where he'd noticed a telephone. He picked it up and heard a dial tone. The device looked new and he guessed it had been freshly installed, no doubt on the instructions of the Ministry. They had evidently moved fast to make sure Bouanga had the means to contact them in an emergency. As he replaced the handset, the former minister appeared, flanked by Delicat.

'I take it we're safe, Inspector?' the minister queried. He glanced at

Claude as he spoke, and added, 'At least, as safe as we can be given the absence of more security personnel.'

Rocco ignored the dig, as there was nothing he could do about it. 'Safe enough, if you keep the windows locked and any shutters you don't use shut tight. Also keep the front gates closed. And I'd avoid sitting for too long in the conservatory, if I were you. You'll make an easy target if your enemies try for a long shot.' He indicated the phone. 'Does anybody from back home know you're here?'

'No. I have not announced my movements, if that's what you are asking. Why?'

'Just a precaution. If you receive any calls and the caller hangs up without speaking, you should let me or Officer Lamotte know immediately. It could be a way of finding out if you're in.'

'Of course. In the meantime, I trust you will pass on my concerns about security to your superiors?'

Rocco nodded. 'I will.' He stepped outside followed by Claude, and the two men went for a walk around the outbuildings. It was a relief to be out of the musty atmosphere and Rocco breathed deeply in the fresh air.

Claude evidently felt the same way. 'If I never have to go in there again it'll be a relief,' he murmured. 'Depressing place, isn't it? If it was me I'd want to throw open all the windows and play some loud music just to stir up the dust.'

'You might think differently,' Rocco said, nodding towards the open fields, 'if you knew somebody was out there waiting to take a shot at you.'

'True enough. Not much of a life, though, is it, stuck out here and waiting for someone with a gun to come bursting through the door?

And that little feller – Delicat? He might be deadly for all I know, but he doesn't look it.'

'That's possibly his main strength,' Rocco replied. He'd come across protectors before, and the really good ones were inconspicuous to the point of being invisible. 'People don't notice him until it's too late. In any case, in Bouanga's position, I doubt he's got a lot of choice. If he's got a lot of enemies, there probably aren't too many bodyguards queueing up to protect him.'

After checking the outbuildings, which had been cleared long ago save for old farming junk like feed troughs and rotting hessian sacks, they walked out across the field behind the house and made a wide loop, studying bushes, trees and dead ground for obvious hiding places. It would be simple for an attacker to lay out here unseen, but getting up and crossing the last two or three hundred metres of open ground would present them with a problem.

Rocco noted the positions of three sturdy trees and a couple of convenient hollows in the ground which would be ideal range markers if they were attacked. They crested a gentle rise of pastureland, the long grass swishing as they walked, and found themselves looking down a long, sloping field with a narrow lane running across the bottom. It was only when Rocco saw a flash of Rizzotti's familiar marker tape and a figure moving along the lane that he realised they were looking down on the ditch where the dead man in the suit had been found.

'I didn't realise we were this close to that road,' he murmured.

'That's your mate Desmoulins, isn't it?' said Claude, a hand shading his eyes. 'Looks like he's been mixing with you too much; he can't keep away from the scene of the crime.'

Rocco grunted, non-committal. The truth was, he wanted nothing more than to be down there with him, not stuck up here looking after a man on the run from enemies half a world away. Maybe Bouanga did need protecting, but whether the threats he feared were real remained to be seen. In the meantime, sitting here wouldn't solve a crime that had happened down there.

He made a decision. 'Claude, stay and watch the place, will you? I'm just going down for a quick look.'

'Of course you are.' Claude smiled. 'I'd have been worried if you hadn't, to be honest. Policing's like being a ball on a roulette table, isn't it? Always moving towards the centre.'

Or a hamster, thought Rocco, as he hopped over the fence. On a wheel.

Twelve

'We could take him here, don't you think?' Romain and Lilou were watching from the van parked down a side track not far from the entrance to the house called Les Sables. 'It's nice and quiet, and off the main road. We could be in and out, job done in no time.'

'Too risky,' Lilou said. 'We don't yet know who else is in the house; we'd be going in blind.' She took a drink from a bottle of lemonade. The inside of the van was growing uncomfortably warm as the sun climbed, the breeze too light to make any impression, and there was still a strong smell coming from the back where the moped had left a trace of its presence. 'It must be nice to have a house like that, don't you think? Big garden, fields, trees… I could live in it quite easily… hold parties and things for all my friends, maybe build a swimming pool if it doesn't have one. Be the country lady – what do you think?'

Romain looked at her with a wry smile. 'No, you couldn't. You're like me; you're too much of a wanderer. You don't like being tied down. Anyway, what friends would that be?'

She touched his face, running the backs of her fingers down his cheek, and smiled. 'That's a bit brutal. But I suppose you're right. I couldn't stand it for long; I'd be bored out of my brain with all that respectability. But it's nice to dream occasionally.' She sat up. 'Maybe after we've dealt with this one we can take time off and go somewhere nice and quiet. We haven't had a real holiday in... well, months.'

'Sure. If you say so.' He gave her a look loaded with doubt. 'We could eat lots, top up our tans and get flabby, like the old folks on the coast gradually dying of inactivity and a lack of excitement.'

'Cynical boy. Oh, look.' She pointed towards the house, where a tiny figure had appeared at the front door and was walking down the side of the building. There was a screen of vegetation in the way that prevented them seeing much detail, but the figure's skin colour was obvious. 'Is that a kid? I thought you said it was just three adults in there.'

'That's what I heard. Maybe the information was rubbish.'

'What was it again?'

'They said Rocco was guarding some VIP minister from Gabon on the run from his enemies. He had to leave the country in a hurry and came here after receiving death threats, apparently. There's a female cook, they said, and a servant. But there was no mention of kids.'

'We need to check that out. We can't go in hard with children about. You know what people can be like: a cop's fair game but someone would rat us out for the price of a drink if a kid got hurt.'

Romain nodded. 'I'll see what I can find out. This place is pretty remote, and if Rocco comes back this way, we might just get a chance to take him. Better than trying for him in town, anyway.'

'What if he doesn't?'

'Then we do it somewhere else. We adapt, like always.'

'Didn't Farek say he could get us some help if we needed it?'

'He did. What are you thinking – a full frontal assault?'

'No. That would take a team with skills. This job is not for sharing.

Maybe we can draw Rocco out with a diversion so we can hit him when he's least expecting it.'

Romain smiled, his eyes lighting up at the thought of some action. 'I see what you mean. That's a good idea. Once I find out what's happening here, we can give Farek a call.'

'And then we can take that holiday I was talking about.' Lilou giggled and fluttered her eyelashes at him, although he didn't seem to notice. But that was fine. She knew he hung on her every word, even though he pretended not to.

Thirteen

As he walked down the hill towards the road, Rocco knew it wasn't just the proximity of this crime scene that was drawing him; like a lot of cops he hated leaving a puzzle for somebody else to unravel. He knew he was going directly against orders, but he figured it was worth the risk if he could get even a tiny clue to pass on to Desmoulins and his team. Return visits to crime scenes didn't always produce results, but occasionally he gained a renewed sense of what might have happened at a particular site and how events might have flowed. That included spotting possible witnesses who might have been overlooked in the initial investigation, although he doubted that was going to work out here in this isolated spot.

By the time he reached the lane his shoes had lost their lustre to the rough grass, and the cuffs of his trousers were showing signs of damp. He stopped short of the fence running parallel to the lane where Desmoulins was now waiting for him. The young detective's car was parked further along under a tree.

'I know I shouldn't be here,' Rocco explained, 'and I'm not trying to tread on your toes. I just wanted to give you a hand.'

'I'm glad of the help, you know that,' Desmoulins said honestly. 'It's too easy to miss something on the first sweep.' He paused, then said, 'It makes no sense to any of us at the station that you've been taken off this work to play bodyguard to some minor foreign bigwig.'

Rocco shrugged to show that there was nothing he could do about it. 'Have you found anything new?'

'Not yet. I just got here. How about we double up? You check the fields on both sides of the road while I do the lane, then we swap over.'

Rocco nodded. 'Suits me. Let's do it.' He made a sweep of the grass some fifty metres back from the fence, looking for anything that might have been used as a weapon. But it quickly proved futile; the grass here was shorter than further up the slope and the men on the original search would have had to be blind to miss anything larger than a razor blade. He stepped over the fence close to where the body had been found. There was little to show what had occurred, save for flattened grass and some scuff marks in the soft edges of the ditch where Rizzotti's men had scrambled to haul out the body.

He moved with care, avoiding the murder spot and crossing further along. He stepped over a thin trickle of muddy water in the very bottom of the ditch and climbed to the top, turning to look back at the field from another angle. He wondered if there really had been a kid up there or whether Matthieu had been imagining things. Maybe he'd have to have another word with the old farmer to see if he could rattle his brains for anything he might have forgotten.

He checked the field on the far side of the lane, even though that, too, had already been scoured, but the ground was clear of all but a few strands of grass and hard-packed. As he stepped back into the lane, Desmoulins whistled to him and waved. He was standing on the edge of the tarmac a few paces away from the murder spot, looking down into the ditch. It was shallow at this point, with grass covering the water at the bottom.

Balanced on the grass was a silver petrol filler cap.

'Could be nothing,' said Desmoulins, 'but worth a look.' He stepped down into the hollow and picked up the cap, and returned to Rocco's side. It was metal, and bore a familiar winged emblem – a capital M and the brand name Motobécane.

'Odd place to lose one of these,' observed Rocco.

'That's not all.' Desmoulins stepped away a couple of paces and squatted at the edge of the lane. He pointed at a circular patch of damp earth which filled a fist-sized hole in the tarmac. 'I spotted this just now but didn't think anything of it. Maybe I was wrong. See the rainbow colours? '

Rocco nodded. 'Petrol or oil.' He bent and pushed his finger into the earth and sniffed it. Petrol; the earth was soaked in it. Not necessarily important, especially where Matthieu's tractor and several police vehicles had stopped recently. He dug down again, wondering how it hadn't dried out completely, and found the hole was like a cup, with a solid base. That explained it; there was nowhere for the petrol to go. As he was about to stand up, he saw something irregular in the muddy mixture. Light-coloured and barely two centimetres across, it had jagged edges.

'Here,' said Desmoulins, handing him a knife.

'Thanks.' Rocco used the knife blade to lift the object and turned it over. The other side was a pale, sludgy green. He wiped off a film of mud for a closer look. He'd seen this colour before, but it took a few moments to remember where. Then it came to him: it was a brand colour used by moped manufacturers and common all over France. If they weren't green they were a dull grey or a vague duck-egg blue.

'So,' said Rocco, 'we've got a moped filler cap and a fleck of paint that could be from a moped.'

'But no moped.' Desmoulins pulled a face. 'Are we making too much of nothing?'

'Could be. But it's more than we had before.' He found an old envelope in his coat pocket and slid the fragment of paint inside while trying to build a coherent picture from the details they had before them. Somehow petrol had been spilled – or had leaked – just here; not a great deal but sufficient to have soaked the small amount of earth in the hole. A fragment of paint had fallen from a moped, too. Or had the moped fallen over and chipped it off? Either way the result would have been the same.

He walked along the lane away from the crime scene, scanning the ground for anything, no matter how insignificant. He'd gone no more than ten paces and was about to turn and go back, when he saw a faint impression in the soft earth at the side of the lane. It was a trick of the light that did it; one step sideways and he'd have missed it. A single tyre track, maybe three centimetres wide. Too wide for a bicycle and too narrow for a car or van. Thanks to the lack of traffic down here, the impression had remained firm enough to be visible.

'I don't believe it,' Desmoulins breathed, eyeing the tracks. 'Sorry, Lucas, I don't know how we missed this.'

'Don't worry – it's easily done. I didn't see it either.'

To Rocco it was a reasonable set of indicators. At some point a green moped had been ridden down this lane, wandering off the firm surface slightly at this point, which was probably easy to do, and onto softer ground. A few metres further on, it had fallen over and lost a chip of paint, also spilling a small quantity of fuel that had settled in a hole in the tarmac.

But where was the moped now?

His attention was drawn to a small tangle of hay rolling along the road in the breeze. Like tumbleweed in a Western, he thought; all it needs is the music and the sounds of jangling spurs. It brought to mind Rizzotti's mention of the straw and hay attached to the dead man's clothing.

'There's a barn or a cowshed around here somewhere,' he said, voicing his thoughts aloud. 'Rizzotti reckons the dead man must have spent the night sleeping out before he got this far.'

'There's one along there,' said Desmoulins, pointing up the road. 'I came down that way just now. It's a ramshackle old place. Do you want to take a look?'

Rocco hesitated, 'Might as well, seeing as I'm here. You never know.'

They walked to Desmoulins' car and drove back up the lane, and soon came to a field with a barn close to the road. Desmoulins was right: it was certainly ramshackle, with gaping holes in the sides where some of the wooden slats had given up the fight and fallen away, and long weeds growing on all sides giving testimony to it having been deserted for a long time.

Rocco climbed out, hopped over the gate to the field, and walked round to the back of the barn and the main doorway. At least, it had been a doorway once; now it was just an opening with a pile of rotting planks where part of the structure had fallen down.

'Have you seen this?' Desmoulins had circled round the barn from the other side, and was squatting down and pointing at the ground, where a patch of mud showed beneath the grass. It was a clear tyre track and half a footprint. 'A moped tyre; could be the same as the one we saw down the road.'

Rocco entered the barn, disturbing a couple of small birds in the roof, and looked around. Most of the space inside was taken up by an ancient two-wheeled trailer with shafts, the wood collapsing into the weeds and hard-packed soil beneath. But at the other end of the structure was a collapsed pile of straw covered in moss, and above it an old manger containing the remains of a hay bale hanging from the wall by a single bolt.

It didn't look promising until he saw that a section of straw had been pulled out and turned over, and revealed a dent where someone had been sleeping.

'Looks like we found his final room for the night,' said Desmoulins. 'But what does it tell us?'

'Not much,' Rocco replied. 'It's a link in the chain, no more than that. What puzzles me is whether the killer knew he'd stopped here, or happened along at the moment he was out on the road.'

'Bit convenient.'

'Or he waited for him to leave. Easier to strike out in the open.'

With no further clues, they got back in the car and Desmoulins drove back to the ditch and dropped Rocco off. Rocco handed him the envelope containing the paint fragment. 'Give the filler cap and this fragment to Rizzotti and ask him to check the colour. It's a long shot but worth a try.'

'Will do.' Desmoulins waved goodbye and Rocco walked back up the slope towards Les Sables, running various scenarios through his mind, discarding the most outlandish. By the time he reached the top, only two solid ones remained.

One: the victim had been on foot and somebody had happened along on a moped and knocked him over. As far as Rocco was aware, there were no sharp, spiked elements on a moped capable of causing such a fatal wound… unless the rider had been a farmworker carrying a fork. It might account for the paint fragment and the spilled fuel. In a panic, the accidental assailant might have rolled the body into the ditch and gone on his way. Result: an accident.

Two: Vieira – and he couldn't now separate the name from the victim – had arrived here on a moped, evidenced perhaps by the tyre track in the barn and the hay and straw which Rizzotti said was on his suit, and somebody had stopped him and killed him. Result: murder.

He shook his head. It didn't explain why or who. And until they found who might have benefitted from his death, that was how it might stay.

He walked back up the slope and climbed the fence into the property, head buzzing with possibilities and improbabilities alike. Everything looked so peaceful here, as it had no doubt for generations. A nice, pleasant spot if you liked a quiet life away from the rush. He caught a glimpse of Claude standing to one side of the house, his shotgun under his arm. Then he noticed his colleague had his free hand against his chest, and was making a covert signal. Moments later Rocco understood why.

Gerard Monteo had appeared at the corner of the building and was striding purposefully towards him.

'Inspector,' Monteo greeted him coolly. 'I decided to come out here for a look at the house, and it's a good thing that I did. Your man Lamotte tells me you were off making a survey of the fields around the house, checking… he said something about an outer perimeter. I don't pretend to understand what that might be, but is it necessary? Under the circumstances I'd have thought you'd be better employed sticking close to Bouanga, don't you?'

'That's one way of looking at it.' Rocco stared down at the Ministry man with a feeling of irritation. Was this how it was going to be – watched, monitored and criticised every step of the way by this suit? If so he was going to have to nip it in the bud, otherwise he'd never have a moment's peace to get on with his job. 'Have you ever protected anybody?'

'No, of course not. Why would I?'

'No reason. It's just that there's not much point sticking close to a target if an attacker decides to stay back at a distance and use a rifle.' He stepped past Monteo and walked towards the house. It wasn't a wise move being so blunt with the man, but neither was taking instruction from a bureaucrat who didn't know the first thing about policing.

He found Delicat in the kitchen talking softly with his wife, who was chopping vegetables. They stopped speaking when they saw Rocco, and turned to face him. The air smelled of a variety of spices and a pot was steaming on a large cooker nearby.

'Monsieur Delicat,' said Rocco, 'did you happen to see any children anywhere near here yesterday morning?'

For a long moment he thought the man wasn't going to reply. His face was a blank canvas and showed no signs of having understood what Rocco had said. Yet he was sure Delicat wasn't quite as dumb as he might be pretending, or as Bouanga had intimated. There was something about the man that spoke of keen intelligence.

'I did not,' Delicat said at last, his voice a thin echo in the kitchen. 'There has been nobody else here save you and your colleague. And now the other man.'

'But you were out in the field yesterday, were you not, overlooking the lane?' He was only guessing, but at a distance, with possibly poor eyesight, it would be understandable if Matthieu had mistaken the small figure of Delicat for that of a child. It would be equally understandable if the bodyguard had witnessed something down in the lane but had no desire to involve himself with a police enquiry in a foreign land.

Another delay in replying, and again Rocco thought the man hadn't understood. But Delicat nodded. 'That is so. I wanted to see what was out there.'

'And did you?'

'There was nothing. A tractor on the road, that was all.'

Rocco thanked him, and was about to leave when he spotted the bow and quiver of arrows through the doorway, now hanging on the wall in the hall. A disturbing thought popped into his head and he gestured towards them. 'May I take one of your arrows to show a friend?' He said it casually, but was watching Delicat to gauge his reaction.

The bodyguard shrugged without hesitation, his face a blank. 'If you wish.'

Rocco thanked him and lifted out one of the arrows as he passed. It was as long as his forearm and slimmer than his little finger. The notched end was fitted with a small feathered flight and the point was plain and, he assumed, fire-hardened, rather than being made of stone or metal. The wood was smooth and elaborately decorated, and he wondered at the hours that might have gone into making it.

He felt a fleeting moment of doubt. Maybe he was tilting at windmills, seeing solutions where there were none. He was also wondering what was really going on here. Bouanga had referred to Delicat as speaking 'barely the basics' in French. Yet from the careful way Delicat had spoken, while it was evident that his French might be limited, he clearly understood enough to engage in conversation. Was Bouanga playing games for reasons of his own, perhaps to keep his staff from being asked awkward questions? It made him realise that he and Claude would be better not talking too freely about what they were doing in front of the bodyguard, in case it was reported back and the ousted minister from Gabon was able to use the information in some way.

Claude was patrolling the stretch of ground behind the house. He turned when he saw Rocco approaching, eyes dropping to the arrow in Rocco's hand. 'Going hunting? You know using a bow makes that thing far more effective.'

'I just had an irrational thought,' said Rocco. 'But I have to check it out. I gather Monteo spoke to you?'

'The tick from the Ministry, you mean? Yes, I think he had a job acknowledging my presence, but he managed to keep a straight face. He seems to think we have glaring gaps in the protective wall of steel you and I have thrown around Bouanga. I said we could always find a gun for him to lend us a hand but he didn't seem keen.' He paused. 'I hear you're taking Mme Denis to the hospital this afternoon. That's very neighbourly of you.'

Rocco looked at him. It was on the tip of his tongue to ask how he knew that, but he stopped himself in time. The village gossip chain made sure that any news worth hearing, and a lot that wasn't, hit the ground running. 'When did you hear that?'

'Last night in the café. It was quite the topic of conversation.' The older man grinned and continued, 'If you're not careful you're going to ruin your reputation as a hard-nosed city cop.'

'I think I can live with that. Can you handle things here while I'm gone?'

'No problem. Excelsiore's been offering me coffee every hour on the hour. From the smells coming out of the kitchen I think she's cooking up a stew for later. I reckon I can put up with that, too, if she's got any to spare.'

Rocco nudged Claude's stomach with the back of his hand. 'As if you need it. And on first-name terms already? You want to be careful; if Delicat thinks you're getting too friendly with his wife he might put that bow of his to good use.'

Leaving Claude with a thoughtful look on his face, and a promise that he'd be back later that night to take over guard duty, Rocco drove to Poissons to pick up Mme Denis as promised. She was waiting, although pretending studiously not to be by flicking imaginary bugs off a row of tomato plants.

'All ready?' he said, as he got out to open the passenger door. She stopped her pretence of gardening and climbed in, settling herself in the seat and clearly enjoying the feel of the leather beneath her. 'I am,' she replied, and placed a hand on his arm. 'You're already doing me a very kind favour, Lucas. Would it be very rude of me to ask if you could drive quite slowly, please?'

'Of course I will.' He wondered how many of her friends would be down near the village co-op, primed to watch as she was driven by. She was sure to have dropped more than a hint that she was getting a lift to the hospital from the neighbourhood *flic*. 'And once we're out of the village?'

'You can put your foot down and drive like a cop in a hurry.' She chuckled. 'Did I tell you you're a very perceptive young man?'

'I'm a detective – it comes with the badge.'

Fourteen

After dropping Mme Denis at the hospital with a promise to collect her later, Rocco drove to the station and went straight to Dr Rizzotti's office at the rear of the building.

'Hello, what are you doing here?' the doctor greeted him. 'I thought you were playing bodyguard to some high-placed foreign dignitary.'

'I am. But how did you know? It's not supposed to be common knowledge.'

'Well, that may have been the intention, but it's all over the station, so I think you can forget about secrecy. Some VIP official from Gabon, I heard. On the run from angry fellow-countrymen and hoping to stay out of trouble with a big cop in a hidey-hole in the Picardie countryside. Good luck with that one.'

Rocco sighed and wondered how long it would take for the news to get out into the wider community and eventually, the press. The idea of a man like Bouanga being in the area and watched over by the police would attract reporters like flies to a jam pot, eager for a story. It wouldn't last long, but the damage would be done.

'I wanted to check something with you, so keep this visit to yourself, would you?' He placed the arrow on the desk in front of Rizzotti. 'What are the chances something like this made the hole in the dead man's neck?'

Rizzotti picked it up with care and studied it in detail. 'Interesting. Where did you find it?' He sniffed at the shaft before replacing it on the desk.

'The dignitary you mentioned has a bodyguard. The arrow belongs to him, along with a bow. Both men are staying in a farmhouse about half a kilometre from the murder site.'

He didn't need to elaborate, Rizzotti was quick to follow his thinking. 'Got you. Proximity and access. But not deliberate, surely? He's only just got here.'

'I agree, but it could have been an accident: out hunting and didn't see the man in the lane. It happens.' Even as he said it, Rocco realised it was a stretch. It wasn't unusual for an accidental shooting to occur, but usually with locals using guns after too much alcohol to celebrate the hunting season. 'Can you match it to the wound?'

'I'll make a comparison, certainly. Unusual item for a bodyguard, though. He's also African, I take it, like the VIP?'

'Correct.'

'Thought so. And is he *un petit* – a small man?'

Rocco grunted. 'He is.'

'I was reading about them a while back. There are various tribes in Gabon and surrounding areas. The Babongo are one such, mostly hunters in the forests, although they're being gradually forced out by the advance of modernisation and the search for a better standard of living. They used to be called pygmies. They still use these weapons to catch their meat. I hope you didn't put this anywhere near your mouth, by the way.'

'I don't usually suck on crime scene evidence. Why?'

'The tips are often poisoned. Stuns the target and kills quite quickly. Not sure what it would do to a big fellow like you, but I wouldn't want to find out.' He stood up. 'It's interesting, as I said, but I doubt this arrow would have killed our man.' He picked it up again. 'Come with me and I'll show you why I say that.'

Rocco shouldn't have been surprised by Rizzotti's breadth of knowledge. He was a very well-read man and seemed to absorb information like a sponge. Now Rizzotti opened a door at the end of the room, and the smell of chemicals filled the air. The adjacent room was tiled, and held three metal tables, a large sink and an array of instruments, the use for which Rocco could only hazard a guess. He'd seen bigger and better-equipped rooms for this kind of work, but on a limited budget Rizzotti somehow managed to accomplish a great deal.

One of the tables held a form covered by a large grey cloth.

'Come and take a look at our only current guest,' said Rizzotti, and pointed at the sink. 'You'd better wash your hands before you do anything else – I wouldn't want to have to explain your sudden demise through handling that arrow to Massin.' He turned and produced a paper bag. 'You'd better put it in this bag just in case.'

Rocco did so, then washed his hands, scrubbing his fingers and nails thoroughly, and dried them before joining the doctor alongside the covered body. Rizzotti flicked back the cloth. The dead man from the ditch was now stripped bare, with the lights turning his skin a sickly shade of grey. Rizzotti held the arrow close to the side of the dead man's neck. The edges of the entry wound were darkened and puckered, and Rocco immediately saw that the size of the opening was considerably larger than the arrow shaft.

'It's an understandable theory, Lucas, and if the size of the wound matched, I'd say you'd hit it on the nail. But I think I might have a better alternative.' He put the arrow down on an adjacent table and picked up an item lying close to the body. He held it up and Rocco immediately recognised it.

'It's a bayonet.' It was little more than a spike with an attachment for joining to a rifle barrel.

'Correct. To give it its full name, it's a number four, mark two spike bayonet, made in Britain during the war. They weren't used extensively here, but a few turn up now and then, popular among collectors. I found this one in the storeroom, confiscated during a bar fight here in town.' He held it against the wound, which matched it for size. 'See what I mean?'

'I do,' said Rocco. He took the bayonet and hefted it. Made for use with a rifle, he knew that commandos had been taught to use them as daggers. So was the person they were looking for a former military man? If so there was no shortage of them around here. 'That's good work.'

Rizzotti shrugged modestly. 'I wouldn't swear to it on oath, but in my opinion it's the most probable instrument we're likely to see. The point is very narrow, as you can see, but the shaft gets broader further up, which matches the size of the wound.' He took the bayonet back and mimed a thrusting motion, then pulled his hand back and twisted. 'The point would have gone in quite easily, and the assailant would have turned the weapon as he pulled it out to free it from the surrounding flesh.' He gave the ghost of a smile. 'Now you're supposed to ask me how I know that.'

Rocco decided to humour him. Rizzotti probably didn't get much opportunity to show off, as most of his reports were couched in neat, unemotional language to be read by people detached from this room and its dark arts. 'All right. How do you know that?'

'See where the edges of the wound are jagged?' He indicated where the flesh around the wound was turned out and raw. 'That's where the weapon was pulled out.'

'But would a bayonet like this have been enough to kill?' Rocco had enough experience of bayonets from his own army service, albeit not this kind, to know that Rizzotti was probably right on the button. But he needed confirmation.

'Absolutely. It would only have needed to go in a short way to have caused extensive internal bleeding into the throat. And the deceased was not a big man, nor was he in the best of health, judging by various other factors which I won't bore you with and which had no direct bearing on his death. If I'm correct, the assailant probably approached the victim with the bayonet concealed in some way, maybe down by his leg or up his sleeve, then stabbed him from up close and to one side.'

'So the victim might have known who killed him?'

'Either that or whoever did it approached him in such a way that it didn't arouse any suspicions.'

Rocco thought back to the murder scene, a picture forming in his mind of a man standing by the side of the lane. 'Like somebody stopping to ask directions.'

'That would fit, yes.'

A nasty way to die, thought Rocco. He'd seen throat wounds in Indochina, caused by bullets, shrapnel and even knives, and few of the victims had survived for long. If the shock and loss of blood hadn't killed them, infection in the hot, humid atmosphere without immediate medical facilities had soon taken their toll.

Whatever, if Rizzotti was right, this made it a certain case of murder rather than an accidental death: premeditated and carried out with cool precision. The body had been stripped of any clues which might lead to the dead man's identity.

Rizzotti walked across to a side table and picked up a small metal dish. It contained the paint fragment found near the murder scene. 'Desmoulins explained where you found this. It's an interesting theory. The colour looks right, but I can check the paint tone with a dealer here in town.'

'And the filler cap?'

'It's old, but not dirty, not like you'd expect if it was lying in a ditch at the side of the road for any length of time. There's not much more I can say except if the two items came from the same moped, your theory might fit. Before that, though, can you wait a second?' He turned and disappeared through another door, and returned carrying a pair of trousers. 'These belonged to our victim.' He laid them out on the next table and indicated a dark patch on the right leg, at ankle level. 'This is oil,' he explained. 'I haven't tested it yet, but if you're right about the paint, I'm pretty sure I don't need to.'

'How so?' Rocco wasn't sure where the doc was going, only that he sounded almost excited.

Rizzotti held the material out. 'The trouser cut is wide in the leg and the material is cheap and light. If he'd been riding a moped or a bicycle, the material would have flapped about in the breeze.' He mimed holding handlebars and pedalling with one leg. 'This oil mark could easily have come from the engine on a moped – possibly an older model or one without a protective casing. If we assume from the clothes that the deceased was a city-dweller, he might not have known that you don't let your trouser cuffs flap about on a moped.

At the very least you'll get them dirty, and the worst is you'll get them tangled in the engine. Nasty way to dismount, if you ask me.'

Rocco looked at him, impressed with the doctor's thinking. 'How do you know that much about mopeds?'

'Because before I became a doctor I was a medical student with no money. My father gave me a moped; it was old and oily and I soon learned to save on cleaning bills by tucking my trouser legs into my socks.' He smiled at the memory – or maybe it was with pride at having figured out this latest piece of evidence. 'It wasn't stylish, I grant you, but it got me about. I loved that old thing.'

It made sense, Rocco had to admit. But it caused another puzzle: if the dead man had been riding a moped, why had he stopped at that particular point on the lane? Had someone waved him down – his attacker, for example? If so, what had happened to the machine afterwards?

'Going back to the weapon,' he said, 'have you ever heard of this kind being used before?'

'No. But I'll ask around. There are probably a few of these in circulation, so it's possible. I'll ring a few contacts and get them to put the word out.'

'You actually have contacts in the business?' Rocco gave him a wry smile. Rizzotti lifted an eyebrow. 'Of course. Why not? I have to get some intelligent conversation somehow.' He nodded at the door. 'Now clear off and let me get on. And don't pick up any more curios with poisoned tips.'

Rocco found Mme Denis sitting on a bench outside the hospital, watching the world go by. She got in the car with a grateful smile and nodded to indicate she was ready to go.

Rocco glanced across at her a couple of times, but she made no move to tell him how the visit had gone. He was happy not to invade her privacy if that was what she preferred, but a small voice at the back of his mind wondered who else would ask how she'd got on. She had a circle of friends in Poissons, but like a lot of her generation she could be stubborn and he wasn't sure how prepared she might be to let others know her private business.

'I might regret this,' he said, after they'd covered a couple of kilometres in silence, 'so do remember I'm driving.'

'What?'

'How did it go? Don't tell me if you don't want to.'

'It was fine,' she replied. 'As I thought, an old woman's back not being as kind as it used to be.'

'You saw the specialist, then?'

'I did. He poked and prodded and tried his best to push my spine and hips out of place, but finally told me I'd got a touch of sciatica and gave me a packet of pills. I probably won't take them, though. I don't hold with modern drugs.'

'Why not, if they help?'

She puffed her lips out. 'When I was a girl growing up in Brittany there was a woman in our village who made medicines from plants. Her remedies went back generations, some as far back as Roman times. They didn't always taste very pleasant, but they worked. At least, none of her patients had any problems until the day they died.'

Rocco had to stop himself from laughing. 'You're serious? That's the best that can be said about her – nobody had a problem until they died?'

She prodded his arm with a finger. 'Don't make fun of the ancient ways, young man. She treated lots of people I knew and cured them, too. So that's what I'm going to do. I'll talk to Mme Evigny – she knows a thing or two about ailments and cures.'

'I've never heard of her.'

'Well, you wouldn't, would you? She's never robbed a bank or tried to assassinate de Gaulle. She lives in Danvillers, if you must know. Now, concentrate on driving, will you – I'd like to get home in one piece.'

When he glanced across at her, he was surprised and relieved to see a smile on her face, and decided that he could leave further interrogation about her ailments for another time.

Fifteen

Rocco's alarm clock dragged him from a brief and restless sleep. It was late and the light was fading, time to take over guard duty from Claude. He dressed quickly, an ear cocked for sounds of the fruit rats upstairs, but they were silent, no doubt snuggled up fast asleep. He envied them. Once the water boiled he made a flask of coffee, checked his gun and set out for the Bouanga residence.

Minutes later he was turning off the main road and following the drive to the house, the car lights sweeping over the fences and trees on either side and catching a fox slinking along on its nightly business. As he passed through the gates the pale shuttered windows flashed back at him, and he spotted Claude waiting by the side of the house. He swung the car under cover in the small barn he'd seen earlier.

'All quiet?' he asked.

Claude grinned. 'I haven't shot anybody yet, so yes.' He jerked a thumb towards the house. 'All locked up and in bed. Can't actually include the little guy in that because I can never keep track of him. He moves like a ghost and scares the devil out of me by popping up out of nowhere when I'm least expecting it. I'm sure he's doing it on purpose.'

'Thanks for the warning. You'd better get home and get some sleep.'

Claude yawned. 'Thanks. I could do with it. It's nice and quiet here, but all that space out there… it's downright spooky. You'd think I'd be used to it spending as much time as I do out at night.'

'I know what you mean. But you're not usually expecting anybody to turn up and start shooting at you.' He leaned back in the car and picked up his service weapon. 'See you back here at six?'

Claude nodded. 'Six it is.' He paused and watched as Rocco took off his coat and strapped on the gun. 'You sound a bit… off. Is everything all right? I can stay here if you like, keep you company.'

Rocco gave him a sideways look. 'You really want people to start talking about us?'

Claude laughed. 'Not really.'

'Fine. You go. We should be all right with one of us on guard for now.'

'Fair enough. How's Mme Denis?'

Rocco still hadn't got round to telling him about the Farek threat. He decided to leave it until tomorrow. Claude would only worry about it and refuse to leave his side, which wouldn't do either of them any good in the long run. Exhaustion through lack of rest made for poor security and could lead to accidents.

'She's fine. Just back pain, if she was telling me the truth.'

'Tell her she should go and see the Evigny woman in Danvillers. She's what they call a herbalist. Very good she is, too.'

Rocco had never thought of Claude as the natural-remedy type. 'And you know that how?'

'Well, I get aches and pains, don't I? It's all that trudging about in the wet.' He grimaced and rubbed his leg. 'I should get danger pay, with all that water.'

Rocco shook his head at the mime. 'Get out of here you old fraud before I change my mind.'

He walked out to the gate ahead of Claude, and closed it once he had passed through and disappeared along the road towards Poissons. The absence of the engine noise left a hole in the night, and he turned and walked back to the house, allowing the darkness to close around him like a cloak.

First he checked the windows and doors on the inside, moving with care through the house. Claude had already done it and would have done so properly, but the first rule of securing a building was to never leave anything to chance. The most vulnerable point was always during a handover of guards, when their attention was momentarily on the colleague replacing them. Anyone choosing that moment to slip inside the cordon would, for a new guard who chose not to double-check everything, pose a fatal threat.

After checking the interior, Rocco stepped outside and closed the door behind him. He went round testing the shutters, which were locked firm. Next he went through the outbuildings, relying at first on his sense of hearing and instinct, and only using a torch inside to check corners and cubbyholes. Eventually he finished his patrol and stood in the rear garden, staring out across the fields, tuning into the night. An owl hooted gently in a tree barely a hundred metres away and, further off, a fox barked, the high-pitched yelp echoing mournfully, like a creature in pain.

As so often in darkness, he was reminded of a place thousands of kilometres from here, where the night had been both friend and foe, providing cover for the cautious and hidden dangers for the unwary. His memories shifted, often triggered by the contrast with where he was in the present moment. Here and now the rush of smells came back to him: of rotting vegetation, the freshness following a cloudburst, or the amazing fragrances that seemed somehow out of place amid all the carnage and death.

He stepped over the fence and walked down the field towards the slope overlooking the back lane where Vieira had died. But he didn't go all the way. Instead he swung in a circle to his right and came up behind and to the side of the house, away from the barn and outbuildings.

As he came near the house, a flicker of movement caught his eye, and he stopped. He was already holding his MAB 38, and took it out of his coat pocket, slipping off the safety catch.

It was Delicat. The bodyguard was standing close to the wall, his features indistinguishable. He was watching Rocco, as still as a statue. Then he turned and slipped away along the side of the building and disappeared round the corner.

Rocco decided to check the front of the building before going in for coffee. He was still feeling fresh after his sleep but he didn't want to lose his edge by allowing tiredness to creep up on him. As he turned the front corner, he saw a tiny flash of light.

He stopped. It had been faint, then gone, coming from the far side of the main road. A trick of the night or was somebody out there? A poacher, perhaps.

He walked down the track towards the gate, sticking to the grass verge, his nerves healthily on edge. He kept his eye as close as he could to the spot where the light had been, but he knew that was at best an unreliable science. The light source could have been a kilometre away across the fields, in which case he'd be wasting his time and leaving the house unguarded.

He arrived at the gate and lifted the heavy latch without a sound, then stepped through and walked the rest of the way to the road, where he studied the darkness for the faintest indication that somebody was out there.

Sixteen

Across the road, in the deep shadows of a thicket, Romain froze in his seat as the gate to Les Sables swung open. It was too dark to discern specific detail, but clear enough to make out the movement of a man on foot. Tall, a large, dark shadow. He knew who it was immediately.

Rocco.

Romain felt a ripple of apprehension in his chest. He'd tried to be careful, using a small torch to check his food box for a sandwich, but had fumbled it. The beam had flicked upwards as the torch fell, the tiniest of flares against the windscreen. He'd quickly grabbed it and smothered the light, but if Rocco had happened to be looking this way it would have been enough.

Which seemed to have been the case.

He thought about waking Lilou, tucked up in the back of the van, but he was reluctant unless he was absolutely forced to do so. Her breathing was soft and rhythmic, showing she was fast asleep. Neither of them had slept particularly well in the past few days, especially in the ratty little cottage they'd found empty in the village where Rocco lived. Wary of making a sound in case the neighbour should scream the place down, the original plan had been to use it as a base from which to hit Rocco, the idea being that he would never suspect a threat coming from within the community. But nerves, and the sense that everybody watched everybody else in Poissons, had left Lilou especially wired and short of energy, and they'd decided to abandon it and use the van instead.

He shifted his legs to relieve the stiffness that came from sitting still for so long. The body and mind needed time to adjust after waking and before leaping into action, and he'd been still long enough for his limbs to have become slow and unresponsive. Soldiers do it because they've been conditioned and trained to move without question, their actions automatic and born of long practice. But this kind of work, especially against an experienced and suspicious target like Rocco, needed careful timing and planning. Anything less would be fatal.

Everything they'd been told about Rocco, his army service in Indochina, his anti-gang activity and his successes against powerful odds, such as the late Samir Farek, made it clear he was not to be taken lightly. Watching the investigator now, walking through the gate and along the track, sent a tremor through him, and when Rocco stopped on the far side of the road Romain found that he'd been holding his breath. He released it slowly, as if the movement of his chest alone might alert the policeman to his presence. While doing that he checked that the van's ignition was ready in case Rocco should step onto the tarmac and head into the bushes towards him.

But that didn't happen. Rocco stopped and stared into the dark like a wild animal on the hunt for a moment, his head swinging slowly. Then a truck appeared in the distance and trundled by. He's a predator, Romain thought, and wondered what it took to develop that kind of skill. Even Farek had seemed in awe of him, although he'd tried not to let it show while giving them their briefing for the contract. Too busy fighting business fires, he'd claimed grandly, otherwise he'd go after Rocco himself. They'd exchanged a quick look at the time, and later agreed that Farek was scared stiff of the big cop.

But then, that was why he'd hired them. Like many of his kind, he had the big talk and the fury, but when it came down to it, he wasn't capable of doing the job himself.

Romain watched Rocco turn and walk back down the track to the house, closing the gate after him. He relaxed, and was surprised to find that he felt nauseous. It brought to mind something from several years ago. He wasn't an animal lover, but he'd once visited a touring circus near Lyon out of curiosity, to see what the fuss was about. The acts had been boring and childish, the clowns uninspiring and the balancing acts performed without great style. So he'd gone for a look around the trailers behind the big tent. He'd ended up standing outside a wheeled cage holding a single, pacing tiger. It was an impressive beast, and had held his gaze in unblinking silence. Seeing it there behind the steel bars, so powerful and steady, he'd felt the same sense of threat and unease that he was feeling right now.

Seventeen

The following morning dawned bright and clear, with the promise of a hot day carried on a gentle breeze off the fields. Claude returned bearing more coffee and a couple of warm brioche rolls, and the two men walked around the rear of the house and studied the surroundings while eating.

'Nothing doing, I take it?' Claude murmured.

'Not a peep.' Rocco didn't mention the light he'd seen during the night. Insubstantial evidence of any kind seen in the dark hours was best treated with caution, and he didn't want to start grabbing at shadows.

'So, what was eating you last night when you got here?' Claude queried. 'Woman trouble?'

'I wish,' Rocco replied, sipping his coffee. 'It would be easier to deal with.' He decided it was time to tell Claude about Santer's call. It was only fair, as Claude might get caught up by association in whatever Farek decided to throw at him; and having the extra pair of eyes and ears of a man he trusted implicitly would be useful if anyone did make an attempt on his life. He gave him a brief summary of the details.

'Christ, you don't make life easy for yourself do you?' said Claude, when Rocco finished speaking. He was aware of the Fareks' history and the connection, such as it was, that Samir, the dead brother, had with Rocco. It had been a bloody business that had come storming out of nowhere, threatening to cost Rocco his life. 'What are you going to do?'

'Deal with it. If I can get a lead on who Farek's likely to send after me it might help. He can't have too many options; most of his men will be crooks and thugs, not assassins. If he wants to use someone he can trust he'll need to deal from a good pack – and it won't be cheap.'

'How do you find that out, though? He won't have the same people around him as Sami did, will he? What was that big guy's name who did all his heavy work?'

'Bouhassa.' It was a name Rocco hadn't thought of in a long while. Sami Farek had relied on him as a bodyguard and killer, but there weren't too many Bouhassas around.

'That's the one. This Farek's hardly likely to tell you what his plans are, so what will you do?'

'I know a couple of people I can ask. You know how word gets around: people talk. Whatever he's planned, it won't stay secret for long.'

'Let's hope you can get a lead on them before they get one on you. What about Massin – are you going to tell him?'

'No. He won't pull me off this job just because of a threat from a gangster. Even if he did I can't hide out forever. Farek will just wait until I show up again.'

Rocco finished his coffee and brioche and walked over to the kitchen where Excelsiore was busy preparing a breakfast tray for

Bouanga. He'd been meaning to return the arrow to the bodyguard and had waited for a convenient moment. As he stepped through the door, he heard soft giggling and saw Delicat standing close to Excelsiore, with his hand gently caressing her bottom.

He coughed, and they stepped quickly apart, looking confused.

'My apologies,' Rocco said, sensing embarrassment. 'I wanted to return this.'

Delicat took the arrow without a word. If he was aware that Rocco had taken the arrow to compare with the wound in Vieira's neck, he showed no sign. He turned and walked away, disappearing through the door to the main hallway, leaving Excelsiore shuffling away into a corner and busying herself at clattering some pots and pans.

As Rocco stepped outside, he saw movement along the track from the road, and a car appeared. The vehicle looked new, a rare enough sight in the area, and came to a stop at the gate. Rocco instinctively reached for his service weapon. He didn't think anyone wishing ill of Bouanga would make such a civilised approach, and even less so in a new car. But you could never tell; assassins came in all guises and the good ones were paid highly because they could adapt to all circumstances. He waited while the driver climbed out and opened the gate, before climbing back in and driving up to the front of the house.

It was Gerard Monteo from the Ministry. Alongside him, looking stiff as always, sat Massin.

'Stand by your beds,' Claude muttered. 'Hut inspection.'

Rocco smiled. He hadn't thought they would get away without some form of check-up; anything involving a foreign dignitary, even one with a questionable background, was bound to be high on the list of things that shouldn't go wrong. And Monteo clearly had an agenda with regard to the Gabonese minister. Part of that agenda would be to make sure everything had been put in place with the local force to make Bouanga as secure as possible, after which he would probably disappear back to Paris and let the cards fall where they may. If anything did go wrong, it would be the local police who would shoulder the blame, not him.

'Make sure he sees your gun,' advised Rocco. 'He's impressed by weaponry as long as somebody else is holding it.'

Claude hefted his shotgun with a smile. 'Will do. Can I shoot something while he's here, just to show we're ready and able? If I do it close enough I might make him wet his pants.'

'Let's not. We have enemies enough in the Ministry, we don't need any more.'

Rocco walked out to meet the two men. He'd been right about Monteo; as soon as the Ministry man's eyes slid past Rocco's shoulder and settled on Claude, who was standing with his gun under his arm, he looked both shocked and anxious.

'What is he doing?' he murmured.

'Don't worry,' Rocco said. 'You've already met Officer Lamotte. He's only dangerous if you try to attack him or go fishing out of season.'

'I'm glad to hear it.' Monteo shot a quick glance at Massin, who gave a nod to Rocco but said nothing. 'This is a nice place. Pleasant spot.' He looked at the house as if doing so for the first time, then around at the fields, and Rocco wondered why Monteo was acting as if he'd never been here before. Somebody else playing games, perhaps, making out this was a big event. Perhaps he was preparing an extensive report for his superiors on how difficult it was arranging protection for a guest of the state.

'It's nice enough,' Rocco agreed. 'Let's hope the opposition don't find it.'

'Of course. But it's very… open,' Monteo continued. 'I hadn't realised.' His statement seemed rehearsed, as if he was keen to let it be known that he was having second thoughts about the viability of the house being secure enough for Bouanga. 'Don't you agree, François?'

Massin didn't respond, but pursed his lips and studied the building and its surroundings. He wore an expression of misgiving as if, seeing it now, he could also see his future career hinging on the possible outcomes of this place and the people in it.

Rocco wasn't prepared to make it easy for either of them. They had agreed to this without fully considering the difficulty of the task involved. It would have been easier to protect Bouanga if he'd been safely locked up in a police cell in Amiens, although that would never have happened. 'Like I said before, all it needs is a sniper up a tree. But I'm sure we'll cope.'

Monteo continued to look doubtful. 'François, are you sure you can't spare anybody else? If anything were to happen to our guest because of… well, lack of resources, it really wouldn't go down well at headquarters.'

Massin gave Rocco a thankless look for his blunt appraisal, but he was in a corner. If he didn't do something, anything, now that Monteo had raised the issue, any failure here would reflect badly on him as the senior local man. His response was to throw the ball deftly to Rocco by saying, 'You're correct, Gerard. Suggestions, Rocco? You know the men well enough to choose. There must be someone else who could assist you – and I don't mean Desmoulins; he's busy.'

'A couple of Godard's bruisers from the *Gendarmerie Mobile* would be ideal. But I don't expect they'll be available either.'

'You're right. They won't.' Massin looked stubborn. 'There have been threats of union trouble at an industrial complex near Compiègne. Godard will need all the men he can muster.'

'If I may,' Claude Lamotte put in, 'how about *Gardienne* Alix Poulon? She's a good shot and knows her way around. She won't fold at the idea of some action.'

Monteo looked at Claude in astonishment, before turning to Massin. 'Did he say Alix? A *woman*? Is he serious?'

Massin appeared to consider it. 'What do you think, Rocco? You know her, I believe?'

'I can't argue with Officer Lamotte's description. She lives not far from here, anyway, so being on hand wouldn't be a problem. She's also good on her feet and has a clear head.' Rocco had worked with Alix Poulon before, and she had proved calm and steady, even in the face of threats. The fact that she was Claude's daughter hadn't seemed to occur to Massin, or if it had he was ignoring it. She had inherited her father's pragmatic attitude, and it was allied with an ability to assess a situation quickly and step in before things got out of control.

'Wait a moment,' interjected Monteo, no doubt sensing the subject getting away from him. 'I can't authorise you placing a woman officer in… well, in danger. What would they say in the Ministry?'

'What could they say?' Rocco countered. 'They're happy to put women in uniform and give them a gun. They even train them to shoot. Or is it just for show?'

Monteo looked conflicted, and Rocco wondered whether it was the idea of taking the news back to the Ministry that worried him more or the potential threat to a woman officer.

'I agree. She would be eminently suitable. She's done good work in the past.' It was Massin, surprising Rocco and Claude. 'I'll get Captain Canet to brief her and issue her with suitable equipment.'

'Like what?' said Monteo, fighting a rearguard action.

'A rifle,' said Rocco, 'would be useful.'

'She's not going to fight a battle, for heaven's sake!'

Rocco nodded towards the fields and distant trees. 'If any threat does come, it won't come knocking on the front door like a carpet salesman. It'll be from out there. If they see a cop with a rifle, they might think twice about coming too close. It's called visible prevention.'

The Ministry man said nothing, giving in in the face of logic.

'All the same,' Rocco continued, eyeing Claude with a faint smile, 'she might need some practice while she's here.'

Claude grinned. 'No problem. I'll set up a few targets for her and she can blow holes in the countryside. Should be fun.'

'It's not meant to be fun!' Monteo snapped. 'This is serious.'

Massin sighed and said, 'I think they're teasing you, Gerard.' He gave Rocco a look of reproach. 'Let's get inside and talk to Mr Bouanga, shall we? I'm sure he'll be relieved to see we're taking this matter seriously. Rocco, I know you're busy here, but I'll see you back in the office. I'm sure Lamotte can take over guard duties by himself for a short while.' With that, he turned towards the house and knocked sharply on the front door.

'That's going to be interesting,' Claude murmured.

'Depends what you're referring to. Those two meeting Bouanga and company or my next meeting with Massin?'

'Neither. I was thinking about having volunteered Alix to help out here.'

'Why? She should be happy enough.'

'She's not going to like it; she wants to be in the centre of things, you see. She's a born organiser and right now she's busy helping out with preparations for the local section of the Tour de France.' He looked at Rocco. 'Will you tell her or shall I?'

Rocco left Claude worrying about who was going to break the bad news to Alix, and drove out of the gate. He stopped on the side of the road and walked into the bushes where he thought he had seen the light last night. The ground here was hard, baked by the sun, and if a vehicle or human had passed this way, they had left no discernible trace. He returned to the car and drove to Amiens. If Massin wanted to see him he might as well be prepared. There had been no indication of what he wanted to talk about, but it was probably going to involve covering his back as usual, and making sure Rocco followed orders to the letter.

He left his car in a space near the station and walked round to the Café Schubert where most of the police took their breaks. It was changeover of shifts and the café was busy. He shouldered his way to the bar and ordered a large coffee, exchanging nods and handshakes with fellow detectives and uniformed officers, before heading for a table near the window, away from the crush.

'Hey – Rocco,' a man in a scruffy suit and ragged tie called to him as he passed by. Émile Anselin was a detective nearing retirement. 'I hear you're babysitting some runaway politician from Gabon – is that right? Nice work if you can get it.'

Rocco didn't bother denying it. Rizzotti had said it was all over the station, but it didn't help having idiots like Anselin shouting it out for all to hear. 'That's right, Émile,' he said with pointed sarcasm. 'Just don't go telling anyone, OK? It's our secret.' He moved away before the man could stretch out the conversation, leaving a few colleagues shaking their heads in sympathy at Anselin's lack of tact.

Schubert, the café owner, brought Rocco's coffee and thumbed the air over his shoulder. 'Rocco? Telephone call. On the wall at the back.'

Rocco was surprised anyone knew he was here. Somebody in the station, perhaps, tracking through all the likely places he might be. He went through to the passage at the rear of the café and found the handset balanced on a shelf. He picked it up. 'Rocco speaking.' He waited but heard only silence. 'Hello?' Nothing. Just the crackle of static down the line.

He replaced the handset and caught Schubert's eye, and raised his hands in query. Schubert looked nonplussed, then gave a shrug before turning back to his work.

When Rocco got back to his table, he found a young woman sitting in the chair opposite, sipping from a glass of water. She was smartly dressed, with short blonde hair and grey eyes, and looked momentarily guilty as if realising she had intruded on someone's space.

'Sorry,' she said quickly, 'I hope you don't mind, but I needed to escape from the crowd.' She nodded towards a crush of new arrivals coming through the door and bellying up to the bar, replacing others on their way out. Most were casting furtive or not-so-furtive glances her way, as if she were a rare species in their world.

'It's not a problem,' said Rocco, sitting down and picking up his coffee. Many cops lacked subtlety when sensing outsiders. It was even worse when those outsiders were attractive single women. 'You picked a bad time to come in here; it's a changeover of shifts at the local station. It can get a bit intense in here, I'm afraid.'

Her eyes widened. 'Oh, are you a policeman, too, then?'

Her gaze was disconcerting in an odd way, almost intimate in its focus, and he nodded, wondering who she was. 'I take it you're not a local.'

'Me, no. I'm just passing through. Did I hear that man call you Rocco? That's an Italian name, isn't it?'

'If so, it's way back in my past. On your way to where?'

But she didn't reply. Instead she finished her water and glanced towards the door again. 'I'd better be going. It's getting busier in here. It was nice meeting you, Inspector Rocco. Thanks for allowing me to share your table.' She held out her hand and he shook it. It felt cool and firm, with the faintest squeeze of her fingers. With that she stood up and was gone, sliding with graceful ease through the crowd and out into the street.

As she disappeared, Rocco felt a momentary sense of puzzlement. It took a few moments as he replayed the conversation before he realised why. She'd called him inspector. How had she known that? Guesswork because he was in plain clothes, perhaps?

Before he could think about it further, a figure stepped up to the table. It was Jouanne, the young officer he'd spoken to a few days ago. He was now in plain clothes and holding a glass of beer, clearly having clocked off duty.

'I see she found you then,' Jouanne said. He had the same knowing smile playing around his mouth that Rocco had noticed before, and seemed to be enjoying the implied familiarity between them.

'What are you talking about?' Rocco finished his coffee and stood up. This place had suddenly got too crowded and there was something about this young officer's over-friendly attitude that got under his skin.

'The woman who was asking for you... the one I told you about?' Jouanne gestured towards the door with his glass. 'You were just talking to her.'

Eighteen

Marc Casparon was thinking about Rocco's call and the best way to acquire the information he was after. Since quitting the job he'd broken off all contact with the underworld figures he'd known, as much for Lucille's peace of mind as his own. The sooner he left that world behind, the better he would feel. Most of his past contacts had operated on the fringes of direct criminal activity. He'd relied on them for snippets of information, even paid them money when needed, but he could hardly call them friends or even trustworthy. Like their fortunes, their loyalties were shallow and fluctuated like the weather.

But there was one man he could approach in absolute confidence. It would come at a price, but that was the free enterprise of the streets; you got only what you paid for. Jean-Luc Madou was the owner of a bar in the Belleville area which was a known haunt used by some of the people around Farek. Madou had let it be known a while back that he was looking to relocate out of the city to safer climes and a slower pace of life, and any piece of income he could generate would help him do that before he got too old.

Caspar finished washing and checked his face in the mirror. The man staring back was less gaunt than he had been, the skin still dark and the close-cropped hair peppered with grey. But even he could see that his eyes had lost the haunted look Lucille had pointed out when they first met. He shrugged on his jacket and left the apartment, and hoped Madou would come up with the information he needed.

He made his way to a side street off Rue de Belleville on the edge of the 19th and 20th arrondissements. It wasn't Farek's home turf, but run by a smaller gang which lacked the muscle to take on Farek's more powerful group, and allowed them to come and go with the minimum of fuss. Caspar knew that using an outside territory was a deliberate policy of the Algerian gangster to filter out any strangers showing an interest in him.

The place he was looking for was the unimaginatively named Bar Madou, sandwiched between a dry-cleaning business and a Vietnamese restaurant. Both these businesses were owned by Farek, part of his growing empire spreading across Paris and run by nominal owners who were happy to play the part in exchange for a stake of the income. All three addresses were served from a narrow cut-through at the rear, giving Farek and his people a way out if the café were ever raided.

Jean-Luc Madou was behind the bar as usual. He scowled when he saw Caspar, his eyes flicking both ways to check who was in before relaxing and giving Caspar a barely perceptible nod which meant it was safe to approach. Safe for Madou, that was.

Caspar checked the room, which was a seedy yellow, courtesy of decades of heavy smokers and little effort in the way of decoration. It was standard for this kind of business, with a football machine, a small jukebox and customer-proof furniture, and a smell of stale beer and coffee. He counted five customers, none of whom he knew. Three old men were obvious barflies, grouped together in ageing solidarity, and the couple in one corner looked like tourists, hunched over drinks while experiencing a taste of the neighbourhood low life to take back home with them to tell their friends and families. He hoped for their own sakes that they left soon and went somewhere more salubrious; hanging around here too long would make them easy targets for the neighbourhood con artists and panhandlers.

Madou leaned across as Caspar climbed onto a stool, and whispered, 'You're joking, aren't you, coming in here? You'll get my throat cut. Anyway, I thought you'd left the cop life behind. What's happened – are you bored?'

'I love you, too, Jean-Luc. And this is a private matter, so nothing to do with the cops. Anyway, I figured you'd skip out the back if I called first.'

'Right, so you've come here to insult me, have you?'

'Don't worry, it won't take long and I'll be gone.'

'You'd better. There's a lot of trouble brewing and I've been getting some odd looks ever since I put this place up for sale.'

'Really? How's that going?'

Madou shrugged. 'Not so good. I've had one or two people show an interest, but the offers were rubbish.' He poured a cognac and slid it across the counter. 'As long as there's a fee involved, that one's on the house.'

Caspar took a sip. The premises may have been careworn and in need of a decent paint job, but Madou had always carried a decent line in spirits. 'If I get the information I need, you'll get paid, don't worry.'

Madou moved along the bar to wipe some beer foam off one of the pumps, a signal for Caspar to follow. He did so and decided to get straight down to business. Madou was evidently unsettled, and a frightened man was only good for a short while before he would say anything to get a guy like Caspar off his back.

'Farek,' Caspar said shortly. 'Who's he using for the heavy stuff?'

Madou looked surprised. 'Christ, you don't want much, do you? Ask me who's moving stolen goods or who's putting a bank team together… that I could tell you.' He hesitated. 'How heavy, exactly?'

'A contract.'

Madou pushed his cheeks out and looked around the bar before answering. 'There's a couple of men he keeps around for heavy work, although I don't think they've done anything like what you're talking about – at least not up this way.'

'Borelli and Abdhoun from down south; I know about them. Anyone else?'

Madou didn't answer immediately. Caspar could see his brain working hard, no doubt filtering through the names of those he could finger and those he should leave well alone.

'Is this to do with a cop?' he asked finally.

'It might be.'

Madou leaned closer, bringing a strong smell of fried onions and neck sweat. 'I hear Farek had a thing about some police captain called Raballe, used to work out of Cambrai. They crossed paths a couple of years ago and Farek always swore he'd take him down. The word around the bars is that Raballe got hit recently. Is that right?'

Caspar nodded. 'Correct. But he's not the only cop Farek has it in for.'

Madou sighed like a leaking balloon and his eyes flickered with nervousness. 'Give me strength – you're not talking about Rocco, are you?' When he didn't get an answer, he nodded. 'It has to be. Raballe was a minor sore to Farek, but Rocco… now there was a major grudge. You know why, right? He did for Farek's brother, Sami.'

'Not true. That wasn't Rocco; it was one of the other gangs looking to take advantage.'

'Who cares? Farek doesn't. As far as he's concerned, Rocco was responsible and he's had a big target on his back from the moment Sami went down.' Madou breathed heavily and stood back as two men walked in.

Caspar watched them in the mirror on the back wall. They looked like Algerians, and he ducked his head into his brandy. He didn't recognise them but the atmosphere in here might suddenly get a little unfriendly if they were Farek's men. However, they barely gave Caspar a glance and called for beers, and Madou went away to serve them. There was no exchange of money, and the two men moved away to sit in the corner. When Madou came back he was looking wary.

'Two of Farek's new guys, just up from the south. Hustlers, the pair of them. The word is he's been recruiting ready to stage a big takeover. Most of them are from Oran in Algeria; men he knows he can trust.'

'Is that what all the chatter's about?'

'Not entirely. Some guys have been lifted and it's thought a snitch with inside information is feeding names to the cops. It's made everyone jumpy.'

'Including you?' Caspar hadn't seen Madou this spiky in a long time. The bar owner was usually laid back, happy to keep his own counsel and stay out of business that didn't concern him. Right now, though, the stress was coming off him in waves.

'Damn right, me too. I've already had a few pointed questions and I think somebody's tried to finger me as a source.'

'And?'

'So far nothing. Just questions from guys connected to Farek, like I say, pointed, as if they were trying to spook me. Farek himself was in here a couple of days ago, in fact, and acted fine. He doesn't do that if he suspects someone's been talking out of turn.' He hesitated, looking around the bar.

'Out with it, Jean-Luc,' Caspar murmured. 'I haven't got all day.'

'Farek's taking a hard line on anyone he suspects might be talking to the cops. Two of his guys, low-level operators he used for muscle work, have already disappeared because of suspicions about them circulating on the street. I think it was bullshit but that's how bad things are.'

Paranoia, thought Caspar. A common disease among the criminal classes – at least those with any kind of imagination. It couldn't happen to nicer people.

'Are we done?' Madou was eyeing the two Algerians. 'Those two will do or say anything if they think it will get them in good with the boss. They don't know you or me from the Pope's cousin, but that won't stop them trying to score a point or two through hearsay.'

'I get it. One more question. I knew about the two you mentioned. Would Farek use them for Rocco or do it himself?'

Madou pulled a face. 'You think Lakhdar would risk taking on that big ape? Not a chance. He might have the ambition but I doubt he's got the balls, no matter how loud he talks. He'll call in someone from outside.'

'Like who?'

Madou hesitated, then said, 'I heard a whisper a couple of days ago that he'd got someone on a retainer, but there's no word on who. A stranger, I heard: a new face. Expensive and very skilled. He won't hang about, though; he'll do the job and get shipped out again immediately. It's the way the pros work: in and out and don't come back. The good ones, anyway.'

'Might it be this new person who took down Raballe?'

'No idea. It could be, I suppose, a sort of dry run for the bigger event. It might even have been Borelli. He's been looking to prove himself up here, get a reputation in the gangs while he's young enough and able to hold his own against the opposition.'

'Why not Abdhoun?'

'Because Borelli wouldn't have stood out in Cambrai, not like Abdhoun.' He grinned, showing a line of tobacco-stained teeth. 'Not many Arabs in Cambrai, so I'm told. I've never been there, so I wouldn't know.'

Caspar didn't bother telling him that Raballe had moved, and had been killed in Dieppe, not Cambrai. It wouldn't have mattered to the bar owner, anyway. What was done was done and it merely proved that Farek's reach was as long as he needed it to be.

'So this new person. Come on,' he insisted, 'I need something.'

'How much?'

Caspar slid his hand across the counter and pushed a fold of notes under a bar towel, where it sat in a puddle of beer. 'A name and a description. Anything you can get. There's a number on the top note. Make it quick, though, because I get the feeling time's running out.'

'Okay, keep your shirt on. I'll call you. Same number?'

'No. I've moved on, too. You won't find it listed anywhere, so don't look.'

Madou nodded, folding the paper into his shirt pocket, followed by the notes. As he did so the door opened and a man stepped inside the café. He was short and stocky, with a bald head. He wasn't looking towards the bar, but had turned to look at a newspaper on a nearby table.

'Christ, no.' Madou hissed. 'It's Achay. Out back, quick.' He made a sharp motion with his head. 'Down the corridor and turn left.' He snatched up Caspar's glass and placed it out of sight beneath the bar, then moved away, scrubbing at the counter with his cloth and making conversation with one of the other customers.

Caspar didn't need telling twice. He turned and walked out, following the corridor and turning left to the rear door. Seconds later he was in a back alley and walking away.

Caspar made his way across the city to Rue Victor Méric, an itchy feeling on the back of his neck. Something about the newcomer to the café had been vaguely familiar, but he hadn't seen his face clearly enough to recognise him. Madou, though, had been seriously spooked, and that meant the man was someone important in the Farek hierarchy, possibly a new face since Caspar's time in the force. He had to switch streets and double back a couple of times and walk through a department store to the rear exit before he began to feel sure that he wasn't being followed.

The area around Rue Victor Méric was familiar because he'd worked it on and off over the years. He was surprised that a low-grade crim like JoJo Vieira had elevated himself to shopping here, and could only assume that he'd been scouting out a possible target for thievery and had happened to see a jacket he liked. The fact that he'd bought it instead of stealing it was a new one, but maybe he'd got cash from a recent informant-fund payout burning a hole in his pocket.

The shop was narrow-fronted, with a single window showing a faceless mannequin in a smart suit, and a selection of shirts, ties and accessories, such as braces and belts. The name L'Homme was curled across the fascia in green-and-gold script, with the name of the owner, H. Aprahamian on a small plaque above the door. The window glass was clean and the doorway swept clear of leaves and dust.

He pushed open the door and was greeted by an elderly man behind the counter, busy pinning the sleeve of a dark blazer. He was thin and stooped, with a wisp of hair over each ear and thick spectacles perched on the end of his nose. The interior of the shop was narrow and long, with an array of drawers and hangers taking up all the available wall space.

'Monsieur Aprahamian?'

'Yes,' the shop owner stopped what he was doing. 'Are you the police?'

Caspar was surprised. With his years working undercover and having to assume personas that reflected the milieu he was moving in, he'd become accustomed to being mistaken for someone on the opposing end of the scales from the police. He wondered if retirement from that world was beginning to soften his appearance in ways he hadn't thought. 'Do I look like a cop?'

'It was just a guess.' The man smiled. 'How may I help you?'

Caspar explained why he was there, and slid a piece of paper across the counter. It bore the invoice number Rocco had given him and the name J. Vieira.

Aprahamian nodded. 'I remember the jacket, certainly. It was a special order which was never collected, so I was forced to put it in the window. It was an excellent garment and was only there for one day before a customer came in and said he wanted it. He did not seem concerned with the price, either.'

'Can you remember anything about him?'

'Most certainly. He was not my usual kind of customer because he seemed ill at ease in my shop. To be honest, his clothes were very cheap and not at all well made, and I was a little suspicious – perhaps unfairly so. However, he had cash and seemed keen to spend it, so I obliged.' He shrugged and gave a wry smile. 'We all have to make a living, do we not?'

'I don't suppose you have an address, if he was a cash customer?' It was a long shot but worth trying.

Aprahamian barely hesitated. 'Actually, I do. Normally, of course, for a cash sale I wouldn't. But he tried it on and asked me to take the sleeves up. To be honest the jacket was a little too big for him, but he insisted, so I worked on it overnight. I offered to deliver it and he agreed and gave me his address, but then changed his mind and said he'd come and collect it.' He gave a faint smile. 'He paid up front, too, which I requested, and came back the following day.' He turned and picked up an order book, leafing through the pages until he found what he was looking for. 'Ah, yes. Here it is. Not too far from here.' He read out an address in Saint Ouen and Caspar made a note. He knew the street, in a ratty area close to the river that had long been marked out for redevelopment but always seemed to miss the call. Just the sort of place somebody like Vieira would call home.

'Is he in prison?' Aprahamian asked.

'No. He's dead.'

'Oh. Then I am sorry for his family.'

Caspar desperately wanted to visit the St Ouen address and get whatever information he could. But he needed to get out to Orly first; he'd already spent longer on this than he'd expected, and would have to deal with it later. If he turned up late for the security review, he'd probably find they'd called in somebody else.

Nineteen

'Are we all set up to go?' Lilou sounded nervous, her voice tight. It was a common reaction when they were ready to do a job, like winding up a clockwork toy. But once they made their first move she would settle into a state of cool control, her mind entirely focussed on what they had to do.

Romain nodded and checked their surroundings. They were in the Citroën van, parked in a quiet side street of small warehouses and lock-ups in the eastern part of Amiens. Other commercial vehicles around them provided useful cover, making theirs just one van among several. Anybody chancing on them would make the obvious assumption: that they were discreet lovers after a little privacy.

The engine ticked and clicked as it cooled down, the only background noise to intrude on their thoughts. Lilou had driven them out to the house for a quick look, then back again to prepare for the next part of the plan. Romain had made the call to Farek earlier, and had just been to a nearby café and called again to confirm the arrangements.

'All set,' he said. 'Farek found four guys, all Congolese illegals. It means they'll do anything to earn some quick cash and ask no questions. They're on their way from Paris right now.'

'What if they recognise Bouanga? He's a public figure – or was. Isn't Congo right next to Gabon? They might balk at lifting him once they see who he is.'

'You think? I wouldn't worry about it. They'll do the job, that's all we need.'

'But I do worry. It's the unplanned events that can screw with our plans, you know that.'

'Lilou, I doubt these people would even recognise their own mothers. They're here without papers, jobs or money. They don't care a *sou* about who their target is. They're cheap thugs looking to earn enough cash to get high then move on.' He sniffed with contempt. 'Cheap and disposable.'

'Can we rely on them to do the job properly, though?'

Romain shrugged. 'Probably not, but they're all we've got. If they foul it up we can always blame Farek; he picked them. They've had their instructions. They go in at midnight and anyone who gets in their way is history. Once they've grabbed Bouanga, they get out and make for the rendezvous. In any case it doesn't matter if they do screw up, they're only there to cause a diversion so we can get to Rocco. What's the worst they can do? We'll be busy doing our job.'

'I suppose.' She gave a faint smile and leaned towards him, breathing against his cheek and humming with pleasure. It was a sign that she was feeling good about the plan, in spite of her concerns. 'It was a good idea to do it this way. Anything that makes our job easier means we can collect the rest of our fee and be gone. Like the man near Dieppe. That was easy money.'

He smiled at her. 'You said the same about Vieira. Getting a little arrogant, aren't we?'

She made a moue at him, her lipstick shiny. 'No. Just saying, that's all. I reckon this Rocco, big as he is, will be just as easy. I have faith in us. In you, especially, my big boy.' She kissed him and laughed, but it was a sound still edged with a brittle quality.

He patted her leg in reassurance, aware that the light-hearted veil was a thin cover for how tightly-strung she was feeling. Up and down like a fairground ride was how he'd once thought of her; up was good but down was wildly unpredictable. Her moods could vary in a moment from joyful and coquettish, to total detachment and frostiness, when even his easy humour would fail to reach her. He had come to recognise which phase was dominant in spite of the outward signs. But to focus too much on it would push things too far and prove disastrous. Like prodding a hornets' nest: if you didn't have to, better to leave things well alone.

Like now, for example. He knew she'd get better as the time to make a move came closer. It was always the same. He had his job and she had hers, and each dealt with the waiting in their own way. Once they set their plan in motion tonight, it would be like a well-oiled machine.

And Rocco would be history.

Twenty

Rocco walked to the station from the café, his mind on what Officer Jouanne had told him about the woman. If she had really asked after him before, why had she not said something when she had found out his name? Nerves, perhaps, on being faced with a policeman in a café full of other cops. On the other hand, she hadn't seemed the nervous type, so what was going on?

He shook it off and made his way upstairs. He had more important things to consider just now, such as what awaited him in Massin's office. He knocked on the door and entered to find a meeting in progress between Massin, Monteo, Deputy-Commissioner Perronnet and Captain Eric Canet, who waved a friendly hand and nudged a chair out with his foot.

'Ah, Rocco,' Monteo said forcefully, as if grasping at a reason to change a sticky topic of conversation. 'Just in time. Sorry to drag you away from your duties. We were talking about this *Gardienne* Poulon who was mentioned earlier. There are some reservations about her being suitable for the Bouanga task. Perhaps you could settle our concerns?'

An air of tension in the room struck Rocco immediately. In contrast to Monteo's suddenly genial and chatty demeanour, the three officers were looking unimpressed. Whatever the discussion had covered so far, it was clearly not going too well.

'What do you want to know?' he said, and sat down.

'Perhaps I might interject here,' said Canet, glancing at Rocco. 'I was about to ask Mr Monteo what was so special about this Mr Bouanga. If I'm expected to take one of my junior personnel away from an important task like the Tour policing and place her in a potentially dangerous situation as a protection officer for a foreign guest, I'd like to think it's worth the risk.' He looked at Monteo, undaunted by the Ministry man's position. 'And from what little you've said so far, he's no longer a minister and not even welcome back in Gabon. So why the special treatment?'

Surprisingly, neither Massin nor Perronnet, the two senior men, offered a comment. Instead, they looked to Monteo for a response.

Monteo scowled at the lack of support, but as they were all looking at him, he couldn't back down without losing face.

'Yes, well. That's a fair question, Captain Canet. Very fair. It's a matter of our responsibilities when looking to the future. Gabon is, it's fair to say, unsettled at the moment, with many contenders ready to assume power if a gap offers itself. That by itself does not create harmony. Quite the opposite, of course. We're actively pursuing talks with the current government, because we have a duty to ensure that the situation remains as stable as possible during the current crisis. But just because a minister – a former minister – has been elbowed out, it doesn't mean that situation will always be so. Mr Bouanga has been a friend of France going back many years, and it's felt in the current climate of international relations, especially with a former colonial partner, that we should not abandon our friends in their hour of need.'

'You mean,' said Massin smoothly, 'he could be back in power at some future date.'

Monteo looked relieved and smiled gratefully for the clean exit from the questioning. 'Precisely, François. As I said earlier, it's simply keeping an eye to the future. It's a fact, of course, that his family in Gabon is highly placed and very influential, in spite of his own unfortunate displacement.' He glanced at Canet. 'Does that explain the situation?'

Canet looked dubious and clamped his jaw shut. He clearly wasn't convinced by the meaningless non-answer but was outgunned by what amounted to an argument he couldn't win. Rocco sympathised. Canet had always been the most welcoming officer here, and had helped Rocco in his early days of being posted to Amiens. Now it was time to return the favour.

'So,' he said carefully, 'it's got nothing to do with Gabon being mineral rich, then, and Bouanga being the Development Minister? Or the fact that everybody and his dog is talking about Bouanga and his presence just down the road from this office?'

The silence which followed was loaded with tension as they digested the statement, and Monteo's mouth opened in surprise. But he recovered quickly by going on the attack. 'I didn't say what his job was, Inspector.'

'No, you didn't. But I was curious, so I rang a friend in Paris.'

Monteo looked ruffled for a few moments, as if it hadn't occurred to him that a simple cop might think to check on the details he'd been given. He said, 'Without question there is a trade element involved, too, quite apart from the personal one of helping a friend of France.'

'What sort of trade?' This came from Perronnet, his gaunt features pointed at the Ministry man like a gun. Rocco had never got to know the man well, but he had heard that Perronnet had a strong moral streak and believed in everything being done by the book. Perhaps using a trade argument to explain providing local officers for the protection of a displaced foreign government minister was something that did not sit right with him.

'Well, it's true, as Rocco points out, that Gabon is rich in minerals.'

'Such as?'

'Um… diamonds, oil – and others.'

'Not to mention gold and iron ore, I believe.' This time it was Massin who chimed in. 'All of which would offer valuable trading rights if we were to protect the right people. Isn't that the way it works?'

'Yes. Quite so.' Monteo dried up, lost for words in the face of their obvious doubts. 'Thank you, François.'

Rocco wanted to smile at the way they had all come together. It probably wouldn't last once Monteo got back to the Ministry, when there would undoubtedly be a few pointed memos coming back this way in retaliation just to show who was boss. However, that was for Massin to deal with. He just hoped the *commissaire*, who was notoriously shy of upsetting his superiors in Paris, didn't suffer a change of heart once the meeting broke up.

'Fair enough.' Canet spoke up after a lengthy pause. 'I'd better brief *Gardienne* Poulon on her new assignment and get her kitted out. Rocco, perhaps you would be kind enough to assist, since you'll be in charge?'

Rocco got to his feet to follow Canet from the room. He didn't need to be asked twice. Anything to get out of here and back to work. If the others chose to continue their discussions, that was up to them.

'Just a moment.' It was Massin, holding up a hand. 'In view of

Rocco's comment about the news having got out about Bouanga, which I can confirm, I think we need whoever's on guard duty to be as fresh as possible. Rocco and Lamotte have already been up there since yesterday, so I propose assigning two officers with guard duty experience to cover the house with immediate effect until tomorrow morning, while Rocco and Lamotte get some rest and *Gardienne* Poulon is brought up to speed on what she needs to do.' He looked at Rocco. 'I've spoken to the Arras office and they can loan us two men at very short notice. They can't take them off duties for any longer than that, so you'll have to manage as best you can.'

'Good idea.' Monteo jumped in. 'Two men should suffice. It's a short-term measure but better than nothing and, as you say, François, it will give Rocco and his colleagues time to rest up and prepare for a longer stint.'

Massin reached for his phone. 'I'll get them in place. They should be there within the hour.' He paused and looked around the room. 'It would be wise to keep this to ourselves, you understand? If it gets out that we've drafted in officers from another station, the press will wonder why and begin making mountains out of molehills.'

'Problem solved, then,' said Perronnet, although the look on his face showed puzzlement at this sudden change of tack.

Rocco wasn't won over by the show of concern for himself and Claude. This was a spreading of the load to cover their backs in case things went disastrously wrong. Monteo, he suspected, was making all the right moves entirely for his own reasons, and couldn't care less about anyone else as long as he'd done everything he was expected to do and was able to make out a convincing report to that effect. Massin was making sure his men didn't fall asleep on the job and cover his own face with egg in the process.

'Did you believe any of that?' Canet said quietly, as they went back downstairs to find Alix. 'What are we doing? Two more men being yanked off duties and assigned to look after Bouanga. From what I heard, he's got a nasty reputation for making his enemies disappear – and we've got the job of protecting him? It doesn't make sense.'

'I'm not surprised,' said Rocco. 'Trade wins out every time. Bouanga could have been the most ruthless man on the planet, but if there's a minerals deal up for grabs, they'll fall over backwards to do whatever it takes to keep in with the powers-that-be.'

Canet shook his head in disgust. 'I'm sure you're right. I'll be surprised if Bouanga goes back there any time soon, though. His seat in government will have been filled already if the history of that country is any guide.'

'But in the meantime?'

'We've got to keep him safe just in case it goes the other way. Makes you glad you joined the police, doesn't it?' He grunted and clapped Rocco on the shoulder. 'Thanks for your help in there. I didn't actually mean you had to come and help me brief Poulon, by the way. You looked like you needed to escape, too. You'd better do as the boss says and go get some sleep.'

By the time Rocco had cleared his desk and driven to Les Sables, he found the two uniformed officers from Arras already in position and patrolling the grounds. Claude was in the kitchen where Excelsiore was pouring him a large cup of green tea. Delicat was nowhere to be seen.

'I gather we're off duty until tomorrow,' said Claude, stirring sugar into his tea, 'so I let the lads get on with it. Suits me – I could do with a few hours extra sleep. How did it go with Alix?'

'No idea. Captain Canet's dealing with it.'

Claude looked glum at the news. 'Ah. I suppose I'll find out when she gets home. She'll probably kill me while I sleep and bury me in the back garden.' He finished his tea and thanked Excelsiore, then picked up his shotgun and went out to his car.

Rocco went in search of Bouanga. Before going home he wanted to make sure the former minister understood what was happening with the two new officers sent to look after him. He found the minister in the conservatory overlooking the rear grounds. He was going through some papers, and Rocco wondered if the man was fooling himself about the possibility of his ever going back to his old position in Gabon.

'Inspector. What can I do for you? I see there are two new men outside. Does this mean the Interior Ministry has recognised my need for more protection?'

'Sorry, Mr Bouanga, but no. They're here while Lamotte and I get some rest and another officer arrives tomorrow morning. From then on, though, we'll be here all the time.' He didn't hazard an opinion as to how long that would last, and instead hesitated long enough to give Bouanga a chance to complain, but the man stayed silent. 'It seems news of your presence in the area has got out,' he continued, 'although possibly not where you're currently staying. But I think it's safe to assume that sooner or later the press will find out and start to ask questions. Once that happens it won't take long for them to fasten on this place. If there is a threat, it will probably come shortly afterwards, before you can move on.'

'I see.' Surprisingly, Bouanga seemed relatively calm. 'That makes sense. What is your advice, Inspector?'

'Take appropriate precautions. Don't answer the door without checking who the caller is, don't wander around outside and don't let anyone inside unless you know who they are and trust them not to kill you. And that includes any of your fellow countrymen who might decide to turn up unexpectedly for afternoon tea.'

Bouanga nodded. 'You don't exactly coat your words in honey, do you, Inspector?'

'I don't see the point.'

'I like that. Too often I hear only what people wish me to hear, never the plain truth. I will make sure Delicat and his wife know, too.' With that he went back to his papers.

Rocco left the house and stopped to instruct the officers to be on constant lookout, then headed for home. With the prospect of sleep, he was suddenly feeling very tired.

Twenty-one

JoJo Vieira's home in St Ouen was even worse than Caspar had imagined. The street was little more than a narrow, cobbled dead end of crumbling houses with sagging roofs, empty windows and an air of something far worse than neglect. The atmosphere suggested that whatever life or hope may have once been here, it had been abandoned long ago, gradually wilting and dying.

Number twelve, he noted, at least had a front door, unlike some of its neighbours, and the step had been swept recently, with a glint of water showing where the accumulation of city dust had been washed away. The windows, too, looked clean. He knocked on the door and it flew open to reveal a woman in her thirties, with the faded look of someone trying hard against prevailing odds to get through life day by day. It was a look Caspar was familiar with, one he'd seen often on family members of those involved with crime. She was dressed in a skirt and a faded man's shirt, spotted with dust and the remains of what might have been a child's breakfast cereal.

'JoJo?' Her voice was faint, barely under control. 'Are you here about JoJo?'

Caspar showed her his business card to show he wasn't a threat, although he wasn't sure she could take it in. He stepped back a pace to give her more room and said, 'I'm afraid I am, Madame. May I come in and talk? Or I can stay out here if you prefer. It's up to you.'

She shivered and clutched her arms together, even though the sun was warm, and he wondered if she had a fever. It wouldn't be surprising in this rotting dump of a place, even in mid-summer. Then she seemed to make a decision and turned to allow him inside.

The interior was a transformation. The front door opened directly into a living room, with a sofa, armchair and a small table, all heavily worn but clean. A number of ornaments were dotted about the place, mostly small china pieces full of colour, as if their vivid contribution might somehow help combat the dilapidated air of the building and the area outside.

The woman gestured to the armchair and he sat down. She took a hard chair next to the table, and clasped her hands between her knees as if to stop them shaking. Strictly speaking this wasn't what Rocco had asked him to do, but Caspar was playing it by ear, which was pretty much what he'd done all his working life as a cop. Sometimes you had to follow your gut feeling, and his every instinct told him that coming here might help Rocco solve the question of why Vieira had been killed so far from home.

'Can I ask your name, please?' he said. 'And your relationship with JoJo Vieira.'

'Miriam,' she replied. 'Miriam Constantinou. JoJo's my brother. He's dead, isn't he?' The blunt question came out in a rush, the words tumbling over one another as if she wanted to get them out before she lost the ability to speak altogether.

'Before I confirm that, can you tell me whether he wore a tattoo?' She gasped, her hand flying to her mouth. 'Yes. A Chinese character, on his left shoulder, at the back. He said it was the symbol for good luck.'

'Then I regret to say that it looks as if JoJo is dead. I'm sorry.' Over the years Caspar had developed a dislike of fellow officers and officials trying to soften the blow of bad news by prevarication, when it was obvious that it was all they had to offer the family. In his experience, most people wanted to hear the news, good or bad, and deal with it the best way they could.

Surprisingly Miriam didn't react other than to look at the floor and nod a few times. 'I knew it. I just knew it wasn't going to end well. JoJo was… he was such a fool with those people.'

'People?'

'He was always trying to make a big score, mostly doing stupid jobs for crooks and thieves who laughed at him behind his back. I kept on at him to stop dealing with them, but it was all he knew. He never had a proper job in his life, just existing on the edges of the gangs and picking up odd jobs and doing a few of his own.'

'What kind of jobs?' Caspar didn't really need to ask, but she seemed to want to talk and he was happy to encourage her. He knew perfectly well that criminals like Vieira rarely worked at anything regular that would earn a steady income. Instead they preferred to perform a string of fetch-and-carry jobs for any criminal who asked, doing the odd break-in or con job of their own to keep their heads – and pride – above water.

'All sorts. Anything that would earn a few francs. But he drank more than he earned and started gambling and getting into debt all over the place. In the end he got kicked out of the place he shared with some other layabouts and couldn't afford to rent a place of his own, so we let him have a room here at the back. It wasn't much but it was better than the street. He was all right for a while, like his old self years ago. He even said he'd paid off some of his debts.'

'Did he say how he'd done that?' Caspar could make a wild guess; it was either through theft or being paid as an informant. But he wanted to hear it from her.

'I asked him that but he wouldn't tell me and got very defensive. I knew he had to be doing stuff – illegal stuff – and then he began acting strangely.'

'Was this just recently?'

'A few months ago. My husband Nico wanted him to move out in case he brought his problems back here, but I argued against it. I didn't mind having him here – not that he was in most of the time. Next thing we knew he said he'd been mugged in the street. He came in covered in bruises, and it was obvious he'd been deliberately beaten up.'

'Who by, did he say?'

'No. If he knew he wasn't saying. He said he'd done a foolish thing to earn some money. He wouldn't say what it was, but I knew he must have been talking to the police; it's the only thing I can think of. The beating was a warning, but that was just the start. In the end it was only going to end one way. He was terrified after that and said he had to get away from here because bad people were going to hurt him… and possibly hurt us. Nico and I have a small boy, Sasha, and that was it as far as Nico was concerned: JoJo had to go.'

'Did your husband know what JoJo had been doing – the police thing, I mean?'

'Yes. I think he'd heard people talking about it and pointing the finger. He said JoJo was a fool and was going to get us all killed. So he lent him his motorbike to get out of Paris, then went to see somebody to try and get them off our backs. I tried to stop him and said it would only make things worse, but he wouldn't listen.' She hesitated. 'I don't blame Nico. When he came back I could see he'd been hurt. I think they forced him to say where JoJo was going.'

So that was how they'd managed to get on to JoJo's trail so quickly, Caspar thought. After that it wouldn't have taken much for somebody to have worked out his probable route and to follow him. Unfortunately, JoJo had stopped along the way for some reason, which allowed the killer to catch him off-guard.

'But why head north? Did he know somebody up there?'

Miriam nodded. 'While Nico was taking Sasha to school one day, JoJo told me that he was on his way to see a policeman who would protect him, and that he had information the policeman would be willing to trade.'

'Trade for what?'

'His safety. But it wasn't just for him. He said the policeman also had a price on his head and JoJo knew things that would help them both.'

'Did he say what they were?'

She hesitated for a few seconds, as if wondering where this was going to end, and whether to trust him or not. 'He said he knew things, serious things, about a man named Farek.' Her voice dropped to a whisper on the final word, as if fearful that she might be overheard.

'Lakhdar Farek?'

'Yes. He said it was information that would put Farek away for a very long time, and because of this the policeman would make everything all right.' She looked up at Caspar and he saw tears in her eyes, the emotion finally welling over. 'He said Farek had put a contract out on this policeman. Is that what they call it – a contract?'

'Yes.'

'JoJo was only trying to do the right thing. What happened to him?'

'I don't know, Miriam. All I can tell you is that he was found on a country road a couple of hours north of here. He'd been stabbed. I'm sorry.'

She nodded and took out a handkerchief, dabbing her eyes. 'I had a feeling he wasn't going to come back. There was just too much stacked against him, what with the people he mixed with, the worthless dropouts he called friends and then the beating. I just hope the policeman he was going to see will do what JoJo said he'd do, and put Farek away for good. He's like a disease in this city, corrupting everything and everybody.'

'I'm sure he'll do the right thing.' Caspar stood up. There really wasn't much more he could do or say. He felt sorry for Miriam, mired in loyalty to her low-life brother and not a hope in hell of getting out of this place any time soon. 'If you think of anything else JoJo might have said about any of this, could you give me a call? It could be important.'

She nodded and followed him to the door. He stopped before going out. 'One thing: I don't suppose you know the name of this policeman JoJo mentioned?'

'I should do. JoJo talked about him as if he was some kind of superhero... you know, like in the comics. Rocco. He said his name was Lucas Rocco.'

On the way home, Caspar stopped at a café for a drink and to call Rocco. He was pleased with the way the day had gone; the security review earlier had gone well, and he now had some answers about

Vieira – especially the identifying tattoo. He relayed what he'd learned and added, 'In the end he was on his way to see you. It sounded as if he thought you were his only hope of getting out of this alive.'

'Me?' Rocco sounded surprised. 'Why? I didn't even know him.'

'You didn't have to. You're the cop who brought down Sami Farek. To a third-rate criminal like JoJo, on the run and desperate, it didn't make him like you very much but it would have made you seem bullet-proof.'

Twenty-two

Rocco thanked Caspar for his help and put the phone down, rubbing the sleep from his eyes. He'd grabbed a quick nap for thirty minutes, and been woken by the call. But he felt elated; they now had confirmation that the dead man was Vieira. It was an enormous step forward, although the revelation that Vieira had been on his way to seek his help had left him feeling puzzled. Criminals, whatever their position on the underworld ladder, rarely looked on policemen as any kind of saviour; they were usually the bringers of their downfall or, at the very least, a constant source of harassment in their daily lives.

On the other hand, he was aware that some criminals had a sneaking, if rarely voiced, respect for cops who had a reputation for honesty and fairness. Where Vieira had got the idea that Rocco would protect him he had no clue but, in desperate times, men did strange things. And there was no doubt that JoJo Vieira had, in becoming an informant, crossed a line that would ultimately lead to his demise. In the narrow world of criminality in which he moved, it seemed he'd formed an inflated view of Rocco's powers of protection.

He made a mental note to pass on the information to Desmoulins. It wouldn't necessarily bring them any closer to finding the killer, but as it was part of the puzzle, it was necessary to include it on the crime report. He was debating whether to go back to sleep ready for the following day, or to get up and do something useful, when the phone rang again. He scooped it up.

'Lucas?' It was Claude, sounding harassed. 'You couldn't come over here, could you? Only Alix is being… difficult about her assignment.' His voice dropped. 'She's just popped outside, but I wonder if you could talk to her for me.'

'I'll be five minutes.' Rocco walked out to the car to drive to Claude's house on the far side of the village, then thought better of it and stepped out into the road. It was a nice day and a good excuse to stretch his legs and see some of the village at a more leisurely pace.

The main road through the village was straight, starting at the church overlooking the square at the end of his road. He passed a group of three people outside the church, all dressed in black. That constituted a crowd in Poissons, he reflected. Two of them were women who nodded amiably enough and murmured a greeting. The third was the village priest who, since discovering Rocco had no religious leanings, had taken to giving him the kind of dark look he might have reserved for the Devil himself. Pulling his soutane around him, he excused himself to the woman and scurried back into his church as if Rocco was about to bring down famine and pestilence on Poissons and the surrounding area.

Rocco watched him go and shook his head. He'd given up worrying about it. The man clearly liked a more impressionable audience.

The main road had a few houses on each side, three farms, a small garage with a single fuel pump and the village school. It was quiet, with the rustle of birds in the trees lining the road, a cock crowing and the distant sound of a tractor engine from one of the farms. It made him realise just how noisy the cities were by comparison, and how he'd come to appreciate the rural setting that was now his home base.

He reached Claude's house and knocked on the door. It was opened by Alix, Claude's daughter. She had a firm set to her jaw and rolled her eyes when she saw who it was.

'Oh, great, he's called in reinforcements,' she muttered. 'How typical.' She stepped back and beckoned him inside. 'Don't think this is going to make me any happier, because it won't.'

Rocco stepped inside and found Claude seated at his living room table, cradling a mug of coffee and looking as if he'd been pinned down and beaten into submission.

'Problem?' said Rocco.

'Yes, there's a problem,' Alix said forcefully before Claude could speak. 'I've spent the last three weeks helping to set up the programme for road closures and crowd control for when the Tour comes through the region. It's taken a lot of time getting the people involved to sit around a table and agree their tasks, and taking on this… this menial bodyguard job means somebody else will be taking over my work. I object to being selected for something without any consultation. I wasn't trained to spend my time out in a field protecting some disaffected and probably corrupt politician who's been forced out of his own country.'

Rocco waited for her to finish, then nodded and picked up a sugar lump from a box on the table, and popped it into his mouth. He crunched it firmly between his teeth and said, 'I sympathise entirely. I really do.'

'What?' Claude spluttered on his tea.

Alix looked both surprised and suspicious. 'You do?'

'Yes. Unfortunately, you're overlooking a couple of things. One, we don't know if Bouanga's corrupt or not, and anyway that's beside the point. Two, being a police officer means following orders – and that includes orders you might not like. You're also forgetting something else.'

'And that is?' Her eyes flashed dangerously at the direction the conversation was taking.

'If being ordered to look after the safety of a visitor valued by the state is something your father and I have to agree to, why should you be given special treatment?'

Her mouth opened to reply, then snapped shut again.

'Well said,' Claude muttered and got to his feet. 'Excellent. Lucas, would you like a glass of wine?'

Rocco shook his head. 'Not for me. I should be getting home.' He looked at Alix, aware that he had probably been a little rough on her. She was an ambitious young woman and was going to make a very good cop. He was already aware that she had the right mix of forcefulness, courage and clear thinking necessary for police work, and had proven herself in a difficult hostage situation where she had been the one being held with a gun against her neck. But she had to learn that in day-to-day matters, none of them had the power to refuse an order.

'Look at it this way,' he said carefully. 'Organising crowd and traffic control on the local section of the Tour de France is important and might get you a thank you if you're lucky. Maybe a small commendation for your personnel file. But I wouldn't count on it.'

She started to say something but he forged on. 'However, special assignments like this one come with the approval and awareness of the Interior Ministry. It won't do me much good because they know

137

me and I've been around the block. But if you do a good job and show that you're not afraid to put yourself out there in what even Monteo thought was a potentially dangerous situation for a woman, it might help you.'

'Dangerous? Nobody said that.'

'Being a bodyguard implies it, don't you think? And what if you have to use force to do your job? What if you have to shoot someone to protect this "corrupt" politician? Could you handle that, or should we get Officer Sabonneux instead? She's a new transfer but I hear she likes a fight – and she's an excellent shot.' He hadn't heard anything of the sort; in fact quite the opposite. He'd heard the firearms instructor saying that she'd have trouble hitting a barn on a sunny day on account of always closing her eyes as she pulled the trigger. But he couldn't imagine Alix checking to see if it were true or not.

She took the bait, nodding reluctantly, as if she was conceding the point but didn't want to be seen to be backing down too easily. 'What if it goes wrong?'

'That's the part nobody ever talks about. Police operations don't always go the way they're planned, you know that. All you can do is make sure your bit goes right. It's all any of us can do. Your father and I will be relying on you to watch our backs, just as we'll be watching yours. We're cops; it's what we do.'

'I understand. I won't let you down.' She looked subdued now, and lifted her chin, her earlier anger dissipated.

He nodded to signal that the conversation was over, and was about to let himself out when Claude's telephone jangled, jarring in the silence.

'Lamotte.' Claude listened for a few moments, his eyebrows lowering in a scowl. He raised a hand to stop Rocco leaving, then thanked the caller and put the phone down. 'That was Mme Duverre. She lives in one of the houses up the Chemin de Fosse. It's a track off the main road a couple of minutes' walk from here. The house next door to her has been empty for a while; it belongs to her sister but she's moved down south to look after an elderly relative. Duverre says she's heard noises coming through the wall, and thinks somebody's using the place without permission. Fancy doing a spot of local detecting? Sorry – but since you're here.'

'Why not?' said Rocco. 'It'll make a change from dead bodies.' He looked at Alix. 'You might want to join us. It can't be too often that all three cops in the village show up in one hit.'

The Chemin de Fosse branched off the main street and was easy to miss. In fact Rocco couldn't recall having noticed it before. Barely wide enough for a vehicle, and probably built in the days of horse travel, the ground level rose as they entered the narrow turning, revealing three cottages linked together down the left-hand side. The track, such as it was, petered out barely a hundred metres further on against a small patch of woodland. The cottages were old, with wattle-and-daub walls, corrugated metal roofs and ancient wooden shutters over the windows. Two of the front gardens were small but tidy, evidently looked after on a regular basis. The third, the one furthest away, was a small jungle of weeds with a neglected path leading to the front door, which had been crudely reinforced with two wooden planks. An elderly woman in an apron and headscarf was waiting for them at the middle cottage. She came forward to greet them, throwing Claude an expression full of dark emotion while he made the introductions.

'I didn't mean to get you involved, Inspector,' she said, her voice loud with relief, and turned and pointed to the end house. 'Only there's someone in there who shouldn't be, I'm certain of it. It's my sister's place although she's not living there at the moment. She's been down south for the last three months looking after a member of the family who's ill. She intends to sell the place, but it's not right that someone else should be using it. I was going to call her on the phone but I knew she couldn't get away so I decided to call Lamotte, here, instead. I had a phone put in so I could keep in touch.'

Rocco held up a hand to stop the rush of information and said softly, 'When did you last hear any movement, Madame?' He was tempted to ask if there were fruit rats in the roof, like his own house, but suspected that might be taken badly. She seemed fairly touchy and reminded him in some ways of Mme Denis, his neighbour. They evidently bred them as a type in these parts, he decided, formidable women not to be taken lightly.

'Yesterday evening. I'd just got back from buying butter at Vestier's farm down the road. It was gone seven and very quiet as always up here. Even the birds had gone silent, so I know I wasn't imagining things. The birds know when something's not right.'

'Can you describe what you heard?'

'A thump.'

'A thump?' Claude lifted his eyebrows. 'Is that all?'

Mme Duverre gave him a scathing look and snapped, 'Isn't that enough from an empty house?' She glanced at Alix for support. 'I'm a woman living alone and I should expect to be believed when I say I heard something. I didn't ring earlier because I didn't want to be thought of as a nuisance.' She threw another glare at Claude as if he'd accused her of a heinous crime. 'It could have been someone hitting another person – you don't know.'

Alix put a reassuring hand on the woman's arm and said, 'That's perfectly fine, Madame. We need to make sure of the detail, that's all. But we're here now and we'll take a look. Do you have a key to the property?'

Duverre stuck a hand into the front pocket of her apron and pulled out a small block of wood with a key attached by a length of string. 'It's to the back door. My sister had to reinforce the front door when the lock got broken. Not that she ever used it, anyway.' She handed it to Alix who set off for the rear of the property before the old woman could launch into another explanation.

Rocco followed, signalling Claude to go round the far side. He had no reason to expect anything out of the ordinary, but it didn't do any harm to demonstrate a show of force when needed.

The back door was reached via a low gate and along a narrow path across a vegetable patch now overgrown and unkempt. The door had a shutter fixed across the usual glass panel, as did the two windows. Rocco tapped Alix on the shoulder and motioned her to wait a moment until Claude appeared on the far side of the cottages. If there was someone living here without permission, they would have surely heard the three officers by now, quite apart from Mme Duverre's greeting them on their arrival. He had no reason to expect this to be anything threatening, but he'd learned over the years that going blindly into an empty property without taking precautions was a quick route to disaster.

He stood to one side of the door and motioned Alix to do the same, then leaned across and rapped sharply on the shutter. The sound echoed dully inside, and raised a couple of birds in the bushes nearby.

No answer.

He nodded towards the lock and Alix inserted the key, giving it a quick twist. But it wouldn't turn. She pushed the door instead and it creaked open, bringing a cry of surprise from Mme Duverre. A rush of dry, musty air came out to greet them, of the kind Rocco had come across all too often when entering abandoned buildings. But that wasn't all. With it came an underlying smell of something much more recent: tobacco smoke.

Twenty-three

Rocco moved forward, reaching for his gun before realising he'd left it at home.

'Well, that's not right.' It was Mme Duverre, who'd crept up silently behind them and was now leaning forward and sniffing the air like an old gun-dog. 'That's not right at all. My sister doesn't smoke.' She glared at them each in turn and jammed her hands into her apron pocket. 'Well, isn't someone going in to look?'

Rocco stepped past Alix and through the door. He was in a small kitchen with a table, two chairs and an ancient wood stove with a large top plate for cooking. Several objects on the table caught his eye: a small metal bottle of camping gas, two empty water bottles, a half-baguette and an opened pack of Camembert with a resident audience of flies.

Cold rations, thought Rocco, eyeing the scene. Whoever had been in here had brought the absolute basics. He prodded the baguette with his finger, the flies lifting off the cheese in protest. A day old, he reckoned, more likely two.

A sink against the back wall gave off the soft plink-plink of a dripping tap. Rocco moved towards a door leading to the front of the cottage and looked through. It was a front room like all front rooms, containing another table, an armchair and a wooden dresser holding an abundance of ornaments and framed photos, snapshots of a time stood still. Everything was unused, layered in dust.

Alix meanwhile had moved to another door off the kitchen. It opened onto a bedroom with a large single bed and a wardrobe. Rocco joined her. The bed was stripped bare but there was a definite dent in the mattress as if someone had been lying there.

'What's behind that wall?' he asked Mme Duverre. She had followed them in like a shadow and was peering around in disbelief at the signs of occupation.

'My bedroom, if you must know,' she snapped. 'Someone's been sleeping in here – I knew I was right!'

Rocco nudged the scrolled wooden headboard with his fingers. It went back without effort and gave off a faint thump as it connected with the wall. She was right. Somebody had sat on the bed and caused it to move against the wall.

'It probably won't produce much,' said Rocco to Alix, 'but check the co-op in the village to see if anybody bought a gas stove and other provisions in the last couple of days.'

Alix nodded and made a note.

As Rocco turned to go, Mme Duverre held his arm. 'Is that it? Aren't you going to do anything else?'

'I'm not sure what we can do. Do you think anything's been stolen?'

She shook her head. 'Like what? My sister wasn't rich, you know. And what about the van?'

'Van?' said Claude. 'You never mentioned a van before.'

'Didn't I?' She looked confused. 'Well, it's been a stressful time, hasn't it? There's been a van out in the main street more than once, which is unusual. It wasn't from around here, I know that.'

'Can you describe it?' Rocco asked.

'I thought I just had. It was grey and looked like a delivery van, that's all I can tell you. One of those square ones. And it had a different number from the cars around here.'

'Which was?'

'Seventy-five. I don't remember the rest. My memory's not what it used to be… although I can remember certain other stuff easily enough.' Her eyes settled on Claude like two deadly gun barrels.

'Paris,' said Claude, ignoring the look. A huge area, thought Rocco, and pointless to even think of looking. Still, it was worth asking around the village in case anybody else had seen it, and he suggested as much to Alix, who nodded. He turned to Mme Duverre and said, 'I think whoever was here has gone, Madame, and won't be back. In the meantime I suggest you get somebody to secure the back door and shutters. That should deter anybody else taking up residence without your sister's permission.'

Leaving Alix to finish off and help close the house, Rocco bid the old lady goodbye and left, with Claude following quickly behind.

'You want to tell me what that was about back there?' Rocco said, as they walked down the track together.

Claude shook his head. 'I don't know what you mean.'

'Liar. You couldn't get out of there fast enough and I could have bitten chunks out of the atmosphere.'

Claude stopped and looked over his shoulder to where Alix was just leaving the cottage with Mme Duverre. 'It's nothing. A bit of history, that's all. Ancient history at that.' He started walking again, but when Rocco failed to catch up, he turned and came back. 'OK, I grant you, there was a bit of an atmosphere. It's nothing to worry about, though. It's been like that for years.'

'Really? Hell, don't tell me you and the old lady used to–'

'No!' Claude looked horrified. 'Certainly not. What do you take me for?'

They were out on the main street before Claude explained. 'She had a niece used to come and visit a few years back. Her name was Christine. We met up in the village one time, got friendly and went out on a few occasions. It was nice. Uncomplicated. My wife had died a couple of years before that, and I thought maybe I was ready for the… commitment stuff, you know?'

'But you weren't?'

'Running scared, if I'm honest. It was all right until she began to get serious. Then I got the sweats and it all went downhill very fast after that. Christine ended up moving away and Madame Bulldog has never forgiven me; accused me of behaving like a *limace* and ruining her Christine's chances of making a decent marriage.'

'A slug? That was a bit harsh.'

'Absolutely. I mean, it takes two, right? Fine, I admit I upset her – Christine, I mean – but she forgave me a long time ago and said it had been nice but we'd never have worked out, anyway, me being a cop. She married a bank manager a while after, so what does that tell you? Anyway, the old lady still thinks I'm the spawn of the devil and should be roasted over a hot pit.' He shrugged. 'I try to avoid her where possible, but in a place this size it's not easy. And as you've discovered, some memories around here are extremely long.'

Rocco nodded. He could vouch for that, all right. And time wasn't much of a healer when it came to remembered hurts.

Claude disappeared inside just as Alix arrived. She turned to Rocco and said, 'I'm sorry about earlier, Inspector. I didn't mean to be insubordinate. I just didn't want to miss the opportunity to prove what I can do, although I can see now that this assignment is a good one for me. Especially as Pa–' She stopped, biting her lip.

'Go on.'

'Papa says I should welcome the chance of working with you because unlike some other policemen he knows, you've never looked down on him. You've always made him feel like a real policeman.'

'I hear you've been investigating an outbreak of house-breaking in the village,' said Mme Denis with a wry smile. She was standing by his garden gate and it was obvious she'd been waiting for him. 'We're getting a very high level of service here, I must say.'

He smiled. As usual, nothing much escaped her attention, and he had no doubts that the three-cop visit to Mme Duverre was already doing the rounds of Poissons at high speed. 'I was nearby and decided to lend a hand.' He pushed open the gate and found the old lady almost skipping along behind him, no doubt anxious to hear all the gory details so she could relay them to her network of friends and gossips.

'I'm surprised Lilliane allowed Lamotte into the house,' she muttered, bending to attack a weed in the path. 'Did you notice the tension between them? What's the word… toxic.' She tossed the weed aside and brushed her fingers.

'I suppose you must know all about what happened.'

'Who doesn't? It was quite the drama, believe me. She decided to make it her life's work never to forgive Lamotte for "breaking her niece's heart". Utter rubbish, of course – it wasn't that serious for either of them. Anyway, Christine forgave him and that should have been the end of it. People move on, don't they? It's what makes the world go round.'

'Really? I thought it was love.'

She scowled at him. 'Now you're teasing. Be careful the same doesn't happen to you, young man, or you'll end up old and lonely.'

'I'll bear it in mind.'

'So who was it, do you think, camping in her sister's house? I've never heard of anyone doing that before.'

'Not out here, maybe, but it happens in cities, where houses or apartments are left empty. The English call it "squatting".'

'They actually have a word for it? Strange people.' With that, she turned and bustled off along the path to the gate.

Twenty-four

Refreshed by a good night's sleep, in spite of the fruit rats' best attempts to keep him awake, Rocco drove out to Les Sables early the following morning, ready to replace the two officers. Just before reaching the turning to the isolated house, he looked in his mirror and saw Claude's 2CV coming up behind him, with Alix in the passenger seat.

As he bumped along the track, Rocco experienced an odd sense of misgiving. He soon saw why: the twin wooden gates, the house's first line of defence, were wide open, something he'd warned Bouanga against allowing.

Rocco stamped on the accelerator and blasted through the gap, skidding to a halt in front of the house. He jumped out, drawing his gun. As he did so, Claude pulled up alongside him in a cloud of dust, he and Alix leaping out to join him.

Rocco stepped up to the front door and pushed. It was already open and swung back.

'*Delicat!*' he shouted. It was pointless being quiet, since their arrival would have been heard already.

Nothing.

'I'll do the other side,' Claude called out, and disappeared round the corner.

'What about me?' Alix queried. She looked pale but determined, holding a rifle which looked huge in her hands.

'Stick with me,' Rocco told her, 'but ditch the rifle. If anybody's still inside you'll need to move fast.' He knew it wasn't her first time facing danger, but searching a house with a rifle could be more of an encumbrance than a help. 'Let's go.'

He moved quickly inside, scanning the hall and alert for any sign of movement. 'Mr Bouanga!'

Rocco stepped across the hall to where the phone had been on a side table, but was now on the floor. He picked up the handset and listened. No dial tone. The line must have been cut. He pointed towards a small room on the right, with the door wide open, and Alix moved quickly to check it out. She came out again seconds later and shook her head. 'Empty.'

He beckoned her to follow and made his way along the hall to the conservatory, which Bouanga seemed to have made his daily spot. Papers were scattered about the floor and on the settee where the minister had sat, and a cup and saucer lay in pieces on the rug. A broken chair lay in one corner below a section of glass starred with cracks, and a large pot plant had been kicked over, spilling dirt and pebbles.

There was no sign of Bouanga or his entourage.

He turned and ran through to the kitchen. It was empty, with a mixing bowl lying in pieces on the tiles. A smear of red stood out on the side of the large table in the centre, but he couldn't tell if it was blood, human or otherwise. Through the window he saw Claude scouting the grounds outside, angling towards the outbuildings.

The stairs were silent and sombre, a host of shadows at the top inviting careful investigation. Rocco's footsteps were muffled by the carpet as he ran upwards, with Alix close behind. He reached the top and signalled for her to go right before turning the other way.

The rooms were empty, with nowhere that he could see for anyone to hide. What furniture there was looked untouched and wasn't large enough to conceal an intruder. He entered a room at the rear of the building and opened the window, pushing back the shutters. It gave him a view of the fields overlooking the site where Vieira had died, and a lot of emptiness save for a clutch of dark shapes where crows were circling and dipping by the fence above the slope.

'Alix?' he called, and was relieved when she appeared from the other side of the house shaking her head. Nothing there.

They hurried downstairs just as Claude erupted through the front door. 'Lucas?' He looked distraught. 'In the barn out back.' He turned and led the way round the side and out towards the barn where Rocco had parked his car the previous night.

The barn smelled musty, of straw long dried and of birds and other small creatures that had made this their home. Dust hung in the air and a butterfly struggled to escape, the sound of its wings the only thing to break the silence. The car used by the two officers on guard stood where it had been all night.

Alongside it lay a body.

It was one of the officers. He had his head thrown back, eyes staring sightlessly at the roof. His sidearm was still in its holster, Rocco noted, and a splash of blood and a scorch mark on his uniform fabric showed he'd been shot in the chest at close quarters.

'No sign of the other one?' said Rocco.

Claude shook his head. 'Nothing in the house, I suppose?'

'Not a thing, but the phone line's been cut. Whoever did this didn't want to risk any calls going out.' He glanced at Alix, who was staring at the dead man with a look of horror. He said gently, 'He's beyond our help. We need to look for the others.'

His words seemed to shake her out of her sense of shock, and she nodded and turned away. 'What do you want me to do?'

'Use the radio in my car. Get on to Massin and tell him it's a crime scene, one dead so far and no sign of Bouanga or his people. This looks like a planned attack. Then stay by the car.' He turned to Claude. 'Stay close by, will you – I'm going across the field.'

Claude nodded. 'You saw the crows?'

'Yes.'

'Take it easy.'

'Crows?' Alix stopped and looked between the two men. 'What does that mean?' But neither of them bothered to explain. She would soon figure out that crows gathering over what appeared to be an empty field could only mean one thing: there was something of interest out there.

'Go on,' said Rocco. 'Talk to Massin. Stay calm and stick to the details.'

Rocco jogged across the field, his body temperature rising quickly in the warm air. Out here in the open, the only sound he could hear was the swish as he moved through the lush grass, and his breathing as the adrenaline coursed through him. Down at ground level and with the field curving away downwards, he couldn't see what was attracting the birds, but it could only be one thing. If Bouanga had been taken and one guard killed, it meant that whoever lay out here was one of three people: the second guard or Delicat… or his wife Excelsiore.

The crows voiced their displeasure when they saw him approaching, rising in the air in a frantic clatter of wings. They wheeled away towards the far end of the field where they sat on a line of fence posts and waited, like mourners at a funeral.

He slowed as he neared the spot, and finally saw a dark shape lying in a shallow fold in the ground.

It was the second officer. He was face down, his arms spread out. A splash of blood showed where he'd been shot in the back. An entry wound, Rocco realised immediately. Unlike his colleague, his weapon was gone from its holster.

He checked the body and was surprised to find the man still alive. His breathing was coming in short, harsh gasps, as if he was struggling to force the air into his lungs. There was a lot of blood soaked into the uniform, and Rocco knew that if he didn't get medical help for him soon, he would be beyond it.

He stood up and whistled, and when Claude looked round, made a circular signal to the side of his head, then pumped his fist. Claude understood immediately, and turned and ran towards Rocco's car and the radio.

Rocco stayed with the wounded man and busied himself removing the man's belt and tying a compress of a folded handkerchief against the wound in his back while making him comfortable. It wasn't much but if he could slow the blood loss it might give him a chance of survival. He gently checked the front of the man's body but could find no exit wound. The guard moaned a couple of times, but showed no sign of coming round, which Rocco thought was probably a good thing for now.

As he knelt alongside him he was transported back to Indochina and the ghastly battlefield wounds he'd witnessed there, and the efforts he and others had made to secure the lives of men hit by bullets or shrapnel. All too often they had lost the fight very quickly. Out of range of immediate help and dependent only on the most basic treatment by field medics, their bodies covered in mud and dirt, they soon fell prey to flies and mosquitoes and the inevitability of infection. Yet amazingly some of the wounded soldiers had pulled through when all hope had seemed lost.

Time seemed to hang still as he waited for the first sounds of emergency help arriving, and he realised after a few minutes that he'd begun talking to the guard without realising it, urging him to hold on and telling him that help was on its way. It was, he knew, the sound of a human voice nearby that often made the difference between someone fighting… or giving up altogether.

He checked the compress to scan the area around him, wondering which way the assailant had gone. There were no other tracks through the grass save for his own, which he could clearly see, and a single, zig-zag line leading right up to the body. It prompted a thought and he lifted the man's jacket, and found that blood had run down the inside of his uniform and puddled around his waistband, soaking into the heavy serge cloth of his trousers and the lower extremities of his shirt. But that seemed to be as far as it had gone. There was none gathered around the front of his body, where gravity should have taken it, and none on the grass beneath him.

Rocco sat back. The blood and the absence of other tracks in the grass meant the guard had been shot somewhere else – probably back at the house. Having lost his gun, he must have run for his life across the field, but had collapsed right here, unable to go any further.

Then he heard a whistle, and looked up to see Claude waving and pointing towards the road, and heard the sound of a siren drifting towards them on the breeze.

'Keep breathing,' he told the guard. 'They're just coming.'

It was all he could think of to say and, just as it had in Indochina, it felt ridiculously insufficient.

Twenty-five

The ambulance crews were soon on the scene and moved with efficiency, determining that the wounded man was not in immediate danger but needed surgery as quickly as possible. They conveyed him gently away, the siren blasting out over the fields and sending up the crows in another flurry. The second ambulance, leaving the barn, was in less of a hurry, its siren unused.

Rocco walked back to the house in its wake. He felt drained, angry and baffled in equal measure. Drained by the speed and change of events, and angry at the way the attackers had simply appeared to drive in and shoot two armed officers, then make off with Bouanga and his people. If they had been sent by Bouanga's enemies, how had they found out so quickly where the ex-minister was staying? Even though his assignment to look after Bouanga was an open secret in the station, it still had to have got out into the wider world somehow. But how?

He was met at the corner of the house by Claude. Alix joined them soon afterwards and said, 'Commissaire Massin said a team is on the way and he'll inform the Interior Ministry. He wanted more details but I said you'd report in when you'd finished attending to the wounded man. I hope that was right?'

He nodded. 'Perfect, thank you.' So now Massin can spare a team, he thought, but didn't say anything. He nodded towards the house and added, 'You did good work in there. While we're waiting, there's a service weapon missing, and the wounded man's cap. Find the cap and you'll probably find the gun. He must have dropped them both trying to make his escape across the field. We need to find them.' It was a time-filling distraction more than anything, but Rocco figured it was better than allowing Alix to stand around dwelling on what she had seen. There would be time for that later.

She said, 'I'll search the grounds.' Then she stopped. 'By the way, I know it might not be the right time, but that business about Mme Duverre's neighbour yesterday evening?'

'What of it?'

'I spoke to Mme Drolet, who runs the local co-op, and she said a man she'd never seen before came in two days ago and bought bottles of water, some bread and a packet of cheese. Camembert. I checked her stock against the wrapping from the cottage. It was the same brand and production batch number.'

'I'd say that ties it down. Did she give you a description?'

'Young, she said. Quite good looking, nice. I asked her if there were any specific details that stood out, but she couldn't think of any. Ordinary, she reckoned, wearing a blue shirt and dark trousers. In fact she thought he was a cop at first, but get this: he was driving a grey van. A Citroën 'H', she called it – the one with the corrugated panels. She knew what it was because her former husband used one for selling fish and vegetables around the villages.'

Rocco was impressed. So Mme Drolet was a witness with a good eye for vehicles, even if not people. It was better than he'd hoped for. Unfortunately, it was a model of van in use all over France, with many thousands on the road. The chances of finding the right one would be low to nil.

'Anything else?'

'She said if you were going to pop in to take a statement, she'd be at your disposal.'

Not a chance, thought Rocco. 'And you said?'

'I told her not to hold her breath.'

'Good answer.' He'd had some experience of Mme Drolet's particular charm, as Alix was probably aware, along with everybody in Poissons. She was a nice enough woman and attractive in a handsome way, but she had what Claude had once described as the aura of a black widow spider looking for a mate on which to feast. He wasn't sure if black widows ate their mates, but he preferred not to be the one to find out.

When Alix was out of earshot, Claude gave Rocco a look of gratitude. 'Thanks for saying what you did earlier about her work,' he said. 'She's holding up better than I thought.'

'She'll do fine. Keep an eye on her, though. It might hit her later.'

'Will do.' Claude motioned towards the barn where the policeman had been shot dead. 'That fellow didn't even have his gun out. Was he asleep, do you think?'

Rocco was trying not to think about it, but it would need airing at some stage when the inquest was held into what had transpired here. 'He was either taken by surprise,' he conceded, 'or he wasn't concerned by whoever was coming towards him.'

'But nobody was expected,' Claude pointed out. 'And he'd have heard a car coming up the drive, so he should have been primed and ready.'

'Unless somebody else was already here, and had sneaked in, waiting for others to arrive?'

Claude scowled. 'You're suggesting the cop knew the person who shot him?'

'It's a possibility. Whatever the reason, he hadn't drawn his weapon.'

'And the other guard?'

'He was shot in the back. He might have been taken by surprise and shot as he tried to get away.'

Claude shook his head. 'Christ, that's wicked. Who would do that?' He stopped short, a shocked look on his face. 'God, Lucas, I just realised something: those poor bastards could have been you, me and – and Alix!'

Rocco said nothing. The same thought had already occurred to him as he was walking back across the field after the wounded guard was taken away. Whoever had done this had been ruthless – and prepared to take out anybody who got in their way.

They heard vehicles approaching and saw clouds of dust billowing up along the track from the road. Rocco turned and saw two cars and a small police van coming through the open gates, no doubt the vehicle containing Rizzotti and his equipment. The cars were shiny and black, and he recognised the plates on one used by Massin. Behind the three vehicles, he saw other cars approaching from Amiens, one bearing the brightly-coloured banner of a regional radio station along the side.

And so the circus begins, he thought.

First out of the front car was Massin, striding across the gravel towards them, an immaculate figure bent on taking charge of a bad situation. Other men disgorged from all three vehicles and got ready to spread out across the grounds, Detective Desmoulins giving them instructions on where to look and assigning section leaders.

Massin didn't look happy and, in spite of himself and the sometimes fragile relationship shared by them, Rocco felt a measure of sympathy for the officer. As top dog here, this was all going to shower down on Massin like muddy rain – *une tempête de merde*, as he'd heard one young officer describing it when bad news was followed by the careful apportioning of blame from above.

'This is a disaster,' were Massin's first words, as he came to a stop in front of the two men. He looked drawn and pale. 'A complete disaster. I understand you arrived here to take over and discovered the two men, is that correct?'

'That's right,' Rocco confirmed. 'And no sign of Bouanga or his people.'

'I've put out an alert to all stations to look out for them. Have you deduced anything from the site?'

'Not much. Whoever did this arrived in a rush, probably taking them all by surprise. One guard was shot dead, the other was shot in the back but managed to get away across the field before collapsing. The house is a mess and they went for maximum impact in taking Bouanga.' He stopped, an image flicking through his mind. Something about the house wasn't right.

'What?' said Massin. 'Rocco?'

'Sorry – I'll be right back.' Rocco jogged across to the house and through the front door. He ran down the hall to where he'd last seen the bow and arrows hanging on the wall. They were gone.

He checked the conservatory and the kitchen, but there was nothing there either. He didn't have to search the rest of the house; he was certain he wouldn't find them.

He walked back to explain his thoughts to Massin. 'Delicat's bow and arrows are gone. I know he had a gun, but his first choice would have been the weapons most familiar to him.'

Massin looked doubtful. 'So what are you thinking?'

'If Delicat took them, it means he wasn't kidnapped with Bouanga. Why would they shoot two cops and leave the bodyguard?'

'Unless he was part of the kidnap plot,' Massin suggested. 'He was an insider. What better person to have on their side, able to tell them where Bouanga was hiding and the best time to come in and get him.'

Rocco couldn't fault his logic. In theory Massin was right, kidnappings were often carried out with the connivance of insiders close to the victim, either coerced or willing. And what did they know about Delicat's background, other than the fact that he'd arrived with Bouanga as part of his small retinue? He could have been put in place a long time ago by the former minister's enemies, to keep an eye on him and to provide information to bring the man down.

Yet a part of him was doubtful. Was it really that simple?

'Either way, he's out there somewhere.'

'Doing what?'

'I don't know. Either helping the kidnap or trying to get his boss back. And that raises another question: why kidnap a man they had threatened to kill? It would have been easier to dispose of him right here and be gone with nobody the wiser until morning.'

'It's madness,' Massin said sourly. 'I heard about the bow from Rizzotti. That's all we need – a maniac firing poisoned arrows at anything that moves.' He turned and bellowed to Desmoulins in an uncharacteristic manner, and everyone stopped what they were doing. Desmoulins jogged across to find out what he wanted, nodding a greeting to Rocco and Claude.

'The bodyguard, Delicat,' Massin told him shortly, 'might still be on the premises. He's likely to be armed so tell the men to proceed with caution but not to fire on him. We don't yet know which side he's on. Understood?'

'Sir.' Desmoulins wheeled away and began passing the message to the men, who dispersed towards their allotted search areas.

'Any further thoughts, Rocco?' said Massin.

'Just one. The wounded man might have seen who shot him and his colleague. It might be a good idea to place a guard on him until he's in a position to talk.'

Massin nodded. 'Good thinking.'

'Where's Monteo in all of this?' asked Rocco. 'I'd have thought he'd be here by now, Bouanga being his responsibility.'

Massin said nothing for a moment, then stretched his chin up and pulled at his uniform as if preparing himself for inspection. 'Gerard Monteo left his hotel in Amiens last night and hasn't been seen since. I believe he's returned to Paris.'

'Odd timing. A family problem?'

'Unlikely,' said Massin. 'He's divorced and doesn't have any other family as far as I know. I've spoken to his office but they're proving most unhelpful.'

Par for the course, thought Rocco. 'What have they got to hide?'

'I don't know. What I did discover is that Monteo has had close relations with certain members of the Gabonese government over recent months, including three visits in the past twelve weeks. Unfortunately, the men he's been meeting are the same ones who ousted Bouanga from power, and the ones who now hold the reins when it comes to awarding mineral mining rights contracts.'

'Is that significant?' asked Claude. 'Sir?'

Massin hesitated for a second, as though unsure about talking in front of a junior officer. Then he said, 'It could be, Officer Lamotte.

On the other hand, there are other factors involved, namely that Mr Monteo has been acting as a *de facto* liaison between the Gabonese government and foreign corporations bidding for mineral rights in the country. As my contact in the Ministry suggested, it's complicated but not unusual.'

Rocco shook his head. He shouldn't have been surprised; as always with high-level officials, there were wheels within wheels, granting favours here for favours elsewhere, often with their own interests at heart. 'What are you going to do?' he asked.

'Nothing, at the moment. I've demanded answers from the Ministry about what, if any, Monteo's position in this affair might have to do with the attack and specifically about the shooting of the two officers. All I can do now is wait.' He turned and watched as more cars appeared along the road leading to the entrance. 'One other thing: the Ministry has despatched an investigations team to take over here. It doesn't reflect on you but is standard procedure for international... complexities. They will report back on their findings. In the meantime I suggest you, Lamotte and Poulon make yourselves scarce; there's not much you can do here and I don't need the press fastening on to one of you and creating a story. What I just told you goes no further, understood? And I want your reports on my desk before the end of the day.'

Rocco and Claude went in search of Alix and found her with two officers marking out a patch of ground at the far side of the house. A gun and police cap lay at the centre of the area.

'It looks like he must have been on patrol round here and happened on the attackers,' said Alix. 'There's a small amount of blood on the grass which they've marked out for Doctor Rizzotti to examine later.'

Rocco nodded. 'Let's leave them to get on with it. We need to get our heads clear and write our reports while the details are fresh. I'll see you both at the office.' He turned and walked back to his car.

'Inspector Rocco,' called a familiar voice, as he was about to get in. 'Is it true the Interior Ministry is involved here?'

'No comment,' muttered Rocco, when he saw who it was. He'd tangled with Serge Houchin before and hadn't taken to the man. A freelance stringer for several news organisations, Houchin always seemed to be on the periphery whenever something went wrong with local policing. Rocco had seen colleagues burned too many times by reporters looking for a scoop, and had learned not to trust them. Houchin was one of the more unappealing of the herd, with the manner and build of a weasel, a thin moustache and permanent smirk whenever he fastened on any story that might be to the detriment of the police.

'Come on, Inspector, give us a break,' the man insisted, his voice an unpleasant whine. 'What about Gerard Monteo? He's been pretty much camped out at the station for days, we know that much. And he's from the Ministry of the Interior – he confirmed that much when I last spoke to him. But where is he now, huh?' He reached out and grabbed Rocco's arm.

It was a big mistake. Rocco stopped and turned suddenly, which had the reporter bumping into him then jumping back with an expression of alarm.

'Don't do that,' Rocco growled.

'Umm… my apologies, Inspector.' Houchin struggled on finding Rocco at such close quarters and looking ready for a confrontation. He swallowed hard, his Adam's apple bouncing and said, 'Can you confirm that Monteo is running some sort of safe house operation here and who he's protecting?'

'That's none of your business. Why are you interested in him?'

Houchin's eyes gleamed, regaining some of his pushy composure. 'Well, it doesn't matter. I know he's been around for days, arranging the protection of a foreign bigwig who was staying here, we know that much. Yet now we hear there's been a shooting with two officers gunned down in cold blood and the mystery guest has disappeared. Surely Monteo would like to make a statement for the press, wouldn't he?'

Rocco wanted to shove the man's notebook down his throat, but restrained himself. It would give the reporter another story to file about police brutality, and there were others crowding around, eager to hear whatever he had to say.

'You'll have to ask the man yourself, won't you?' he said bluntly. 'Or speak to your contacts if they're so good. Now, I'm a little busy at the moment, so you'll have to excuse me.'

He climbed into his car and slammed the door, nearly taking off Houchin's fingers in the process.

Twenty-six

Romain was trying hard not to be sick. He'd never been shot before and the pain was excruciating. That infernal cop at Les Sables had got off a lucky shot that had caught him in the fleshy part of his waist just above the hip. He'd hardly noticed it at the time, with the thrilling adrenalin rush following the shooting of the first cop in the barn, it had come as little more than a punch to the gut. But at least he'd paid back the one who'd shot him. He'd made the mistake of thinking Romain was down for the count, and had turned to check on his mate. More fool him; Romain had shot him in the back. He'd run off, dropping his gun as he went, and Romain had started to follow him but had figured he wouldn't get far, so why bother?

He'd waited for Lilou to go to sleep before lifting his shirt and removing the towel wadding he'd placed there to soak up the blood. He hadn't told her about the wound yet, blaming the way he was holding himself on one of the cops having taken a swing at him with a shovel. Now he knew he couldn't hide it any longer and would have to own up soon or she'd know something was wrong.

At first the sensation had been little more than a dull throb, constant but not debilitating; no worse than the injury he'd suffered playing rugby at school once, when half the opposition pack had jumped on him for bringing down one of their teammates with a deliberately high tackle round the neck. They'd waited for the other kid to be stretchered off, then turned on him while the ref's attention was elsewhere. It was brutal and had put him in bed for a week. But this was different; the wound was now beginning to ache with every movement of his body, as if someone was reaching inside him to grab a handful of his guts and giving them a vicious twist.

He pulled out the first-aid box from under the front seat and found a tin of sulpha powder and some tablets in a bag. He wasn't sure how effective either of them would be, but he had to do something quick about the damned pain or he'd go mad. He'd got hold of the sulpha from a guy who'd used it in the war, and said it was good for preventing infection in wounds. He had no idea about the tablets but they seemed to help Lilou's headaches, so they were worth a try. Anything was better than the crippling agony that was threatening to tear him inside out.

He took two of the tablets and washed them down with water, then turned to the wound. The sight of it terrified him and almost made him throw up again; it was swollen and ugly and a thin trickle of blood was seeping slowly down his side. He grabbed the sulpha powder and sprinkled some across the opening, then replaced the towel wadding, folding it carefully into place and wincing when he caught the edge of the wound where it was most tender. It would have to do for now. As long as he didn't have to move too much he could stand it for a while longer until he figured out what to do.

Lilou was moving in her sleep in the back of the van, as she often did, and he waited for a sign that she'd noticed what he was doing. But after a moment her breathing became quiet and steady.

That wouldn't last once he told her, he realised. She was already stressed enough over not finding Rocco at the house and him shooting the two cops, saying that they should have known about the first and that the shooting had been unnecessary. How she'd react when she heard he'd caught a bullet didn't bear thinking about. He felt the tablets beginning to have an effect, his eyelids becoming heavy. The pain was receding to a bearable but constant ache, so maybe it wouldn't be so bad after all. He'd find a friendly doctor willing to treat him in exchange for some ready cash and a promise of silence, and they'd be off into the blue just as soon as this last job was done.

The job, he thought, his mind wandering. They still had to complete the job. But they would. Rocco couldn't hide forever. All they had to do was come up with a new plan. Lilou would help. She was good at planning.

As sleep took over, he was thinking about the different ways he could finish Rocco off. That would make up for the pain like nothing else; that and the admiration of Lilou as he completed their assignment.

Twenty-seven

The atmosphere at the station was like a morgue, with every available officer out in search of the abductors of Bouanga or setting up road blocks and questioning motorists. In Rocco's opinion it was too little too late; if the people who'd done this had any brains, they'd be a long way beyond any cordon by now, or keeping their heads down in a remote location and waiting for the dust to settle.

It lent the normally busy office a faintly surreal atmosphere, as if all the usual inhabitants had been lifted out and spirited away *en masse*. Even the air smelled almost clean, with none of the usually heavy fog of cigarette smoke hanging overhead. Claude and Alix followed him in shortly afterwards and made for separate desks to write their reports, both as surprised as he by the quiet. It gave Rocco a chance to write his, sticking to the basic facts without adding any unnecessary details.

In spite of his efforts at clear thinking, Rocco soon found the events of the past few days intruding like flashes of lightning. Each one, it seemed, from the cottage break-in, the mystery woman in the café who had pretended not to know him, the murder of Vieira and the threats to his own life, and now the disappearance of Bouanga and the shooting of the two officers, seemed to be ganging up to confuse the hell out of him.

He thought them through one by one in an attempt to break the puzzle down to its separate components. He couldn't do much about the mystery woman, which was odd, but not worth losing sleep over. If she had something to say, but was cautious, maybe even frightened of coming forward for any reason, there was little he could do about it unless he saw her again. Until then, he pushed it to the back of his mind.

The squatting at Poissons was hardly earth-shattering, although the village inhabitants, especially Mme Duverre, would no doubt disagree. In such a small and remote community, it would stand out purely because it was so unusual. It wasn't the first shocking event to hit Poissons, and certainly not the worst; that dubious honour belonged to the murder of a young woman in the *marais*, followed closely by the death of a local scrap metal man who'd blown himself up with some wartime ordnance after trying to kill Rocco. Those two, in police terms, ranked much higher in the order of magnitude. Fortunately, since nothing appeared to have been stolen from the cottage and the only offence was one of trespass, it would have to take its place on the long list of odd events that went unsolved in every police district throughout the country. Burglaries were a common factor in most towns and cities, and were only likely to become more common in the country as time went by and populations spread out from the urban areas.

As for the alleged threat from Lakhdar Farek, there was little he could do about it other than to keep his eyes open and be on his guard.

With the Bouanga affair, the despatch of an Interior Ministry investigation team had taken that out of his hands. Unless he was tasked with joining in to help with the search, it looked certain that it was going to be kept that way, no doubt because, as Massin had said, there would be political ramifications once the details got out that Bouanga had been here. He had fled his own country in questionable circumstances, and been offered secret protection in France, which Rocco could only guess might mean some difficulties between the two countries in future trade terms. How that might compare with the reaction from the general population once it was known that France had harboured a man of Bouanga's alleged reputation was anybody's guess.

Which left the murder of JoJo Vieira. It was unusual enough that the dead man had arrived as if by magic and been dumped in a ditch not far from Poissons. It had an added dimension, however, with Caspar's revelation that Vieira had been on his way to seek Rocco's protection from the same Lakhdar Farek.

He stood up and walked over to the large wall map of the area. Someone, probably René Desmoulins, had stuck a pin in the spot where the body had been found, along with a slip of paper showing the basic details of the time, cause of death and location, and a file number for further reference. Rocco picked up another pin and stuck it in the spot where Les Sables was located. It didn't help clarify his thoughts, merely indicating the regularity with which unexpected and seemingly unconnected events occurred in close proximity to each other.

He traced a route from Paris across country to where Vieira's body had been found. It wasn't a straight line by any means, and a city rat like Vieira would have soon been out of his depth on the narrow roads and in open countryside. If he accepted that Vieira couldn't have known where Rocco lived, it was more likely that he'd been making for Amiens, which was about the same distance and on a more direct line than Poissons.

Yet whoever had killed him had managed to find him down a narrow country lane. Was that pure chance or had the killer followed him with extreme patience, waiting for his chance to strike?

He took a walk around the office, stopping for coffee on the way. What kind of killer did Farek have on his books who would have that kind of patience? From what Caspar had said, neither Borelli nor Abdhoun sounded as if they possessed that level of self-control. Like most killers they preferred to let anger and machismo dictate their actions. The Corsican had beaten someone close to death in a rage over a woman, even though he must have known whom he was dealing with in such a small community; and the Algerian, Abdhoun, sounded younger and even more volatile so even less likely to wait patiently for the ideal opportunity to strike a target. He would be more likely to go in hard and messy just to get a name for himself.

That left a professional hunter; somebody capable of following a target undetected, of planning their moves and melting into the background even in open countryside. Someone who was accustomed to biding their time.

He picked up the phone and dialled Santer's number.

The captain answered immediately. 'Lucas. I hear all hell's broken loose in sunny Picardie. What are you doing up there?'

'I wish I knew,' he replied. 'But that's not why I'm calling. Can you run a check on a couple of names for me? I need to know if they've been out of town in the past few days.' He gave Santer the two names, Borelli and Abdhoun, and what little he knew from Caspar's description.

Santer grunted. 'Yeah, I've never had the pleasure but I've heard plenty from one of the gang boys. They're a nasty addition to the other thugs and miscreants up here and looking to move up the chain. Not that it'll do them any good. Last I heard the Algerian's already upset Farek's second-in-command, Seb Achay, which won't do him any favours; Achay's a tough nut and wants to hold on to his position. Borelli's a bit too handy with his fists, which could bring down too much attention from the local cops. Why are you interested in these two, anyway? You're not thinking they lifted your politician-in-hiding, are you?'

'No. From what you and Caspar have said it doesn't sound their style. I'm just looking at the murder of JoJo Vieira. If they never left Paris it lets them off the hook.'

'I see. That's not good. Still, I'll ask around, just in case anybody's heard. Give me twenty minutes and I'll get back to you.' Santer rang off and Rocco sat down and waited while ruminating on the puzzles before him.

Santer was even quicker than he'd promised. 'Good news – and bad. Abdhoun's out of the picture. He's been in hospital for the past five days with serious stab wounds to the chest and stomach. He got in a bar fight with a couple of past acquaintances from Oran. According to my guys on the street he's lucky to be alive and certainly not in any condition to travel anywhere, much less kill anybody.'

'And Borelli?'

'He's still around and been seen on a regular basis strutting with Farek's crew. If he's been out your way, he's found another form of travel that takes no account of time or space, if you know what I mean.'

'Thanks, Michel – I owe you a meal sometime.'

'That you do, my son. In fact, now you mention it, I know of a nice place which serves an excellent langoustine in garlic butter followed by smoked salmon, and a decent chilled Chablis to go with it. You'd like it, I promise.'

Rocco grinned. Santer never forgot his stomach for long. 'I'll bear it in mind. You said you had some bad news.'

'Well, only by implication. If we've discounted these two no-goods being responsible for Vieira's death, it means there's somebody else out there who knows what they're doing. And if they're acting on Farek's behalf, you could be next on the list. It's a pity you don't have the inside track on what Farek's been thinking.'

Rocco had already been thinking about how to get that information. It occurred to him that JoJo Vieira would have been close enough to Farek's circle for a while, at least, to have picked up any rumours and bits of gossip about the crime boss's intentions. He would certainly have stayed as close as possible because his own safety was at risk as long as he was providing inside information to the police. At the first hint that he was suspected of talking to them he would have headed for the hills, as was finally proven by his flight from Paris. Unfortunately, Vieira was no longer in a position to provide the answers Rocco wanted. But it prompted a thought.

'Do you know who was handling Vieira as an informant?'

'I do, actually. The team is headed up by a mate of mine. They're deliberately isolated from normal duties while it's going on, because the outcome is potentially so high-profile. Bringing down Farek will also bring down a raft of others. Why do you ask?'

'I'd like to talk to him. He might have something he hasn't thought relevant. And frankly, at the moment, I'm treading water.'

'I'll see what I can do.'

'Thank you. I need to get this done quick, though, so I'd rather it wasn't cleared through channels.' Any kind of inter-departmental clearance would take days, not hours, and would probably end in a refusal on jurisdictional grounds.

'Still ready to bend the rules, huh? Leave it with me and I'll call you with a time and place.'

Rocco dropped the handset and walked back to the map on the wall. He placed another pin, this time on the town of Dieppe, in Normandie. A channel port, it was roughly eighty kilometres from Amiens and just over an hour away.

Did the same person who killed Raballe also kill Vieira? It didn't sound like the same *modus operandi*, with one shot and the other stabbed; but who knew?

There was only one way to find out: he'd have to take a look for himself.

Twenty-eight

The town of Dieppe sat quiet and settled in the late morning sun, the light glancing off the roofs and windows and forming a haze out over the channel. Sea birds formed clusters, wheeling against the sky in their search for easy pickings down below. Beyond the town the sea was a glistening blue-grey backdrop dotted with boats inshore, while further out was the smoke trail and flashing wake of a ferry headed towards the English coast.

Rocco had been here once before, but not in connection with his job. Then he'd hoped to enjoy a few days' vacation, looking to unwind away from the city with Emilie, his wife. Now ex-wife. He experienced a momentary regret as he recognised some of the landmarks, and, beyond the town, the dark blue of the water. Back then he'd been trying to mend the increasingly visible cracks in their relationship, cracks that seemed to widen almost daily. After returning from military service in Indochina, he'd joined the police force much against Emilie's wishes. She'd been living with the danger in his military life, she'd said tearfully, and the possibility that he wouldn't come home one day. Now the police. It had been a step too far.

The stay had been a long way short of successful, and painfully short-lived. They had separated not long afterwards.

He shook away the memories and focussed on finding the town's Hôtel de Police. Parking outside in a reserved spot, he flashed his card at a uniformed cop on the front entrance, who nodded him through. He approached the desk and asked for Detective Franck Joncquet, with whom he'd had a strained conversation before leaving Amiens. Joncquet had announced himself as the detective in charge of investigating Raballe's death, but had lost no time in making it very clear that he didn't appreciate a detective from another force showing an interest. The matter was, he'd insisted, being dealt with and would soon be wrapped up.

Rocco had met men like him before, keen on protecting their bailiwick and anxious to keep outsiders away. For them, it was tantamount to calling into question their capabilities.

Ten minutes later, after an apology from the desk sergeant for being kept waiting, Joncquet appeared, chewing on a baguette and in no apparent hurry, his belly straining against his shirt front. He was in his fifties, but looked older, with a scrub of greying hair and an over-blown moustache. His suit had seen better days and Rocco recognised a man coasting down to his retirement and anxious not to push himself too hard along the way.

'So you're Rocco?' Joncquet stopped in front of him. He viewed Rocco with evident displeasure, no doubt for the benefit of the desk sergeant who was watching with interest. 'I've heard about you: the big shot from the city come to clean up for the country *paysans*, is that right?'

'If you say so.'

'Well, you're wasting your time with this one. Raballe was killed in an accidental shooting, probably by a two-two calibre. It hit him in the throat. No way back from that.'

'I'd like to verify that, if I may.'

'Why? I even know the kid who did it; little shit's been told before about shooting off his rifle in the open but he doesn't listen. His papa's a councillor and he thinks he's untouchable.' He took another bite of his baguette, crumbs cascading down his shirt front and scattering on the floor.

'Let's hope you're right, Detective.' Rocco agreed calmly. 'But this case has possible connections to the disappearance of a foreign government minister from a safe house just yesterday and the shooting of two cops, one of them dead. It's being investigated by the Ministry of the Interior. I think you at least owe me the courtesy of showing me what you've got so far. Don't you?' It wasn't quite the whole truth, but Rocco was counting on this mess of a man not questioning it. What he was also counting on was the police grapevine having passed information along about Bouanga's disappearance and the shooting of the two officers, something Massin would certainly have put into motion.

'What?' Joncquet stopped chewing and threw a glance at the desk sergeant. 'How can there be a connection? We're a long way from your patch. Anyway, it's the first I've heard of it.'

There was a dry rustle of paper and they turned to see the sergeant waving a telex. 'We got a call earlier today,' he said, 'and a level red bulletin just came in an hour ago about the two cops. I sent copies around the building.' He nodded at a notice board on the wall. 'It's up there, too.'

'Yeah, I saw it.' Joncquet looked annoyed and threw the sergeant a nasty look. It was evident that there was little liking or respect between them. It put the detective in a difficult situation. A level red bulletin was an all-eyes notification which he should have read as a matter of urgency and clearly hadn't. He was also in danger of word getting to his superiors that he wasn't being helpful to a fellow detective, which might make his retirement look suddenly less exciting.

'Detective Joncquet, I don't want to cause waves here,' Rocco said easily, to give the man an out. 'But if you can tell me what you've got so far, and allow me to look at the body and talk to your pathologist or whoever wrote up the forensic report, it would help our investigation and I can report back to the Ministry and close the file to everybody's satisfaction.'

Jonquet took the bait. Without a word he gestured with his baguette and led Rocco back the way he'd come. As Rocco passed the desk, the sergeant gave him a look which said 'nicely played'.

Joncquet took him through to a separate section of the building, where a technician in a white coat and rubber boots was hosing down a metal table, the water sluicing into a drain in the centre of the floor. The room would have made Rizzotti green with envy, Rocco thought, seeing the equipment on display. But it remained to be seen if the work done here was up to the doctor's same high standards.

At Joncquet's bidding the technician stopped what he was doing and turned off the hose. He went to a heavy door set in one wall and pulled it open. Seconds later he wheeled out a gurney bearing a form covered in a white cloth.

'We have a visiting pathologist who comes up from Rouen,' Joncquet explained. 'Unlike Amiens, I expect, we don't run to our own.'

Rocco didn't bother responding to the dig. Instead he signalled to the technician to lift the cloth. The man did so and stepped back, allowing Rocco to move in and inspect the body.

Former Detective Raballe had been heavily built, with skin mottled by a series of moles across his arms and shoulders. He had a faint and not very well executed tattoo of a dagger on one forearm, which Rocco guessed had been done in the army, and another smaller one on the opposite bicep. But it was the side of his throat which he was interested in. A dark wound had been punched through the skin close to the carotid artery, with the edges showing ragged and bruised.

Just like Vieira.

Rocco looked at the technician. 'Seriously, a gunshot wound?'

The man nodded, but appeared unsure, and glanced at Joncquet for support. 'That's right. The pathologist said it was consistent with a two-two round. There's no exit wound and he says the deceased probably choked on his own blood.'

Rocco went round the other side of the table and checked the dead man's neck. No exit wound and no sign of bruising. 'Did he determine the direction of the entry wound?'

'Straight through the side at right-angles. The bullet must still be in there.'

'Why hasn't he dug it out to make sure, then? I'm sure Raballe wouldn't object. It's been a week or more – it should have been done by now.'

'He couldn't.' The technician shuffled his feet. 'He's in hospital, collapsed with a heart problem. We've asked for a stand-in but they couldn't find one available until tomorrow.'

'May I check the wound?'

The man shrugged. 'I guess so, although I can't let you cut into the body.' He turned to a jar containing swab sticks on a side table, and picked one out. 'Help yourself.'

Rocco took the stick and inserted it into the wound. It went in with little difficulty, and showed the wound going through the throat at right angles as the technician had said.

'Joncquet? What do you think? A bullet to the side of the throat, with no exit wound? Why – there's nothing to stop it, even a two-two calibre.'

Joncquet was looking queasy, although Rocco doubted it was at seeing the body at close quarters; a man of his experience would have seen plenty in his career. He could probably see what Rocco was driving at and couldn't find an argument.

'I see what you mean. A bullet would have gone straight through,' he conceded. 'Unless it was deflected, of course.' But he didn't look convinced. 'So what was it made the hole, then, if not a bullet?'

Rocco pointed at the ragged edges to the wound. 'That tearing of the skin is caused by a weapon being pulled out. I suggest you get somebody in authority to phone Dr Rizzotti in Amiens. He'll verify what I'm saying.'

'Damn,' Joncquet breathed, and looked at the technician. 'You'd better get someone in here as soon as possible.' He turned to Rocco. 'What else do you want to see?'

'The scene of the killing.'

Ten minutes later Joncquet stopped his Renault at the side of a narrow road bordered on one side by fields, and on the other by a thick stretch of conifers. Rocco pulled in behind him and climbed out, and walked to meet the detective, who was standing next to a metal police tripod on the grass verge.

'The body was found here,' said Joncquet, 'by another dog walker. It's always quiet along here, especially early in the morning, apart from people with dogs and a few tourists who like trees. Most of them prefer the sea.'

For a split second Rocco saw a flash of the similarity between here and the lane where Vieira had died. The scenery around them couldn't have been more different, with trees rather than open fields, but there was the same sense of isolation and the stillness was the same: a quiet spot, with nobody around and the victim taken by surprise.

'Is the witness credible?'

'Very. He's a retired chemist, name of Palmet. He started training as a doctor, then switched courses. He's been here all his life and is well-respected. Ex-council member, too. He said he checked the body but there was no sign of life, although it was still warm to the touch. He reckoned it couldn't have happened very long before he arrived because the air was cool. There's a breeze off the sea sweeps right through here. Another half hour and it might have read very different.'

'And the body was right here? There was no sign of movement, or having been dumped?'

'That's correct. He reckoned Raballe had bled out right here.' Joncquet demonstrated by moving the tripod sign to reveal a dark patch in the sandy soil beneath the grass. Rocco didn't need to dig down to know that the chemist had read it perfectly. Serious blood loss.

'Did he report hearing a shot?'

Joncquet looked nonplussed. 'No. He didn't. I think that was a wrong assumption on our part.' He had difficulty meeting Rocco's gaze, and the admission had no doubt been difficult to make. 'If it wasn't a gun, what was it?'

'Our pathologist's best bet is a spike bayonet. If you've got a war museum here in town, you'll probably find one in their collection. You should borrow one and check it out.'

Joncquet's eyes flickered. 'I know the type you mean: they were used by commandos.' He was referring to local history. Dieppe had been the target for a spectacular raid during the war, when British commandos had found themselves thrown up against superior forces in what some had seen as an impossible obstacle. It had not been their finest hour and they had lost many men. 'I don't understand, though, who would use such a thing, and why?'

'I don't think the why matters that much,' said Rocco. 'It's probably just a killer's sick quirk. It's the who I'm interested in.' As he'd discovered early in his career, some killers chose an unusual weapon for no other reason than to be different, to build a reputation and stand out, as if the tool of their trade would grant them a special cachet among their peers. The reality was, more often than not, that their vanity in selecting something so specific and identifiable eventually led to their downfall, a signature they could not, in the end, shake off.

Rocco looked around. To his right the road ran inland through the trees on the edge of the forest; to his left was the road back towards the town.

'Are there any houses further along here?'

Joncquet nodded and pointed away from the town. 'There are a couple of workers' cottages round the bend, about three hundred metres away, but they would have been out of sight of what happened here.'

'Is that what they said?'

'Not exactly, but that's how it looks.' He flushed red as he said it, a sure giveaway to Rocco that Joncquet hadn't bothered to check.

'What about Raballe's place? Is that out of sight, too?'

'Same side of the road about half a kilometre further on. It was his brother's, but he died over a year ago. Raballe took it over and has lived there by himself ever since. As far as I could make out, other than walking his dog he's been pretty much a recluse.'

'Wouldn't you be,' said Rocco coolly, 'if a major criminal took out a contract on your life?'

He walked away towards his car, signalling the detective to follow. He didn't really care whether the man followed him or not, but it would reinforce the fact that he should have already tried what Rocco was about to do, instead of cutting corners.

Twenty-nine

He pulled up outside two small cottages, stone built with rough tiled roofs and heavy wooden shutters, with Joncquet close behind. Stacks of logs stood outside, drying ready for winter, and both properties had the same air of rural utility and a lack of sophistication that was common around Poissons.

He knocked on the door of the first cottage. It was opened by a tiny lady in a dark floral dress and a white apron, drying her hands on a small towel. 'Can I help you?'

'Sorry to disturb you, Madame,' said Rocco, and showed her his card. 'Could you tell me your name, please?'

She squinted at the card and said, 'Whatever that says, you'll have to read it to me, young man – I don't have my glasses with me. And my name is Huguette, thank you for asking. Are you from the town hall, only I've been expecting someone from the council about the state of my roof.'

Rocco explained who he was and his reason for calling. She listened carefully, eyeing Joncquet in the background, then shook her head. 'I'm sorry, but I don't recall seeing anybody. There's Palmet the chemist, of course, who walks down here every day – I see him fairly regularly, just in passing. I say chemist, but he hasn't been one for some time; it's more of an honorary title now although I'm not sure who decided that.' She squinted up at him and said, 'It's like military people, isn't it, who keep their titles even after they've retired? Why do they do that?'

'I'm afraid I don't know. Was there anybody else? It doesn't matter how insignificant it might seem to you, it might be important.'

She shook her head. 'I'm usually in the kitchen at the back, so I don't always see anyone unless they knock, like you just did. I heard about the dead man, though. Isn't it awful? And right on our doorstep. He hadn't been here long but it's still a tragedy.'

'Did you know him at all?'

She shook her head. 'I don't think anybody did really. He kept to himself and only spoke to be polite. His dog seemed to be his only companion. What happened to it, do you know?'

'It was found wandering along the road,' Joncquet put in, 'and taken to a rescue centre in town.'

'Poor thing. It's not as if you can explain to an animal what's happened to its owner, can you? They're the innocents in this kind of thing.'

'Is there anybody else here who might have seen something – your husband, perhaps?' Rocco asked her.

'My husband died six months ago, bless him.' She took a deep breath, the memory obviously vivid, then said, 'Try next door. Her name's Edith. Edith Capelle. She's always got her eyes on the road – and doesn't miss much, either.' Her voice dropped almost to a whisper. 'She's always been a bit of a busybody ever since school. She was class monitor, too, and nosey even then.'

'Do you mind if I do this one?' Joncquet murmured, as they walked back out into the road. 'I haven't done much else of any good on this case, have I?'

Rocco nodded, happy to let him regain some lost ground. 'Go ahead.'

They walked to the next cottage and Rocco waited while Joncquet went through the ritual, this time with another elderly lady. She scowled at both men and shook her head. 'Not me, sorry. You're talking about the man Raballe, aren't you? Is it true he was a policeman? Everybody in town is talking about it.'

Joncquet responded with a question. 'You didn't know him, then?'

'Only to nod to, you know, like you do. He didn't always speak, though. To be honest he always looked as if he had all the world's problems and none of the pleasures. But there are people like that, aren't there? It's sad, really.'

'Did you see anyone else in the road that morning?'

'The usual ones, people walking their dogs at that time of day, but that's about it. Not that I spend all my time looking – I have things to do. The tourists come a bit later in the day... walking or on bicycles, enjoying the forest. But apart from that, no. If that's all, gentlemen?' She began to close the door.

'How about vehicles?' Rocco asked quickly, before she could retreat.

'Well, there's never much traffic down here, certainly not early in the morning. When was this, last week? Dreadful business. Makes you frightened to go out.' She shivered at the idea. 'I didn't see any cars, anyway. A lorry from the co-operative down the road – I remember that because the driver, Emmanuel, is the son of a good friend of mine. There was a van, as I recall. But no cars.'

'A van?'

'That's right. Like the market people use. Only it wasn't one of them because there was no trade name that I could see and the local traders wouldn't stop there, anyway.'

Rocco stepped forward. 'Pardon me, Madame Capelle. My apologies, I didn't introduce myself before. Inspector Lucas Rocco, Amiens commissariat. I wonder if you could cast your mind back and describe exactly what you saw or remember about the van? It would be a great help in our investigation.'

The old lady looked him up and down, and half smiled at his courteous approach. 'Well, of course. Let me see... yes, I'd come out here to clean my front step, as I do a couple of times a week. We don't get too much dust and dirt from traffic, but I like to keep it looking nice, unlike some around here.' Her eyes flicked sideways towards the house next door. 'Anyway, as I was sweeping it, I heard the noise of a car door slamming. I looked up and saw a man just along the road there.' She pointed towards the bend in the road. 'He was standing by a van.'

'Was he doing anything?'

'No. Just standing there and smoking. I could see the smoke in the air above his head. But he kept looking the other way towards the town as if he was waiting for somebody. I thought perhaps he'd stopped to let somebody use the bushes, you know, like they do – and I was right.'

'How so?'

'Well, a woman appeared from in the trees further down. They must have been in a hurry to be somewhere because she was almost running. As soon as he saw her the man threw his cigarette down, which is a stupid thing to do around here with all the pine needles and the ground so dry. Anyway, they both climbed in and away they went towards town.'

Rocco already had a picture building in his head. If they had been waiting for Raballe to appear on his morning walk, it would have made sense; choose a quiet spot out of sight of any of the houses, then post a watcher and wait further along the road with the van out of sight of their target. To a walker, especially one with a good reason to be watching his back, a van being driven along the road looks a lot less threatening than a car waiting on the verge. The moment they saw him coming, they were on the move with the execution spot already picked out.

'Can you describe the two people or their van?' said Joncquet.

'Well, like I said, it was like the market traders use. But they weren't traders, I could see that from the way they were dressed. She was wearing smart clothes, a jacket and trousers, which you don't see every day around here, and he was dressed in a blue shirt and dark trousers. In fact,' she raised a finger, 'I thought he was a policeman at first. But of course a policeman wouldn't be driving around in a van with a young lady, would he? It wouldn't be right.'

'Could you see what they looked like, these two people?'

'Not really. A man and a woman, both reasonably young, I'd say – although everybody looks young to me. But I couldn't see their faces, not at this distance. Sorry.'

'Caspar? Wake up, man – it's Jean-Luc!'

Caspar rolled out of bed and trailed the phone line through to the kitchen where he wouldn't disturb Lucille. He'd had a late night reviewing security during a night shift at Orly, and with nothing specific on today, he and Lucille had decided to sleep in. It was now gone midday and his head felt stuffed with cotton wool. But he recognised Madou's voice immediately and that was enough to get him up.

'Go ahead.' He poured a slug of cold coffee from a battered aluminium cafetière to shake loose the remaining cobwebs and hoped the bar owner had something useful for him.

'What you were asking,' Madou said, his voice low, 'about who Farek's brought in to do his heavy work? You were ahead of the rush. It's not solid, you understand, but I've heard things from more than one source since you came in. In fact there's talk going round the bars like it's the biggest thing since Le Havre AC won the Coupe de France in 'fifty-nine.'

'Let me have it.' Caspar wasn't surprised by the rumour mill. In the minds of the kind of people frequenting Madou's dive of a bar, talk about a professional assassin on the loose would be too good to pass up. You could always catch up on the latest football news in the papers, and it wouldn't vary much week to week, but the idea of a professional killer being brought into the city to make a hit was rare enough to be exciting. You had to filter out the wild speculation from what was real, which was par for the course in the underworld, but that was why people like Madou were useful: they knew who had the inside tracks and were astute at sifting through to the gold dust.

'First, I was wrong about it being one person; it's two – a team. One's a spotter, the other is the trigger man. Word is, the spotter is a woman, but that's all I know.'

'Names?' He drank more cold coffee, the liquid gritty and bitter, and began to feel more awake.

'That's the problem – there are none. Farek must be playing this one really close to his chest.'

'Not surprising, is it? If he broadcasts who they are, they could end up coming after him instead.'

'Sure. These two come from down south, apparently. There's a story going round that the trigger is ruthless, and moves around a lot. He's even operated in Milan and Geneva and some are saying he goes under the label of Nightingale.'

'Seriously? Nightingale?'

'Hey, don't blame me for the silly name. The guys on the street love all that code stuff. Makes them go all gooey – and they're going stupid over this one, I can tell you.'

'How long have they been in town?'

'Well, that's the strange thing. I thought they must have only recently rolled in because there's been no solid mention before apart from the odd snippet, which frankly wasn't worth listening to. But now everybody's talking about it and saying they've been in the area for several days. And guess what?'

'Go on.'

'Word is they hit that cop, Raballe. Only it wasn't in Cambrai, but somewhere on the coast near Dieppe. It was a dry run, somebody suggested, practice for the real thing.'

'But using a live target.'

'Yes.'

'How solid is this information?'

'I'd put it at ninety-eight percent. Anyway, it's all I've got. For this you owe me a bonus, right?'

Caspar grunted. Ninety-eight percent from Madou was about as solid as it could get. The bar owner wasn't given to over-egging his information, even for the promise of more money.

'I'll put it through your door later today. Thanks, Jean-Luc. You'd better get out of town before it's too late.'

'I'm ready to go, don't worry.'

Caspar put down the phone and put the kettle on to boil. He now had a headache and needed more coffee, preferably hot, fresh and with plenty of sugar; but first he had to ring Rocco.

Thirty

Rocco followed Joncquet to Raballe's cottage further down the forest road. It was similar to the two he'd just seen, although not so tidy and in need of repair. Retired cops could be divided into two sorts, he thought, eyeing the jungle of a garden. There were the obsessives, who devoted all their time to a hobby or a new job, anything to drive away the memories they wanted to bury deep of the daily stresses that came from dealing with criminality, threats and violence; and there were those who, once they lost the cocoon of the police brotherhood and its routines, basically gave up and allowed themselves to die a slow, disintegrating death. He hadn't known Raballe, but he got the feeling the ex-cop had more or less slipped into the second camp, although his solitary existence may have been fuelled by his desire to hide away from whatever vengeance he suspected was going to follow.

Joncquet led him round the back of the cottage, past grimy windows and grey curtains, the shutters hanging open and loose on their hinges. He stopped at the back door.

'We came here to make sure it was secure,' he explained, 'but at that stage we didn't have any reason to suspect foul play.' He pulled a face at his own lack of diligence. 'I wish I'd done more, you know?'

Rocco said, 'Let's take a look inside, shall we?' He wasn't about to go softly on the man; any feelings of remorse might just make Joncquet play the game properly for however long he had left in the job.

Joncquet took a key from his pocket and opened the door. The air rushed out, heavy with the smell of rotting food and burned cooking oil, and dragging with it the musty aroma of neglect.

Rocco clicked the light switch inside the door, but it didn't work. Disconnected, he guessed, through non-payment or because the news of Raballe's death had reached the power company. In any case there wasn't much to see in the gloomy interior. A few dirty items of clothing had been left lying around where they'd been dropped, dirty dishes were piled in the sink and some stale crusts of bread lay scattered on the kitchen table with a line of ants making off with crumbs across the floor to a hole in the wall. A number of wine bottles were gathered in one corner like pins in a bowling alley, uncorked and empty, a testament to at least one of Raballe's regular habits. A dish containing a few segments of dried meat and some dead flies sat on the floor alongside a cereal bowl of water and a misshapen cushion layered with dog hairs.

Rocco moved through the house to the bedroom. Retired cops didn't spend a lot of time sleeping unless they hit the bottle or had done a hard day's work. In Raballe's case the bottles in the kitchen dispelled any notion of sleep or labour. For many, the bedroom was a kind of comfort, as alone with whatever thoughts troubled them as they were with the dark memories that undoubtedly dogged their waking hours.

A service weapon hung in a cracked leather holster from the back of a hard chair against one wall. He checked it; it was cleaned, loaded and ready to go. At least one habit that had stuck. Inside the wardrobe was a meagre collection of clothes on hangers and two pairs of stout black shoes. A single long drawer in the bottom held a jumble of underwear and socks, and a broken wristwatch with a browned face. Alongside it sat a box of ammunition.

'Looks like he was expecting trouble,' breathed Joncquet, eyeing the gun then the box. 'Odd, though, that he went out without his weapon.'

'Maybe he thought he was in the clear,' said Rocco. More likely, he thought, he simply got careless. Living out here, isolated from any contact with his old world, he might have grown to believe that any threat was now behind him.

They finished checking the rest of the house but there was nothing to suggest Raballe had been troubled before being attacked out in the road. In the end Rocco had seen enough. Given that the killer or killers must have known where he lived, if they had been fed the information by Farek's inside contact on the police force, they would have had plenty of time to watch him and nail down his routine carefully before moving in for the hit. All they'd had to do first was pick their time and place.

It was odd, though, that they hadn't chosen to deal with him here at the house. It was quiet and secluded, and unlikely to get much in the way of visitors. Unless the idea of a dog had deterred them. But the more he thought about it, and the similarity to the way Vieira had been dealt with, maybe it was the killer's preferred method: out in the open.

He said goodbye to Joncquet. The detective promised to write a revised report and get another pathologist to confirm the cause of death, then stuck out his hand.

'I'm sorry for everything, Rocco. That doesn't mean much and I don't blame you for thinking it.' He looked awkward and shifted his feet. 'I wasn't always a shit cop. I hope you can believe that.'

Rocco nodded. 'I can. How long before you hand in your papers?'

'Four months.'

'Then make sure you leave with a clear conscience. Get this written up properly and make sure the kid you thought had shot Raballe has a clean slate, too.'

Rocco was twenty minutes out from Amiens when he thought to switch on his radio and call in. There was a burst of static followed by background voices, then the familiar voice of the radio operator.

'Inspector Rocco, I have three messages for you: one is to call a Marc Casparon – I believe you have his number. Another is from Captain Santer about a time and location you requested. And Commissaire Massin wants to know where you are. This one is most urgent. Over.'

'Casparon. Got that. Keep the information from Santer until I get in, and please advise Commissaire Massin that I'm on my way.' Rocco switched off the radio; he could do without being peppered with more messages. He spotted a small village up ahead and decided to call Caspar from there. As for Massin, he would have to wait. Too much had been left to chance already and he didn't want to repeat the mistake by not picking up on any information Caspar might have found out about Vieira.

He pulled in alongside a *bar-tabac* near a crossroads and went inside. It was empty apart from one old man in a corner, reading a newspaper. The air was heavy with cigarette smoke and the lingering aroma of the lunchtime menu. Rocco ordered a coffee and asked to use the phone. The lady behind the bar dropped a *jeton* on the counter and pointed to an alcove at the back of the room.

Caspar answered immediately. 'I hope you're keeping one eye on your back, Lucas.' He relayed what the bar owner had told him about the hit team Farek had brought in, including the alleged shooter's tag name of Nightingale.

'Is it for real?' Rocco wasn't bothered by what name the killer liked to be called, but it might be useful to feed the name out there to see what it brought back. If it was known in criminal circles in Paris, it would be known elsewhere.

'Madou's information is usually solid, and he's desperate to get out of the game, so I don't think he'd sell me any duff information. The fact that this man has operated in Milan and Geneva sounds pretty genuine, too. If so, Farek's spent a lot of money to get these jobs done.'

'Thanks, Caspar. I owe you. But this ends here for you, right? Stay away from any of Farek's contacts from now on in case he decides to lash out even further.'

'Will do. From here on in, I'm out of sight.'

Rocco hung up. So, a two-person team; the shooter named Nightingale, the spotter a woman, names unknown. It fitted with the two people the old lady, Edith Capelle, had seen where Raballe had been killed. He was surprised by the presence of a woman. They weren't unknown in criminal organisations by any means, but they were usually used as runners, as fronts to cover for criminal activities or were simply willing but silent accomplices to their man's criminal career. He'd never come across one as an active member of a hit team before.

He drank his coffee, paid the bill and hit the road again for Amiens. He was going to have to tell Massin about this turn of events, before the rumour mill got there ahead of him.

Thirty-one

'Is there any reason why you kept this from me?' Massin was looking at Rocco with a flat stare after hearing about Farek's threat and his rumoured move to bring in an assassin to kill Rocco. 'One of my officers being threatened is a serious matter. Yet you decide to keep it to yourself. What the hell were you thinking, Inspector?'

'I needed to be sure that the rumour was credible,' Rocco replied calmly. He'd come straight in to see Massin and tell him everything he knew about the threat on his life. Massin reacting the way he did came as no surprise, and Rocco understood that. Senior officers didn't like being kept out of the loop, even though it was sometimes better for their own peace of mind. 'The criminal world lives and breathes rumour, you know that. The idea of a cop being targeted would have them feasting on it like flies on honey. But it wouldn't mean the rumour was correct.'

Massin didn't look mollified. 'That's for me to decide and for others closer to Farek and his activities to prove. As for this man – Caspar you say? How much faith do you place in his version of events?'

'I trust him implicitly.'

'But he was retired from the police on health grounds, wasn't he – a breakdown?'

'That's right.'

'So how do you know that in the state of an unsound mind he hasn't made up the whole story?'

'Because he was a very good officer with an excellent record of working the gangs in Paris and beyond. Captain Santer in Clichy will confirm that. I asked Caspar to look into it for me because he knows the people concerned, especially Lakhdar Farek himself, and he still has contacts in that world. He says his source is reliable and I believe him.'

'I see. And the detective Raballe was also on Farek's list?'

'Yes. Raballe had crossed him in the past and disrupted his activities, and Farek swore he'd get even. It took a while but it looks as if he finally carried out his threat.'

Massin took a walk around his office, hands held stiffly behind his back. 'I suppose it's no surprise that a career criminal like Farek blames you for the death of his brother, no matter how twisted his version of events. You're not exactly unknown following your previous work in Paris. No doubt Farek hopes to gain some kind of tortured kudos from carrying out his threat on a high-profile officer. What I don't understand is that hundreds of officers throughout France disrupt the activities of criminals every year, yet they don't get targeted. Why was Raballe singled out?'

'You mean why not hit me directly?'

'If you must put it that way, yes.'

'Caspar's source believes Raballe was a dry run.'

Massin's eyebrows shot up. 'Seriously? That's monstrous. Why would they do that?'

'Because practice makes perfect, I suppose – and Farek had a score to settle with Raballe, anyway, so why not take the opportunity to be done with it?'

Massin didn't respond immediately, but frowned for a moment, absorbing the statement.

'The official report on Raballe's death says he was shot with a small calibre weapon. But you believe differently, is that correct?'

'He was stabbed in the throat. I believe the killer waited for him to walk his dog as usual along a country lane, and drew up alongside him. Raballe either thought he was safe or he'd got careless; he'd left his gun behind in his cottage.' He took a deep breath and added, 'Also, I don't think Raballe was the only one.'

'You mean the man Vieira.' It wasn't a question. The next one, however, was. 'Did you verify the fact of Vieira's death with Rizzotti, by any chance – even though you'd been assigned to watch over Antoine Bouanga at the time?'

Rocco ignored the obvious hole he was digging for himself. It was too late to back out and in any case he had nothing to say that would change whatever was in Massin's mind. Instead he ploughed on calmly and said, 'Yes. But don't blame Rizzotti – that was my doing. Both deaths used the same approach, the same type of weapon and in a similar isolated location. I'm certain the killer was the same man.'

Massin nodded. 'So, let me get this straight, Inspector; you followed up the killing of Vieira, even after being told to hand it over to Desmoulins; you approached your mystery source, this former officer Caspar in Paris, and got him to verify your suspicions; then you drove to Dieppe and bluffed your way into their investigation to prove that Raballe was the victim of a pre-arranged assassination. Am I correct?'

'Yes.'

Massin came and stood right in front of Rocco, and stared him in the eye. A pulse was beating in the senior officer's cheek and he looked ready to explode, his breath hot and smelling faintly of oranges. 'Tell me, Rocco, what makes you think I shouldn't suspend you with immediate effect for disobeying my orders, or for going beyond your jurisdiction and intruding without official permission on another force's investigation? Either would be ample grounds for disciplinary action.'

Rocco stayed silent. There were times to speak and he judged this wasn't one of them. If there was to be a fall-out, he'd have to take it on the chin and hope to argue it out afterwards, but making matters worse by arguing the inarguable wasn't going to help.

Massin turned away and went behind his desk. 'I allow you a great deal of leeway, Rocco, I hope you realise that. It might not seem so at times, but it's true. You're a thorough investigator with exceptional instincts… although you push the boundaries of your authority to the limit. Would you agree with that assessment?'

Rocco nodded. 'I suppose.'

'Well, I'm glad we can agree on something.' Massin straightened a blotter on his desk. 'The only reason I'm not suspending you is because the local magistrate in Dieppe has been in touch about your visit. It seems the officer who investigated the murder of Raballe has admitted to not pursuing his duty thoroughly in following up all available leads in the case. That officer has also revealed that their resident pathology expert wrote up an incomplete and essentially false report on the cause of death which could have resulted in a wrongful arrest and conviction had you not intervened when you did.' He sniffed and stretched his neck against his collar. 'The magistrate has asked me to pass on his thanks for your assistance, and says the official reports will be amended to reflect that. It pains me to do so, Rocco, but it would be churlish to do anything else.'

'Thank you.'

Massin sat down and gestured to Rocco to do the same. 'The fact is, you now have a professional killer on your trail and we have to do something about it. That takes precedence in my mind. Members of the police force are not here to be used as target practice or for settling old scores. If that got to be the norm we would have open warfare on uniformed officers by any criminal with a grudge. But we also have the matter of Bouanga's kidnapping still completely unresolved, in spite of the Ministry's investigation team being on the case.'

'I have a question about the attack on Les Sables that's been bothering me.'

'Really? Just the one? Enlighten me.'

'Shooting the two officers seems almost… extreme.'

'I agree, it does. But officers get shot – it's one of the risks of the job, as you know only too well.'

'But why? One man didn't even have time to draw his gun, the other was shot in the back. The dead man clearly wasn't a threat, but he was killed anyway.'

'Your point being?'

'Lamotte said something earlier that's just come back to me. He said it could easily have been him, *Gardienne* Poulon and me on the ground, instead of the two men from Arras.'

Massin considered the suggestion seriously, his expression grave. 'They were easy targets for criminals without morals.'

'No. I think they *became* the targets. Shooting them was more like an execution – a vindictive reaction. The killers couldn't find me so they shot the officers instead.'

'That would suggest the kidnappers might not have been employed simply to kidnap Bouanga, but to dispose of you, too. It's a bit wild, isn't it? You and Bouanga aren't connected except by your current assignment.' He stopped speaking and stared at Rocco, eyes flickering with concern. 'You're not suggesting there's a connection with this Nightingale, are you?'

'Maybe. Nobody outside of this office other than the Arras division would have known about the change of guard. You issued instructions about keeping it quiet.'

'So you're suggesting they attacked the house expecting to find you there because they had no reason for thinking otherwise.'

'I know, it's crazy. There's just something about this that doesn't add up.'

'I agree it's odd. But we'll know the real answer when we find the kidnappers. Get them to talk and we'll have what we need.'

'If they know anything. I take it there's been no sign of them?'

'Not yet. As we don't even know what vehicle they were driving, we're probing in the dark, although the investigation team from the Ministry found what appears to be part of a headlight unit from a Simca by the front gate, where it was rammed open. But as there are plenty of those cars about, it's not going to be easy stopping and checking them all. I feel sure something will turn up, though.' He tapped his desk. 'I suggest you go home and get some rest and wait for developments. It's no good you driving around the countryside as well, and we don't yet know to what extent you might be being watched. Offering yourself as an open target would be pointless.'

'Actually, I was thinking of going to Paris.' Rocco explained that he'd been thinking about the Vieira killing, and how it might tie in with Raballe's death, simply because the orders would have come from the same person.

Massin gave him a sharp look. 'If you're suggesting going to speak to this Farek man, Inspector, I forbid it. He's already the subject of an investigation and I can't have you getting involved.'

'That wasn't my intention. I'd like to speak to the unit involved with handling the flow of Vieira's information. Vieira may have been a street thief, but he was no fool. By one account he was on his way to see me to give me some information in return for his safety. If he'd heard something about the planned assassinations, he might have mentioned it to the unit but it hasn't filtered out yet. I gather they've been keeping things close to their chests to prevent Farek finding out the name of their informant.'

Massin chewed it over, eyes scanning his desk in search of answers. Finally he nodded. 'Very well. Do it. But don't tread on anybody's toes.'

Twenty minutes later, after a call to Santer to confirm details of the meeting, Rocco was on his way to an address in Neuilly, in the north-western outskirts of Paris, to see the head of the unit dealing with JoJo Vieira and the Farek investigation.

'His name's Georges Kopa,' Santer had told him. 'His unit's been billeted out in an abandoned print works to keep them away from other officers and allow them free rein to pursue their investigation in isolation. He'll give you whatever he can, but he can't promise much.'

Rocco wasn't expecting answers to drop into his lap, but right now, any activity was better than none. Sitting down and waiting for Farek's killers to call on him was a surefire way of ending up with the same fate as Raballe.

He found the print works, surrounded by wooden hoarding and plastered with notices announcing the imminent development of the area into shops and housing. He knocked on the door and waited. Two minutes later it was opened and he was asked for his card by a surly individual in workman's clothing and boots who directed him to an office on the first floor. It held three desks and some old filing cabinets, all of which looked as if they'd been there since the building was first put up. An older man was working at one of the desks, sorting out a pile of papers.

'Rocco?' Inspector Kopa was a slim man with thinning hair and doleful eyes, wearing a gun on his hip. He stood up from behind a battered desk covered in paper, and shook hands. 'Santer says I can trust you, which is good enough for me.' He smiled, adding, 'You wouldn't have been allowed inside the building otherwise. He also said to remind you that you owe him big for this, although I don't need to ask what that means. With Santer I figure it has to involve food.' He indicated his colleague. 'Jules, my number two.'

Jules nodded but said nothing. He had the sour look of a man who'd been disappointed too many times and learned not to trust anybody at first or even second glance.

Rocco nodded back and took a seat while Kopa poured coffee. 'This place is a bit out of the way, isn't it?'

Kopa shrugged. 'It had to be. You heard about the mole who fed out Raballe's address to Farek? Don't worry – it's common news down here. The thing is, we figured Farek was clever enough not to have just one insider; he'd have another in reserve. So we got permission to isolate the unit from our usual office and keep everything to ourselves while we were building a solid case. Santer told me about your history with the Fareks and how you took down Sami, so I reckon you know they've got their tentacles everywhere.'

'Pretty much. But it wasn't me who took down Sami.'

'Yeah, I think everybody knows that. But I doubt Farek cares. In fact I think he's already dealt with the two men who arranged it.' He took a sip of coffee and lit a cigarette. 'You know what it's like with vermin like him: he's been shouting the odds about you for so long it would look bad for him if he suddenly changed his tune and let you off the hook. It's all about face with people like him. Any sign of weakness and the other rats will move in for the kill. Anyway, how can I help?'

'You heard about Vieira's murder?'

'I did. That was a shock. We thought JoJo would stick it out but being beaten up must have spooked him. One minute he was around, the next he'd dropped out of sight.' He stubbed out his cigarette, leaving a plume of grey smoke rising in the air and ghosting off the ceiling. 'To be honest we'd got as much as we were likely to get from him, anyway. I know that sounds harsh, but you know how it works with informants.'

'I do. They don't last long.'

'Not if they can't keep their mouths shut. We figured JoJo had already pushed his luck by talking to the wrong people and splashing his money around. We'd warned him to back off but he wouldn't listen. Any ideas on who did it?'

'That's what I was hoping you might help with. The word I've picked up is that Farek's brought in a professional team from somewhere down south.'

'Do you know who?'

'A man and a woman. The man goes under the name of Nightingale. I think he did for JoJo and Raballe, using the same weapon and MO.'

Kopa whistled softly. 'If we could prove that, Farek would be in line for the guillotine. And you think JoJo knew something?'

'Possibly. I know he was coming to see me because he thought I could protect him, and he had information to trade.'

Kopa lifted an eyebrow. 'Who told you that?'

'His sister told a friend of mine that he'd mentioned my name just before disappearing.'

'Miriam? I know her. She's dead straight.' He looked at Rocco, his expression suddenly tight. 'A friend, you say? You sure it wasn't you she told?'

At the desk across the room, Jules had stopped shuffling papers and was watching, the atmosphere in the room suddenly tense.

'Not me, I promise. I was busy in Dieppe, checking Raballe's death.' Rocco waited it out, knowing what was happening. They were suspicious that somebody – namely himself – had been intruding on their turf unannounced. For normal cops it was a discourtesy and, as in Joncquet's case in Dieppe, might be seen as acceptable if it pushed forward their investigation. But for men like Kopa and his colleague, who were operating in a bubble of strict secrecy and close to wrapping up a big case, it was dangerous and a potential threat to weeks, maybe months of work if word of what they were doing got out.

'Who's this friend, then? He must be local to have got to Miriam.' Kopa sat back in his chair, a clear indication that if Rocco didn't answer, their meeting was over and done.

Rocco hadn't wanted to mention Caspar's help if he could get away with it, but he saw no way round it. Some cops instinctively distrusted colleagues who'd been laid off with stress-related illnesses, as if they, too might become infected. It was illogical, but it was the way things were. 'Marc Casparon.'

Kopa nodded. 'Caspar? Yeah, I know him. He was a good man. I thought he'd gone private.'

'He has. He does me a favour now and then when I need it.'

Kopa relaxed. 'Fair enough.' He leaned forward and shuffled some papers for a moment. 'JoJo mentioned you, as it happens. He asked about you a couple of times, in fact. Did you know him, maybe from when you worked up here?'

'No. I never met him.'

'It was a bit strange. We just thought he was reaching, you know – looking to get some kind of credit by saying he knew this top cop who'd taken down Sami Farek. But he never said he'd try to get to you or why.'

'As a crook, JoJo was strictly third-class,' said Jules, speaking for the first time. 'He did low-level criminality and wasn't particularly good at it. It was like he'd never really got the knack, you know? Like a sheep dog that doesn't understand what he's supposed to do. Good at running but crap at following the whistle.'

'But he must have had his uses?'

'Absolutely. I'm not denying he brought us some useful stuff. He was sneaky and clever at being in the background around people like Farek and his scummy *potes* without being noticed. If he had a strength, that was it.'

'Part of the fittings,' said Rocco. He'd known others who could merge into the background like that; hell, Caspar for one, and he was a cop.

'Exactly. It's how he was able to pick up information the way he did. It wasn't always gold dust by any means, but it helped fill in the picture. He also knew which buttons to push to get us listening and chasing our tails. That was his downfall.'

'How so?'

'He got greedy. In the end he'd spun us one too many lines, telling us what he thought we wanted to hear, and was running out of chances.'

'Like what?'

'He was taking up way too many man hours, checking out some of the rubbish claims he was making about potential jobs Farek's crews were involved in. His information was getting sketchy, too. I reckon it was because he was being excluded once they figured he might be a snitch. I'm amazed he wasn't dumped sooner, to be honest; Farek doesn't usually waste time dealing with people he doesn't trust.'

Kopa said, 'Jules was all for cutting him loose and so was I in the end.'

'But you still used him?'

'Less and less. The information always sounded right, but he was a good talker. A few of the rumoured jobs were genuine but low level, not even worth following up because we knew Farek would have covered himself. The others were JoJo just pulling our strings with make-believe to get some extra money. We were on the point of dropping him when he took off.'

'See this?' Jules picked up a fistful of paper, mostly scrap, of the sort you'd find at the bottom of a waste basket in a busy office. 'He brought that in the day he went and dumped it on us. Said it had some real gold we could use if only we could be bothered to look. Cheeky little sod.'

'And did it?'

'No idea. He was pissed at the time and started getting hands-on with a female colleague. He also stank the place out as if he hadn't washed in a week, so we showed him the door. If you ask me, he'd outlived his usefulness.'

Rocco felt a touch of anger at the callousness shown by the man, but held back from judging him. Dealing with people like JoJo Vieira was never an easy ride. Criminals lived and breathed cynicism in their everyday lives, saw themselves as being marginalised and hounded by the police and their own kind, so when they did encounter people who might be able to help them, they harboured nothing but suspicion because that's how they saw themselves judged by others.

In the face of this apparent dead end, Rocco felt his enthusiasm beginning to drain away. He'd had no idea what to expect from these men, but he'd been hoping for something – anything to forge a link between Farek and the murders of JoJo Vieira and Detective Raballe.

Jules huffed in ill-concealed irritation and stood up. He dropped the papers on the desk in front of Rocco and said, 'Here. You know the kind of stuff we're looking for. Take a look for yourself while you're here. Who knows, you might find something useful to take back to whatever-it-is backwater you've come from.' With that he turned and walked out of the room, slamming the door behind him.

Kopa looked nonplussed. 'Sorry, Rocco. That was uncalled for. He's having a tough time at the moment, with retirement coming up in six months. He hates fishing and gardening and can't stand the idea of working with guard dogs and building sites. And I heard yesterday his wife threatened to kick him out if he doesn't get another job.'

'Too much time spent on this case?'

'This and others. He's a career cop, same as you and me, and can't let go at five o'clock like an office worker. It's what gets most of us in the end, right?'

Rocco knew the situation all too well. 'You're right.' To show willing he picked up the papers Jules had dropped and began to leaf through them. Most of it was fit for burning: scribbled notes to or from unnamed people suggesting times and places that seemed to have a code of their own; receipts for meals, mostly involving several people but no names; copies of shipping or consignment notes for goods brought into a warehouse district out towards Orly airport; crumpled bills... and an envelope holding half a dozen black and white photographs. Rocco leafed through them. Most were unfocussed and contained nothing of any worth.

But there was one that brought him up short.

It was a shot of the interior of a restaurant, with lots of fancy mirrors and ornate ceilings, and waiters in the background in white aprons and dark bow ties. Very Parisien, very *chic*. The kind of establishment frequented by the rich and influential and much too expensive and exclusive for the masses, he guessed. He turned the photo over. There was nothing on the back, no indication of where or when it had been taken.

He held it up for Kopa to see. 'Do you know this place?'

Kopa peered at it and nodded straight away. 'That's Place Carnot. It's along Boulevard Malesherbes in the 17th arrondissement. Very high-end and supposed to be nice if you can afford it, which I can't. Why?' He stood up and came round the desk, sensing something important.

Rocco was looking at the faces. Four men and two women, all dressed smartly for a party. The odd thing was, none of them were looking at the camera, but at a waiter to one side holding a large menu board, as if in the act of reading out the specialities of the day. 'Do you know these people?'

Kopa pulled a face. 'Farek, of course, you know,' he said, pointing at a man on the far left of the photo, dark-eyed and smiling as if he owned the world. He was dressed in a smart dinner jacket and Rocco immediately saw the resemblance to his dead brother, Samir. 'His current number two, Seb Achay, is next to him.' Achay was short and balding, with a prize-fighter's nose and sharp, button eyes. He was standing slightly back from the others with his arms folded, which Rocco thought was telling; maybe he didn't want to be there.

'He doesn't look happy.'

'Achay? He never does. He was born miserable, the little runt, and came out nasty. Rumour has it that he sees himself as the next boss but Farek's not moving over.' He tapped the photo. 'I don't know the two women, so they're probably just sweet filling for the evening. The next man is a moneylender named Tuquet. We're pretty sure he's been bank-rolling Farek's expansion plans. If so he probably knows more than anyone else about his network. I wouldn't mind being able to get him in a cold dark place and see what he could tell us. I don't know the young guy, though. One of Farek's minders, probably, staying close to protect his boss.'

Rocco took a deep breath, of the sort that always came up when he sensed himself on the brink of something important. 'I thought you'd know all his current crew.'

'We should, you're right. But this one's a new face. Hang on – Jules!'

Seconds later Jules appeared in the doorway, munching on an apple. 'What?'

'Take a look at this, will you. You know Farek's people. Who's the young guy on the far right?' He took the photo and held it out. The man he was talking about was about thirty years of age with dark eyes and hair, and the kind of looks some people might have classed as handsome, were it not for a weak slant to his mouth.

Jules looked at it carefully, then shook his head. 'No idea. Doesn't ring a bell, anyway. He looks Italian. The restaurant's Place Carnot, I can tell you that. A member of staff, maybe? Where did you get it?'

'Among those papers you gave me,' said Rocco. 'Any idea from the people in it when it might have been taken?'

Jules dropped his apple in a nearby bin, his interest stirred. 'Yeah. Not from the people, though. They had the interior remodelled just recently. It was finished about three weeks ago, with all those fancy mirrors put in instead of paintings. Must have cost them a fortune.'

'So it would have been taken sometime since then?'

Jules scowled in frustration, no doubt at the knowledge that he'd had this photo close at hand and had never looked at it. 'You're right. Why the hell did Vieira bring it in here?'

'Good question.' Kopa was watching Rocco carefully. 'You know something, don't you?'

Rocco nodded. 'Not something, but someone.' He took the photo back and pointed at the young man and, next to him, a young woman. The last time he'd set eyes on the man, he'd been standing in Café Schubert in Amiens, telling Rocco that the woman next to him in the photo had just walked out of the door of the café.

'I believe this young woman is an associate and spotter for the man next to her.'

'A spotter? Does that mean what I think it does?' Kopa looked surprised. 'So who's the man – or should I say, what?'

'He's a professional assassin known as Nightingale.'

Or, as Rocco knew him, Officer Jouanne, recently on guard at the Amiens station.

Thirty-two

Rocco headed back to Amiens as fast as conditions would allow. Late afternoon traffic was already building, and he was conscious of being away from the office for too long in case of any breaking news. He'd left Kopa and Jules staring at the photograph from Place Carnot after getting Jules to run off a few extra copies.

'The thing I don't understand is,' Jules had said, 'if this Nightingale is a pro, why would he allow someone to take a photo of him? That's professional suicide for an assassin, surely.'

'He probably didn't know it was being taken,' Kopa had countered. 'They're not even looking at the camera. I bet this was Farek playing smart: get a picture of his new hitman just in case he ever needed to trade it in, a favour for a favour. He's a man who thinks ahead.'

'I agree,' said Rocco. 'Somehow JoJo must have got hold of the photo among some other bits and pieces and brought it away hoping he could use it. From what you say he was an opportunist.'

'Unless he actually knew who the man was,' said Kopa.

'Knew or suspected. If he was as adept at picking up scraps of information as you say, he might have heard about the meeting and was looking for something in case he could do a trade with you.'

'Or you. He was on his way to see you, you said.'

'He was taking a hell of a risk, though,' Jules muttered. 'He wasn't the brightest button in the box, and always had that shifty look about him. I'm amazed he wasn't found out earlier.'

'He was just trying to save his own neck.' And in the end, thought Rocco, it hadn't worked.

Jules was tapping the photo. 'And this woman is the killer's spotter?' He didn't sound convinced. 'She doesn't look the type.'

'You're right. But isn't that the whole point? She leads the way and gathers information, and sets up the target for the killer. Who better than a young woman?' Rocco was recalling their brief conversation in the café in Amiens. He'd taken her for an office worker, smart, attractive and utterly normal. Yet she'd been sizing him up as a target. He related the details to the two men, including the fact that the man had passed himself off as a policeman by bluffing his way into the station as a new transfer.

'He's got balls, then,' Jules murmured. 'Her, too.' He still sounded unsure, but his mood had mellowed. 'Sorry about my response earlier, Rocco – that was unprofessional. It's been a long haul and it looks like being for nothing if we can't take this any further.'

Rocco dismissed it. 'Forget it. If we can make these links stick, you'll get your result.'

Kopa was silent, staring at the photo as if it were the Holy Grail. 'Rocco's right,' he breathed at last, looking at Jules. 'This proves Farek has had a meeting with an assassin. If we can prove that's what this Nightingale does, and place him at the scene of the murders, we get him *and* Farek all tied up with a bow.'

Rocco wasn't sure if it would work out quite as simply as that; pros like Nightingale were usually very good at keeping their real identities secret, especially from their clients. They were, after all, employed by people who wanted others killed for their own ends. Trusting them was foolish: people like that would not hesitate to turn in the assassin if the need arose. But he understood Kopa's excitement at the prospect of success. Months of work trying to nail a high-level career criminal often ended with the suspect walking free because of a hole in the available evidence or a lack of concrete proof. If the man he knew as Jouanne was actually the assassin Nightingale, Farek might find it a little hard to walk away from this if all the links could be put together.

On arrival back at the office he went in search of Captain Canet. There was something he needed to confirm before going up to Massin's office, and it couldn't wait. If the outcome was what he was expecting, the balloon would go up in no uncertain manner, and Canet would need to know beforehand. He found the normally genial officer at his desk, staring at a sheet of paper in his hand as if it might burst into flames at any moment.

'Problem?' said Rocco.

'Bloody new intake,' Canet muttered. 'I'm missing my wife's birthday party for this. They seem to think they can come and go as they please. I've got two new officers off sick and now another one seems to have vanished like a puff of smoke. With everything else kicking off *and* the Tour coming up, I need absentees like a hole in the head. Where the hell do they get recruits these days? Is it the uniform they like, do you reckon – or the opportunity to chase villains and crack a few heads?' He stopped, aware that he was rambling. 'Sorry, Lucas. Was there something you wanted?'

Rocco handed over one of the photos from Place Carnot. 'Is this man one of your absentees?' He pointed at the figure on the right.

Canet stared at it in surprise and jumped up from his chair. 'Christ on a bike – it's Jouanne! And isn't that–?' He searched for the name, snapping his fingers. 'I've seen his picture somewhere.'

'Lakhdar Farek.'

'The gangster, that's it. Samir's brother – the one you had a run-in with. But what's Jouanne doing with him?'

'Jouanne is what he calls himself at the moment. He's not a real cop, he's just adept at passing himself off as one. I'm pretty certain he's actually a professional killer known as Nightingale.'

'Wha–?' Canet stared at him. 'You're kidding me! A killer?'

'Yes. The photo was taken less than three weeks ago, at a restaurant called Place Carnot in Paris.' He explained briefly about the covert unit who'd been running JoJo Vieira. 'The other men in the photo are Seb Achay, Farek's number two, and a money-man associate. I believe they were having a meeting to discuss, among other things, the killing of JoJo Vieira and Detective Raballe... and me.'

'And the woman?' The colour had drained from Canet's face as he absorbed the information, and he seemed too stunned to comprehend fully what Rocco was telling him.

'The woman next to Jouanne is his spotter. They work as a team. Jouanne told me a couple of days ago that a young woman had been asking questions about me, and made it seem as if I had an admirer. I didn't realise it but the same woman turned up in the Schubert and we had a brief chat. She said she was in town looking for work. When she'd gone, Jouanne had the neck to tell me she was the one who'd been asking after me.'

'But why? What were they playing at?'

'Mind games, I expect. Maybe they get a kick out of getting close to a target before carrying out the hit. Nobody said assassins were normal people.'

'Hang on, Lucas. Don't get me wrong, I'm not discounting what you say, but where's this coming from? Let's say Jouanne is an imposter, he wouldn't be the first sad lunatic to get a kick out of passing himself off as a cop. But an assassin as well?'

'Why not? What better way of picking up details that only cops would know – like my movements and routine?' Rocco told him about the cop in Clichy who'd passed information to Farek about Raballe's whereabouts, which had led to his murder. 'It's probably not the first time he's played cop, either. He certainly has some nerve.'

Canet said, 'But he had the right paperwork – I saw it!'

'Did it check out?'

'Well, I didn't do it myself, I left it to...' He stopped. 'Oh, God, I don't believe it.'

'What?'

'I gave it to our office supervisor to get signed off upstairs, but she's been off sick ever since. What with everything else going on, it's probably still on her desk.'

'I wouldn't bet on it,' said Rocco. 'If this Jouanne was clever enough to bluff his way into a position here with fake papers, he'd have made sure those papers disappeared the first moment he got.' He gestured upwards. 'I've got to report what I've found to Massin. You want to come with me?'

Canet nodded, his eyes blank. 'I think I'd better. Christ, how do I explain this away?'

Rocco had no answer for him. The truth was they'd all been fooled by an expert, and would have to learn from it. For now, though, it was best to be open about what had happened and let Massin know.

They walked upstairs and were met in the corridor by Massin. The senior officer was staring out of a window as if contemplating his future. He said nothing when he saw the two men, but turned into his office, beckoning them to follow. He seemed surprised by Canet's presence, but all he said was, 'Do you have anything to report, Rocco? Only I've been getting questions from the Ministry about our lack of progress. It would be nice to have something to report to get them off my back.'

Rocco was surprised by this change of tack for Massin. He was normally so uncritical of the Ministry. Maybe the pressure of this business was getting to him. Before he could speak, however, the door opened again and in walked Gerard Monteo.

'Where the hell have you been?' Massin demanded, almost as if the words were out before he could stop them.

'I've been busy,' Monteo replied. 'I was called back to the Ministry at short notice. There have been developments in Gabon which couldn't be left unattended, and I was the only one who could deal with it. I won't bore you with the details.' His eyes swept across all three men and came to rest on Rocco. 'I hear you've lost Bouanga. Bit careless, wasn't it?'

Rocco wondered if drop-kicking the little tyke down the stairs could be done without losing his job, and decided not. Maybe he could put sugar in his petrol tank... or something stronger. Instead he said, 'He was taken sometime during the night. Two officers on guard were shot, one dead, the other seriously wounded. If you dismiss that as simply "careless", you're a bigger ass than I thought.'

'Thank you, Rocco.' Massin said quickly, as Monteo's face registered shock. He continued, 'I'm sure Mr Monteo didn't mean to be insulting, although,' he paused and looked at the Ministry man, 'an apology wouldn't go amiss.'

'Why? I don't see what I have to apologise for. There's clearly been some lack of co-ordination here if somebody could simply walk in and take Bouanga hostage. Have you any idea of the work I've put into this project? Now it's all ruined–'

'Enough!' Massin held up a hand to cut off any further talk. 'This is outrageous. May I remind you that *you* refused to help with any budget for this "project"; *you* insisted that we take it on without considering the ramifications for this office and the men and women in it; it was *you* who made sure that your part in this was kept entirely clean while any faults or failings would fall squarely on this office and my staff. So don't talk to me about your hard work. The only hard work you've performed is on your own image in the eyes of the Ministry!'

'I say, François–'

'I haven't finished.' Massin cut him off. 'Your lack of consideration and poor management has cost one officer his life and another to suffer serious injuries that may well cost him his job.'

'What? You can't lay the blame for that on me.'

'Are you saying you didn't give an interview to Serge Houchin, a local reporter?'

'Yes. I mean, I did, but I didn't tell him about Bouanga.'

'You didn't have to. The man's a reptile but he's not stupid. He knew you wouldn't be here checking our stocks of pencils and paper. So it had to be something important. Are you sure you didn't drop a hint about Bouanga?'

'Absolutely. If he says I did he's lying.' But Monteo's voice had dropped and his face flushed, a clear signal that he wasn't sure.

Massin pounced. 'And here you are after having disappeared without the courtesy of informing anyone where you were going,

219

suddenly turning up and heaping the blame on my staff – and, by implication, me!' He reached down and picked up a folder. 'Just for the record, I have a full and detailed set of notes of our meetings and every word uttered by you, including your refusal to provide adequate funding or resources. Every page has been signed and dated by my fellow officers. Should I drag Houchin in here as well and ask him what he learned from you? He's never been known not to brag about his inside connections.' He leaned forward. 'Now what do you have to say for yourself?… Or do I have to send this folder off to the Ministry by courier today?'

Monteo's mouth opened and closed as if to object, but faced with Massin's verbal onslaught and the folder being thrust in his face, he back-pedalled rapidly. 'Of course, I apologise. That was insensitive of me.' He raised both hands in surrender. 'I can only plead exhaustion from my travels. I wasn't briefed about any shooting, just the abduction. I'm sorry.' He turned to Rocco and said, 'Please accept my apologies, too, Rocco. I was out of order.'

Rocco nodded without comment and turned to Massin. 'I need to discuss the Farek situation with you. Shall I come back?' It was as clear as he could make it that he didn't want to talk about his trip to Paris in front of Monteo. He didn't trust the man not to find some issue with jurisdictions in a bid to puff up his own importance.

Massin, though, seemed in no mood for discretion. With a stern look at Monteo he said, 'I'm sure anything we discuss here will not go any further. What did you discover?'

Rocco gave a summary of his meeting with Kopa and Jules, and placed the photo taken at Place Carnot on the desk. He ran through the known names of those present, including Jouanne, and the roles of Farek and his colleagues.

Massin didn't react to the officer's name, but Rocco wasn't surprised; in a busy station with new people arriving recently, it would have been hard keeping up with everybody. Rocco's tone when he used the name was enough, though, to tell Massin that there was something significant about Jouanne.

He tapped the photo. 'Do we have any further information on this man?'

Rocco looked at Canet, who stepped forward and relayed what he now knew about Jouanne. By the time he'd finished, Massin was looking stunned. He stepped out from behind his desk and walked around his office, shaking his head. Monteo opened his mouth to speak but a swift wave of the commissaire's hand silenced him.

'How?' Massin demanded of nobody in particular. 'How could this happen – a killer simply strolls into this station and assumes the position of an officer on guard?' He returned to his desk and began leafing through a folder, scattering sheets of paper until he found what he was searching for. 'Hell and damnation!' he swore softly, and tossed two sheets of official-looking paper onto the desk, with a black-and-white photo of Jouanne attached by a paper clip. 'These made their way up here for countersigning by me. This one even carries the official Ministry stamp!' He slapped the papers with the back of his hand.

'Impossible,' muttered Monteo, peering past Rocco at the papers. 'Clearly forgeries, anyone can see that.'

Rocco and Canet looked down at the papers. It was a transfer authorisation for Junior Officer Romain Jouanne to be attached to the Amiens *commissariat* as part of his training period. Massin's signature was on the bottom.

'They look authentic to me,' said Rocco. 'Especially with the stamp.'

'They are,' Massin confirmed. 'I've seen enough of them in my time. Somehow this Jouanne was able to get hold of a genuine transfer document.' He slid the paperwork back into the folder. 'I'll have to report this to my superiors; if it's stolen paperwork they'll want to hold an internal investigation to find out where it came from. It would have serious security ramifications for all forces if this became widespread.'

Monteo cleared his throat, clearly wanting to join in, but a warning look from Massin stopped him from speaking.

'I'm sorry, sir,' said Captain Canet. 'I should have checked with the issuing office and Jouanne's supposed last posting.'

Massin waved the apology away. 'It wouldn't have made any difference, Captain. There was no reason why any of us should have checked, although,' he gave Monteo a cold look, 'clearly the Ministry needs to review its procedures.' He looked back at Canet. 'Do we know where this Jouanne was staying?'

Canet shook his head. 'His file says he was staying temporarily in a small hotel in town until a room became available in the *gendarmerie* barracks. We have an arrangement with them for personnel on assignment. When he didn't check in for his shift I rang the hotel. They don't have a record of anyone of that name staying there.'

Massin was about to speak when there was a sharp knock at the door, and it opened to admit a uniformed officer waving a telex.

'Apologies, sir, but you asked for immediate sight of any information on the missing man, Bouanga.'

'What is it?' Monteo demanded, but Massin snatched the telex and scanned it quickly as the officer left.

'There's been a development.' He handed the telex to Rocco. Officers on traffic duty on the outskirts of Arras, to the north of

Amiens, had stopped a Simca Vedette being driven erratically. The car, which was large and modelled on sweeping American automobile lines, contained a number of men and a woman. The front seat passenger had produced a handgun and threatened to shoot the officers. In spite of that, they had managed to pull the man from the car and arrest him. As they'd done so they'd heard screams coming from the back and noted an older man and a woman struggling to get out. The car then drove off before they could stop it. The gunman was later found to be a Congolese national, and confessed that three other men in the car were, too, but the identities of the man and woman were unknown.

Bouanga and Excelsiore, Rocco thought. It had to be. But there was no mention of Delicat. He wondered why the kidnappers had stayed in the area. Arras was less than forty minutes away from Amiens, perhaps even less at night on quiet roads. If Bouanga's enemies were responsible and intent on disposing of him as they'd threatened, why hadn't they done so at the house or shortly after taking him, before disappearing? They would have had a head start and been well away before anyone had been any the wiser. And why use Congolese nationals? None of it made sense.

'You look puzzled,' said Massin.

'They didn't go far after kidnapping them,' Rocco replied. 'Why not? Kidnappers usually get clear of the immediate area to avoid police cordons. And this gang had plenty of time to do that – hours, in fact. They could have been on the other side of Paris by now: away and clear.'

'We'll probably never know. If they're driving around so openly and producing a weapon at a road block, they're clearly amateurs.' He stopped as his phone rang, and snatched it up. He listened for a few moments, then thanked the caller and put the phone down. 'That was a follow-up report from Arras. The officers on traffic duty were on foot with their prisoner and weren't able to mount a pursuit, but an officer going off duty saw what happened and followed the car to a factory complex outside Cambrai. He confirmed that at least one of the men was armed and a man and a woman seemed to be their prisoners.'

'I know the place,' said Canet. 'It's a network of old buildings and warehouses from the twenties. It hasn't been used in years. It's like a rabbit warren in there.'

'Fine,' said Massin. He picked up his phone and issued rapid orders. Then he turned to Rocco. 'I'm authorising you to take Desmoulins and join up with *Sous-Brigadier* Godard and a unit of his *gendarmes mobiles*. They're already on their way to the site to assess the scene. I'd like you to give them every assistance. Men from Arras are also on their way. You know what Bouanga looks like, so you can brief everyone in case there's any resistance. The last thing we need at this stage is one of our officers seeing a black face and shooting dead the man we're trying to rescue.'

Monteo finally pushed himself forward. 'I would like to be present as well, Massin. Bouanga is, after all, my responsibility.' He pushed his chin forward and squared his shoulders.

Massin looked at Rocco. 'Inspector?'

'Better not. The wrong people can get shot on these operations.' The look he gave Monteo left the man in no doubt that insisting on joining them would be a very bad idea.

'I agree,' said Massin. 'Anything else?'

'No.' Rocco felt relieved. At last, something positive to do. He'd worked with Godard before and trusted him and his team. They were professional and skilled at their jobs. He headed for the door with Canet hard on his heels, no doubt as keen as he was to get out of the toxic atmosphere between Massin and Monteo.

'Oh, and Inspector...' said Massin, as Rocco turned the handle, '...something else Arras mentioned from events at Les Sables: an inspection of the injured officer's firearm shows it had been discharged.'

'So he got off a shot?'

'It would seem so. You'd better be going. Let's try to keep the body count down, shall we? With the Tour coming through the region shortly, a massacre nearby would cast an unfortunate shadow.'

Thirty-three

Rocco headed out to the rear car park, where he found Desmoulins waiting and ready to go. Godard's men had just left to scout out the site near Cambrai, the blue fog of diesel from their heavy operations van clouding the air.

'I've put some gear in the boot,' said Desmoulins, grinning at the prospect of some excitement. 'A couple of rifles and ammunition and some smoke grenades, although if we have to use those, we'll probably be too late. Just in case Godard doesn't have any, I mean.'

Rocco pulled a face and got behind the wheel. He didn't much care for rifles unless it was going to be outright warfare, but it paid to be prepared. And the likelihood of Godard forgetting any tactical equipment was remote. The man lived for knowing what was where and having everything at his fingertips. If these kidnappers were indeed armed and had killed and injured police officers already, they clearly had little concern for the law and the consequences of breaking it. With Godard on the case, it was probably going to be their most costly mistake.

As he drove he brought Desmoulins up to date on events so far, including the similarities of Raballe's murder to that of Vieira.

'Sounds like Farek's got himself a couple of hot-shots on the job,' Desmoulins concluded. 'And a woman? That's unusual.' He was looking at Rocco with concern. 'Doesn't it bother you, having pros on your tail?'

'Well, I'm hardly pleased about the idea. But there's not much I can do to stop them coming unless I spot them first. At least I now know what they look like.'

'I suppose. And you say you actually spoke to both of them. That's… that's bizarre, like they were playing some kind of game.'

'What's bizarre is that they didn't take the opportunity to finish me there and then.'

'And Jouanne's a professional killer? I can't believe it. I never got to know him, just said hello in passing.' He paused, then added, 'I suppose it might be because of what you've just told me about him, but the couple of times I spoke to him I got the feeling he was enjoying a joke at everybody else's expense, like he knew something we didn't.'

'You weren't wrong. It's precisely what he was doing.'

They drove on for a while in silence before Desmoulins spoke again. 'Having a team around this long, though, it's risky, isn't it? I thought the top guns usually kept on the move, in and out again, job done and back to their hidey-holes.'

'Usually. But Farek must be making it worth their while to extend their stay. Caspar thinks Nightingale's an international operator, which will only increase Farek's profile and serve as a warning to the rest that he won't be messed with.'

To Rocco, hiring such a person was also an indication of how untouchable Farek thought himself to be now. But he knew the gangster wasn't only motivated by arrogance; beneath the veneer would be a desperate desire to maintain face among the criminal community by being seen to settle scores with people who had dared cross him, on both sides of the law. Either way, such a high-profile strategy was taking a huge risk. Even top-rated assassins had limits when it came to the code of never talking to the police. If the killer was caught, faced with a one-way visit to the guillotine, he might decide to negotiate a lesser sentence in exchange for the name of his current employer.

They arrived near the old factory complex, which lay at the end of a weed-strewn metalled surface off the main road, and found Godard's men and a number of other vehicles from the Arras section clustered in a group. An officer Rocco didn't know came forward to wave them down.

Rocco showed his card and the officer nodded. 'Thank you, Inspector. *Sous-Brigadier* Classens, Arras Division.' He waved them through.

Godard approached as they climbed out of the car. 'Here we are again,' he said cheerfully. 'I've sent a couple of men around the perimeter to scout out access points and report back. I'll send them back once we decide to move in, just in case the kidnappers try getting away across the fields.' He looked up at the sky. 'It's still light at the moment but it's a big perimeter to keep under observation if they decide to slip out under cover of dark. Once they're out in the field we'll never find them.'

'A good reason not to let them get too settled, then,' said Rocco.

'That's what I was thinking. As long as we don't scare them into harming their hostages, maybe we can play with their nerves a little.' He eyed Rocco, who was checking his semi-automatic. 'Is that all you're taking? I've got some heavier stuff if you want it. It could get messy if they've got a lot of ammunition.'

'This will do fine.' Rocco put the gun away and studied the complex. It was an extensive and ugly collection of buildings and rusty machinery, set in an area the size of three football fields and surrounded by a three-metre-high fence. In between the buildings ran a spider's web of what he took to be conveyors and walkways, while at ground level there were piles of unnameable detritus dotted about, some several metres high, leftovers from an attempt to break down the site ready to be carted away. Since then, the owners had abandoned the job to the mercy of the elements: what ground had once been concreted over around the buildings was now cracked and broken, with weeds pushing through in wild clumps and even small trees growing into the walls of the buildings.

'Does anybody know what state the buildings are in?' he asked Classens, who was standing nearby.

'Unfortunately not. The fences and structures are supposed to be checked every couple of years to prevent intruders getting in and hurting themselves, but the owners of the site went into liquidation some years back and it's fallen between the cracks.'

From where they were standing the fabric of the buildings looked dangerously fragile, with boards flapping beneath the corrugated roofs and holes in the cladding where sheets had been ripped away by nature or local scavengers. The surrounding fence, in a cruel twist, seemed to have withstood the ravages best, and remained rigid and impenetrable. To Rocco, as potential nightmares went, it looked the worst kind to be facing. Riddled with nooks and crannies, a single gunman, if skilful or desperate enough, could hold off any attempt to penetrate the inside by picking off targets at leisure.

'Is this the only way in?' He nodded at a pair of metal-grilled gates, partially pushed open and sagging on their hinges.

'I'm afraid so.'

He shook his head. All the men inside would need was a clear view of the road and they would be able to watch anyone trying to enter slowing down to get through the gap in the gates. If they had a rifle it would be like a duck-shoot.

'Has there been any activity so far?'

Godard nodded. 'One of the Arras boys was the first one here. He said he saw the Simca being driven down the back and turning into one of the buildings, and a couple of guys standing around and waving side-arms in the air like they were gangsters on a film set. It sounds like they're anticipating trouble.'

'Sounds like they don't know what they're up against,' said Desmoulins moodily, although with a slight grin. 'Pretty stupid driving around in a Vedette, too. Not many of them around in these parts.'

'You've got that right.'

'Inspector Rocco?' It was Classens, who'd stepped away in response to one of his men. 'I've had a message for you from the station. The man they captured is talking and they think you should hear what he has to say before we go in.' He gestured towards a police van nearby. 'My colleague has the radio.'

Rocco nodded, climbed into the van and took the handset from the driver. 'Rocco.'

'Inspector Rocco. This is Captain Hugo Batisse, Arras division. Thank you for your assistance.' The officer's voice was clipped, as if he were making a recording, and Rocco put it down to perhaps having an audience behind him.

'What have you got for me, Captain?'

'The prisoner is a Congolese national, like the others, which I think you know already. We were led to believe they were employed to kidnap the ex-minister Bouanga by his enemies in Libreville. But this man denies it. He says they were paid to take a man they later learned was named Bouanga and keep him captive until they received instructions to release him. In fact he claims to have no idea who Bouanga is, nor the woman with him. Later they would be told to release the man and would get the rest of their money and return to Paris where they came from.'

'Does he know who paid them?'

'Not by name. He said a white man. He's anxious to talk, and I think he's beginning to realise his position.'

'Good. Can he describe the man who paid him?'

'I asked him that already. He said young rather than old and, get this, he was wearing a blue shirt… like a cop.'

Jouanne. It had to be. Rocco could feel it in his bones.

'How did he meet this man?'

There was a rumble of conversation, and Batisse came back. 'He says he was contacted by a *chef* in Paris and told to go to a bar in Amiens where they would be met by the young man and paid half their money, the rest on their return to Paris.'

A *chef* – a boss or leader. Was that a gang boss?

'Do you believe him?'

'He sounds genuine, although he's still intoxicated on something so it's not easy to tell. He says he and the others have been chewing something called *ncassa*. It's a leaf of some kind, but nobody here knows what it is or what it does. He says it makes people happy and brave. If waving a gun around and shooting my two officers is happy, God help us if they get brave. You'll be going in hard, I take it, and will punish those bastards for what they did?'

Rocco's priority was getting Bouanga and Excelsiore out safely without loss of life. Faced with trigger-happy men in the grip of some narcotic substance, the likelihood of this business ending in a happy outcome was slim. Going in hard, as Batisse put it, like a cavalry charge, wouldn't guarantee anybody's safety, least of all the hostages.

'Thank you for the warning, Captain. We're hoping to find a way of getting the hostages out to safety. Beyond that, we'll see what develops and keep in touch.' He cut the call before Batisse could say anything else, and passed the handset back to the driver.

As he walked over to re-join Godard and brief the men on what to expect, two of Godard's men appeared from along the side of the complex. Their legs were covered in thistles and fragments of greenery where they had been walking through long grass.

'There's a section of fence down on the right-hand side,' said the first man. 'It's unsighted from inside the factory behind a storage tank, so I reckon we can go through there and spread out without being seen.'

'Nowhere else?' said Godard.

'No.' The second man stepped forward. 'I went down the other side and we met at the far end. The fence is solid all the way down and there's no cover anywhere. Anyone trying to climb over or cut through it would be a sitting target. Near the storage tank is better.'

'Did you see anyone?' Rocco asked.

'Three men, all carrying handguns, and an older man and a woman, both with their hands tied. The man looked like he was trying to protect the woman and getting a kicking in the process.' He gestured to his colleague and added, 'We talked about it on the way back up here and we don't think they've even considered the possibility of us getting inside. They're busy shouting and laughing like they're having a party. It's crazy. At least they won't be able to shoot straight in that state.'

'They're crazy all right,' said Rocco. 'The party's inside their heads and whatever they've been chewing is making them think they're fireproof. But that makes them even more dangerous, not less.' He looked at Godard, who was ex-military and experienced in these kinds of operations. 'This is your speciality, so we'll follow your lead. But let me say this to all of you: the older man and the woman are hostages. They're Africans, like the kidnappers, so don't mistake them for the kidnappers. The moment you find them, put them somewhere secure until we can gather up the three gunmen.' He heard some muttering from among the Arras officers and knew what they were thinking. They wanted revenge for their dead and wounded colleagues. He decided to nip that idea in the bud. 'You have something you want to get off your chests?'

'Just one thing, Inspector.' It was Classens. He was short and pugnacious, and looked ready for a fight. 'These three are animals. Delfour, the one they killed, had three kids and the docs are saying Noel Vallet might never walk again.'

'I know that. What's your point?'

'You sound as if you want us to be gentle with them after what they did.'

'I know how you feel about them, *Sous-Brigadier*; they shot your colleagues. I understand that. But remember this: we're professionals and we need to know who paid them to kidnap Bouanga. Killing them out of revenge won't tell us who did that.'

'The mad bastard we caught in Arras will tell us,' said another man. He looked at his colleagues with a smirk. 'At least he will if I get five minutes alone with him!'

Rocco waited for a ripple of laughter to subside. They were venting, he understood that. Like any soldiers about to go into battle they were nervous, but it was tinged with an anger and hate that demanded to be satisfied.

'I'm not saying take silly risks to take a prisoner,' he said. 'I'm saying we need to verify the facts. I want to take down the man who paid them, because he's just as much to blame for the death of your colleague as they are.' He turned to Godard, anxious to get on with it instead of arguing semantics. 'Desmoulins and I will go in through the main gate. If we cause a distraction, they'll think it's a frontal assault and give you a chance to find out where they're hiding the hostages. You all right with that?'

Godard nodded with a grin. 'I appreciate that, Lucas. Some noise will be good. Just don't draw all the fire.' He pulled a folded sheet of paper from his map pocket and opened it. It was a hand-drawn schematic of the factory site. He looked at the two officers who had completed the recce. 'This is a rough idea of the factory layout. If you can mark the broken stretch of fence on here, we'll have a better idea of where to go in. We can split up as we see fit once we're inside.' He handed over the sheet and a pen, and the first officer placed a cross against the fence two-thirds of the way down.

Godard took it back and held it so everybody could see. 'The two men who did the recce, you know the ground, so you lead the way and stay on the outside and watch for anyone breaking out. The rest, let's go.'

Rocco watched the men set off and gave them time to get down towards the breach in the fence, then nodded to Desmoulins. 'You ready? We're about to make some noise.'

Thirty-four

Before going through the gates, Rocco inspected the hinges. They were in a very poor state and pretty much held on by rust. One good tug and they'd probably fall apart. He took a length of rope from the boot of his car and tied one end to the towbar and the other to the centre of the gate.

'You go through first and stay out of sight,' he told Desmoulins, who was checking his rifle. 'I'll follow and take the gate with me. If anybody's waiting to jump out it should test their nerves.'

'Will do. How do you want to handle it when we're through?'

'The noise will distract them from Godard and the others going through the fence. We leave the car and go through the buildings on foot. If anyone's waiting up here to catch us out, we deal with them first.'

Desmoulins jogged away and slipped through the gap in the gate, disappearing quickly on the other side behind some giant bobbins that had once held steel hawsers or coils of wire. Rocco gave it a count of thirty, then eased the Citroën carefully through the gate, which was open just wide enough to avoid scraping the sides. Once through, he let the car drift under its own momentum until he'd taken up the slack in the rope. Then he put his foot down and the heavy car surged forward.

There was the slightest tug of resistance and the gate came off its hinges, skidding along on the bottom of the frame until it toppled over and hit the ground with an enormous crash that Rocco felt vibrating through the car's tyres. It bounced once before hitting the ground again and he slammed on the brakes and turned the wheel to avoid the gate sliding up behind him and hitting the rear of the car.

He turned off the ignition, jumped out, and jogged across to join Desmoulins.

'If they didn't hear that,' the young detective murmured, 'they must be deaf or dead.' He pointed ahead to the first large building, which appeared to have been some kind of warehouse with a delivery bay and an old elevator track coming out through a hole in the wall. 'We could get in through there, I reckon. It might give us better cover than going along on the outside.'

'Good idea. Let's go.' Rocco led the way, his gun in his hand, and keeping a careful eye open for any sign of movement. If one of the men was guarding this end of the site, they might have only a split second to take evasive action.

They reached the delivery bay and Rocco jumped up onto the concrete platform and headed for the elevator track. He stopped by the wall and listened, but all he could hear was the flapping of birds' wings inside, no doubt nesting close to the roof. It was a good sign; if there were birds, there was a good chance there wouldn't be men with guns.

He crept through the gap alongside the track, and found himself looking at a vast empty space with a large pool of scummy water in the centre of the floor. The ceiling was crisscrossed with gantries and hung with lights, all the colour of rust and spotted with white bird droppings. Directly across from where they were standing were two doors which looked like access to offices, and in the centre of the back wall a set of wooden sliding doors on runners.

Rocco signalled Desmoulins to take the door to the right, and headed forward across the floor to the one on the left. He was halfway there when he saw something on the edge of the water. A footprint. And it looked recent.

He dropped to the ground just as a shot rang out, echoing around the warehouse and sending up a volley of wild flapping from among the rafters and gentries overhead. A thin puff of smoke drifted from an open spyhole in the sliding door, and he felt the snap of the shot going by and heard it impact somewhere behind him. At almost the same moment he heard numerous shots coming from deeper in the complex, then footsteps running away.

Things were hotting up.

He ran forward to make it harder for the gunman to sight on him, slamming up against the sliding door, and turned to see Desmoulins doing the same. It was pointless shooting when they couldn't see a target, especially with the other officers now in the factory.

Rocco tested the office door nearest to him. It opened only a short way before coming up against something solid. He pushed through and saw a large filing cabinet, mangled and lying on its side, blocking the way. He guessed that the room he was in was an old production or shipping office, about ten metres by five. Whatever furniture had been here was long gone, save for the filing cabinet.

He scooted over the cabinet, feeling the grit of dirt and flaking paint on his hands, and dropped to the other side in a crouch. Another door was in the wall across the room, which he guessed must lead to the rest of the complex.

He nodded to Desmoulins, who had taken up a similar position and was facing a door of his own. He mimed pushing forward, then held up his hand and counted down from three. Desmoulins got the message and watched him. The moment he hit the one, they charged forward simultaneously until they reached the doors at the same time, kicking them open and running forward into the room beyond.

Empty. It was a carbon copy of the room they'd just left. But a door on the far side was just bouncing back, having slammed behind whoever had just opened fire on them.

Rocco didn't care to be so close to the gunman in the confined space. Once through the next door there might be nowhere to hide. He gave a soft whistle to attract Desmoulins' attention, and nodded towards a gaping window opening on to the yard outside. Desmoulins got the message and scooted across to join him.

'I'll go first,' said Rocco. He bent and picked up a lump of featureless metal and handed it to Desmoulins. 'He might be waiting for us to move beyond the door. Give me a count of ten and throw that, and I'll see if he shows himself. If there's no reaction you should be all right to go through, and I'll cover you.'

Desmoulins nodded. 'Got it.'

Rocco dropped through the window space to the ground and crept along the wall to the next window. As he reached it, he heard a bang from inside as the lump of metal hit the door.

Nothing.

He stood up and whistled, and Desmoulins appeared inside the next large room, which looked like some sort of assembly area.

The man had gone, presumably to join his colleagues holding Bouanga.

Rocco looked around, feeling the familiar itch of being watched by unseen eyes. It was probably meaningless. Had it been one of the gunmen, he would have opened fire by now. A building across the way was joined to the others by a suspended walkway some ten metres up, its windows all gone along with most of the floor. Anyone trying to cross that gap would be insane. The rest of the structure was like a ghost building and looked ready to fall down.

Rocco beckoned to Desmoulins to follow but to stay low. So far they'd heard nothing from the other men, and figured that they were taking each building with care and searching for Bouanga and Excelsiore. He was concerned that they were now getting too close to the other group for comfort. The worst thing to do would be to come upon each other by accident and for one group to open fire on the other.

Then he saw one of the Arras officers jog out of one building and duck behind a large pile of bricks and rotting wood. He was holding a rifle. Seconds later a voice called out and a dark figure appeared from a small doorway in the next building along. He stood there for a moment, looking around, and called again, the words unintelligible.

It was one of the kidnappers, armed with a handgun. He walked out into the open and stood there as if he were taking the sun, except that his movements were oddly uncoordinated and he was swaying as if drunk. He was also shaking his head and seemed unable to stand still. Without warning he bent and vomited noisily, but held onto the gun.

The Arras officer stood up, his rifle held into his shoulder. '*Police! Throw down your weapon!*'

The other man's response was immediate. He turned and opened fire immediately, pulling the trigger again and again and screaming in defiance. Wherever the shots went, they didn't touch the officer, who calmly stood his ground and pulled the trigger. The kidnapper staggered and spun round, then lurched back inside the building clutching his shoulder.

Rocco gave a warning whistle, and the officer turned, ready to open fire, until he saw who it was.

Rocco and Desmoulins moved forward to join him, and Rocco said, 'Where's Godard?'

'Inside,' said the man. 'He's trying to get to the hostages but these idiots are shooting at anything that moves. Did you see what just happened?'

'I did. They're definitely high on something.'

As if confirming the officer's words a sustained volley of gunfire came from inside the buildings, the flashes lighting up the window spaces like a ghostly pyrotechnic display. The noise was intense and Rocco could only guess what it was like for anybody inside. More gunfire and someone shouted orders to pull back. Rocco recognised Godard's voice.

'Can you get Godard out here?' said Rocco, 'or do we have to go in?'

'I wouldn't,' the man said. 'It's easier for him to come out. Hang on.' He made a double whistle, which Rocco recognised as a signal. Moments later the tall figure of Godard appeared in another doorway and jogged across to join them.

'That's not us firing,' he reported. 'Those people are nuts. They must have enough ammunition for an army. All they're doing is running around making holes in the night.'

'How many men have you counted?'

'Three. But they're not staying still for long and keep changing positions. It's a bloody strange kidnapping, if you ask me. They haven't even tried to negotiate or make demands.'

Rocco had to agree with him. In fact, the more he thought about it, the less he thought it was about kidnapping at all. 'Have you seen Bouanga and the woman?'

'They're held in a large room in the main building, with a man who's doing a lot of the shooting. I think he's trying to bolster himself because he's firing at shadows. I keep hoping his gun will overheat and jam but it hasn't done it yet. We can't shoot back because of the hostages.'

Rocco was getting worried. The longer the man stayed in there with Bouanga, the more danger they were in. If he was drunk or on drugs, he might eventually start to come down off his high and decide to finish them off and get out of there.

'We need a diversion to end this,' he suggested. 'Can you show me any of the windows to the room?'

Godard nodded, and led them round to the rear of the building, tramping through a tangle of weeds, long grass and nettles. He pointed out a large window set in the wall, with one of the giant bobbins lying on its side just beneath it. He said softly, 'I took a quick look through there earlier, but I couldn't see enough to risk going in. The entrance is on the opposite wall. There's another door set in the far end, but that's being guarded by another man.'

'And the hostages?'

'Just the other side of this wall, I think, down on the right. What do you want us to do?'

'Do you have any flash-bangs?'

Godard smiled. 'We certainly do.'

'Good. Let off a couple outside to draw his attention, then give it a count of three and lob a couple just inside the door. We'll use the flashes to spot our way in and confirm where Bouanga and the woman are, then we'll go inside. Give us three whistles when you're ready to begin and we'll do the same once we've got the hostages.'

'You've got it.' Godard disappeared back the way they'd come, while Rocco and Desmoulins climbed up onto the bobbin and waited. Desmoulins had put his rifle down and pulled his sidearm instead. There was no glass in any of the windows, and the openings were easily big enough to climb through. As soon as the flash-bangs – which were like large fireworks, only much louder – went off, they could make their move.

Thirty-five

Two minutes passed agonisingly slowly, with only intermittent shots coming from the gunmen. Rocco was just beginning to think something was wrong when three whistles sounded, followed by two flash-bangs going off in quick succession on the far side of the building. The explosions and flashes of bright light raised a lot of shouting and more shooting from the men inside. Three seconds later, two more explosions followed, this time within the room itself and rattling the fabric of the building.

Rocco and Desmoulins were already on their feet, ready to go, and in the light spotted a gunman by the door, firing wildly into the darkness. It was now or never. Rocco went first, slipping over the windowsill and dropping to the concrete floor of the room. Even as he dropped he knew that Bouanga and Excelsiore wouldn't be able to make an exit this way; it was too high up to climb and there was nothing to stand on. They would have to leave through the main door, which meant getting past their guard.

He turned to check them out and saw them sitting close to one corner, but in the poor light and the drifting smoke from the flash-bangs he had no idea if they were still alive. He focussed instead on the gunman, who was reloading his gun and shooting out into the night. Then the man seemed to sense the threat and spun round, bringing up his gun and shouting a warning.

Desmoulins opened fire first, knocking him off his feet, and Rocco ran to see to the hostages. He was relieved to see they were alive and moving, if terrified, with only their hands tied. He lifted them to their feet.

'We're going out that door,' he said clearly, pointing to the entrance where the gunman had fallen. 'As soon as we get the all-clear, follow me and keep going. Don't stop unless I tell you and don't look around. Understood? You're going to be all right.'

They both nodded, eyes wide, and clung to each other.

Desmoulins had run over to check the body of the gunman and kick his gun away. He signalled to Rocco to bring the hostages to the door, where they huddled against the wall.

By now the shooting had died down, with only intermittent shots from either side. Rocco waited for a beat of more than two seconds' silence, then gave three long, loud whistles.

'All opposition down!' It was Godard's voice. 'It's safe to go.'

Rocco slapped Bouanga on the shoulder as his signal to move and led them out of the door to join two of the Arras officers waiting outside to usher them up the yard towards the main gate and safety.

Rocco saw Godard and Classens outside the next building, and went over to join them. Two officers were standing inside the building, weapons drawn and standing over two men on the floor. One was dead, the other had a wound to his shoulder and was moaning softly, his arms outstretched and his face to the floor as if he was trying to blend into the concrete.

'The dead one ran out and opened fire,' reported Godard. 'Classens put him down. The other one was already down without a weapon. Good luck for us but not for him.'

'Well done. There's another one inside, also dead.' He looked at Classens. 'You'd better get an ambulance on the way here and tell your boss it's all over.'

The officer seemed to have trouble tearing his eyes away from the wounded man on the floor, but he finally nodded. 'What about this maggot?'

'What about him?'

'He gets a cushy bed in hospital, does he? It won't bring our mates back, though, will it?'

'No, it won't. But he's going to be the one who provides information on the others, and on the man who paid them. You've done your bit by your mates, so let it go.'

Classens sighed, then backed down, the sharp light of anger fading from his eyes. 'Yes. Sorry. I'll call it in. The brass will be on their way already, I expect, after all the gunfire.'

The last thing Rocco needed right now was a collection of senior officers getting involved. He signalled to Desmoulins and took him to one side. 'Take the wounded man to one of the smaller rooms. The grittier the better.'

Desmoulins nodded. 'Will do. There's an old workshop next door. It's empty but grim. What are you going to do?'

'I want to talk to him. Once he's in the system he'll be untouchable. I want to get what I can out of him before the Ministry or the lawyers get involved. He might know something the man in custody doesn't.'

Desmoulins looked worried. 'You're not thinking of leaving him with the Arras guys, are you?' He looked around and his voice dropped. 'They're pretty strung up about their mates being shot. I reckon give them half a chance and they'll send him to join his friends.'

'We can't let that happen. He's our only hope of finding out what's behind this. I want him unsettled so he'll talk. It's ten to one he knows nothing about how we treat suspects in France, so he'll be wondering what's going to happen.'

He went over to Godard, who was checking through the contents of the kidnappers' pockets.

'Have you found anything?'

'Not much. A few sweets, some leaves which I'm guessing is the *ncassa* stuff they chew, some cigarettes, and three identity cards that look fake. There's hardly any money, though, just a few francs. If they were paid to lift Bouanga, they wouldn't have had time to spend any, so where is it?' He handed an identity card to Rocco. 'This is the one who survived.'

Rocco looked at the card, which gave the man's name as Patrick Pembele. The printing was sub-standard and the photo faded and grainy. It certainly looked fake, but it was all he had for the moment.

'Perhaps there wasn't going to be a final payment. I doubt they're the brightest buttons. They probably took a token down-payment with the promise of a big pay-out on completion. Let's see if we can find out. Do you have any camo paint among your equipment?'

'Sure. Always do, although we haven't had cause to use it recently. Why?'

Rocco told him what he wanted, and Godard smiled. 'Don't worry – I'll get Lavalle togged up. Aside from me he's the biggest and ugliest. Give me a few minutes and we'll be with you.'

Rocco walked towards the workshop Desmoulins had mentioned. Before entering he pulled his coat collar up around his chin and took out his gun. Then he stepped inside.

Desmoulins was holding a flashlight and standing over the

prisoner, a young man with a wasted frame and a bony face. He was in handcuffs and sitting on an old wooden storage box. He looked frightened, one leg bouncing uncontrollably. His eyes went wide and rolled away when Rocco appeared with his gun held down by his side.

'What are you doing with me?' the man asked, his voice a dry croak. He held up the handcuffs as if he expected Rocco to release him.

Rocco waved a hand and made a shushing noise. The man's shirt was wet, he noticed, and the air smelled strongly of vomit. His upper arm was covered in blood.

Rocco stepped around the room, deliberately taking his time as if inspecting the structure for signs of wear and tear. It was filthy dirty after many years of being abandoned, with swathes of cobwebs hanging from the walls, a liberal scattering of rodent and bird droppings and a deep chill in the air in spite of the warmth of the dying day. A large iron pedestal which he guessed had once held a drill stood at one end, and scarring on the oil-stained concrete floor showed where a lathe or similar machine had stood, the retaining bolts still protruding like fingers pointing at the ceiling.

'Why am I being kept here?' the man asked. His French was heavily accented, but good. 'This is not right.'

'Why not?' Rocco countered, still walking around.

'Because this is not a police station. You have no right–'

'Really?' Rocco cut him off, this time turning to face him. 'Do you think we should treat you to coffee and cake, perhaps? Offer you a hot shower and a nice big meal? Mr Patrick Pembele.'

'I don't understand.' The man's eyes welled up and he swallowed hard, staring at Rocco's pistol. 'I don't understand what you want of me.'

247

'Pembele. That's your name, isn't it? It says so on your identity card.'

'Pembele. Yes.'

'So why did you kill the policeman?' The words seemed to bounce around the room, but that was as far as they went, the thick walls absorbing the sound like blotting paper.

'What? Policeman? I did not kill anyone, I swear! That is a lie!'

'At the big house – where you kidnapped Bouanga and the woman. Two policemen, dead.'

'No. No.' He shook his head, the word dying off in a keening sound. 'I did not. Please.'

'So who did it? One of your friends? Tell me which one and you'll be allowed to go.'

'No, not me... not my friends.'

'Really? But you were all high on... what do you call it – *ncassa*? How would you remember what you did? Do you really want to stay here in this place?'

Pembele looked up. 'No. You cannot do that.'

'Give me a name and I'll let you out of here.'

There was the sound of footsteps outside the door. Rocco turned and saw two tall, dark figures standing in the gloom, belted, booted and buckled, carrying guns. Their faces were streaked in camouflage paint, which made them look cold and threatening. Godard and Lavalle, huge, intimidating and without expression, their eyes fixed on the prisoner.

Behind him Pembele gave a faint cry of despair and began to sob. Rocco turned back to the prisoner and signalled for the two men to go. Their job was done.

'You attacked the house, Mr Pembele. Yes?'

A long pause and a sob. 'Yes.'

'And the policemen were shot, yes?'

The man nodded slowly. 'But not by me, Mr Policeman. We did not kill anybody, I promise you.' He swallowed again, then whispered, 'It was the other.'

'Other?'

'The man who was there before us. The white man.'

Rocco exchanged a look with Desmoulins. At last they were getting somewhere.

'What was this man's name?'

'I do not know. He did not tell us that. He was very angry and waving his gun and we thought he was going to kill us all. He had already shot the two policemen and we were frightened we were going to be next.'

'Can you describe him?'

'He was white and… young, I think. It is not easy for me to tell. He was in blue, like the policemen, but not the jacket. A shirt only.'

'Blue?'

'Blue, yes.'

It tallied with what the prisoner in Arras had said. To make absolutely certain, Rocco took out the photo from the Place Carnot and held it in front of Pembele's face. 'Is this the man?'

Pembele scanned the photo, squinting in the poor light thrown by Desmoulin's torch. 'Yes. This one.'

'Point.'

Pembele did as instructed, moving his hands awkwardly together. His finger came to rest on the face of Jouanne. 'But there was another with him, also,' he added.

'What?'

'Another person, but we did not see him. He was in the van.'

'What van?'

'I could not tell the colour – it was too dark. But it was outside the gates when we arrived. The man, this white man, he was waiting for us by the front door. He had already placed the old man and the woman in a room and locked the door. These, he said, were the ones to be taken. One of my friends went to relieve himself and that's when he saw the dead policeman in the big shed.' The words were flowing now, unstoppable and desperate, and Rocco could tell the man was finally spilling everything he knew, eager to please.

'Why was the man angry – did he say?'

A shake of the head. 'No. Only that it had been a waste of time. I do not know what he meant and was too scared to ask. It was none of our business. We just wanted to have our money and do what we had been told in Paris.'

'That's where you were hired?'

'Hired?'

'Promised money if you did this thing.'

'Ah, yes. In a café near the Gare du Nord. Café Terminus. An important man, a *chef*, said we had to go first to a café in Amiens, where the angry man would be waiting to give us money.'

Chef. A boss or leader. To men like this, any man with the bearing of authority and offering money with a promise of more would fit that title. It confirmed what the man in custody had said. 'Then what?'

'Then we would go to the house in the night and take the old man and keep him somewhere until we were told to let him go. It would be two, maybe three days only, he said, then we would be paid in full and could return to Paris. But we did not know this angry man would be here also.' He nodded at the photo.

'Did you know Mr Bouanga before you came here?'

Pembele frowned. 'I do not know this Bouanga person. The *chef* said the other man would give us instructions. If his name is Bouanga, then he did not say.'

'How did you know him, then – when you met him in Amiens?'

'We did not. But he knew us. He asked if we were from Congo and we said yes. That was all.'

A simple password, thought Rocco. But it worked. 'This *chef* who gave you instructions, do you know his name?'

Another shake of the head. 'No, but he is there in that photo. You did not know this?'

Rocco didn't need to look to know who he was talking about.

'Point.'

Pembele did so, his finger resting on the face of Lakhdar Farek.

Rocco looked up to see someone standing in the doorway. It was Godard.

'I just checked on the hostages. They've been examined by a medic at the gates. Bouanga's a bit knocked about but nothing's broken. I've sent them back to Les Sables with two of my guys. They will stay with them overnight until we get replaced. I suggested a hotel to Bouanga but he asked to go back to the house.'

'Thank you.' He sensed Godard wanted to say more. 'What?'

'The Arras guys are getting restless.' He nodded at Pembele. 'They want to know why you're keeping this one in here instead of handing him over. They see it as their collar.'

'You heard what he said?'

'Enough. A white man was the shooter – is that true?'

'Yes. You might want to tell the men that before they do something they'll regret.'

251

Godard smiled. 'They won't, don't worry. Not while I'm here.'

'Good. You can also tell them that we know who paid him, too. This man's evidence will get the killer convicted, and the man at the top responsible for the whole sorry business. But he has to make it into court to testify.'

'Is it anyone I might know?'

'You've heard the name Farek? His brother.'

'I remember. So why was he involved? I thought this was a political job.'

'No. It was a convenient smokescreen. This was aimed to get at me.'

Thirty-six

'*God, it hurts, Lilou! You have to do something!*'

Romain's breath was coming in short, sharp gasps, a hand clutched to his side, the other thrust against the window and his head pushed back against the cab of the van. His fingers were covered in blood and smearing the glass, and the clothing around his waist was a deep, dark red. Outside, darkness had fallen and they were alone with the sounds of the night and the smell of stale water.

'Let me look.' Lilou eased his hand away from his body and switched on the inside light. It wasn't very bright but it was sufficient to tell her that what Romain had claimed was nothing but a flesh-wound was far more serious. By his pallor she could tell he was losing blood at a steady and alarming rate

'I don't understand,' he muttered, his voice high, like a child. 'It didn't hurt all day, and now it's… God, it's agony!'

Lilou didn't know what to say. Since the kidnap of Bouanga, Romain had seemed fine, other than sounding as if he were drunk after shooting the two cops. When he'd told her how he'd been caught by a chance shot from the gun of the second policeman, he'd waved it off as a graze, of little consequence. At the time she'd been happy to believe him, and he'd relaxed. But as the day had gone by and his colour had begun to change, she'd suspected he was either in shock or hiding the true extent of the wound in some sort of silly show of machismo for her benefit. Now it looked as if an infection was setting in. If she didn't do something soon, she was worried that it would be too late. But the question was, what?

She held the torch close and slid her fingers gently around behind his back. She was hoping to find an exit wound, some indication that the bullet had glanced off a rib, that he might be lucky and not still have it inside him. But there was nothing. The bullet was still in there, and getting bullets out wasn't the kind of skill she possessed. She wouldn't even know how to begin.

She sat up and placed a hand against his face. 'Shhh,' she hushed softly. 'It's fine, Rom, really. You're just experiencing some after-pain from the bruising around the wound. I'll put some cream on it to cool it down and you'll feel a lot better. I've got some more tablets you can take, too, to help you sleep.'

'Sleep?' He blinked hard and shook his head. 'I don't want to sleep – I need this pain to stop, Lilou.'

'I know, I know.' She turned to a box on the floor by her feet and took out a roll of bandages and a tub of ointment. She'd never had to use the first-aid pack before now. They'd put it together thinking it was the thing for people in their line of work to do, in case they should ever, you know, run into some trouble and have to fight their way out. As to the contents, they hadn't given it much thought. Romain had heard about the sulpha powder; she'd added the tub, and the selection of tablets because she needed them, anyway, for her recurring headaches and hayfever. She figured the ointment might be good for its cooling effect and would help ease Romain's discomfort. She applied it gently with a piece of gauze, easing it carefully around the wound.

After an initial jump and a cry of protest, Romain began to quieten down and his breathing became more normal. She tied the bandage in place with a fresh wad of material to stem the bleeding, then gave him two painkillers with a drink of water to wash them down.

'If you hadn't shot the two cops,' she said tersely, as he swallowed with difficulty, 'we could have kept them prisoner in the house until the blacks had taken Bouanga, then left and nobody would have been any the wiser. Now we're stuffed.'

She was trying not to get stressed but it was threatening to take over the way it did sometimes.

Romain's eyes jerked open. 'But we haven't got Rocco yet. He was supposed to be there, wasn't he? You said we could use the blacks as a diversion and finish him off there and then. Isn't that what you said?'

Lilou bit back on a rush of anger at his accusing tone, as if it were she who had brought them to this situation. 'I know what I said. But you were supposed to check on his movements throughout the day and night. If you had we'd have been able to track him. You never said he was being replaced that night, otherwise we'd never have wasted time going there.'

'I didn't know because they didn't tell anyone!' he muttered, his teeth chattering feverishly. 'It was all kept very quiet. I told you, I asked around the station but nobody knew where he was so I thought he must be at the house. What could we have done if we had known, anyway?'

'We could have waited and tried again later, don't you see? Rocco wasn't going anywhere. He's a conscientious idiot who follows orders. Sooner or later he would have come back and we'd have had him exactly where we wanted him. If you hadn't been so keen to use that gun we could have waited for him to turn up.'

But Romain was no longer listening to her, drifting off instead and justifying his actions. 'They'd seen our faces – well, my face. There was nothing else I could have done, don't you see? I had to do it because they knew me. Anyway, they were just a couple of lowly *flics*, nobodies in uniform, so where's the harm? It seemed the best thing all round to protect us… to protect you.'

'Really? You think the rest of their tribe are going to write them off as nobodies? I've told you before, you never kill ordinary uniforms. If you plan it properly, you should never have to.'

'But Rocco–'

'Rocco is different!' she snapped. 'Rocco is no ordinary cop and this was going to be our biggest score. If it had worked out we'd have been able to go into hiding for a few months to let the dust settle, maybe get some easy jobs elsewhere for a while.'

'But we still can, can't we?' He looked at her and reached out for her hand, a child seeking approval.

But she hadn't fully worked out her mood. She snatched her hand away. 'And how could those two cops have identified you? They were strangers, you said, isn't that right? They weren't even from the Amiens station, you said, but some other hick town.' She sat back from him and shook her head, her voice trembling with emotion.

'They were from Arras, actually.' Romain hung his head, his voice tinged with righteous resentment like a punished schoolboy. He inhaled sharply as another stab of pain ran through him. 'I'd never seen them before.'

'Right. So you'd never seen them before and you were just a face in the dark, you said, which means they couldn't have identified you anyway. Which is it?'

'I don't know… I'm trying to think. It was all confusing. Maybe…

they might have caught a glimpse, when I first went in and told them I was there to help. I had to let them see the uniform shirt to get me in and up close, don't you see?' He coughed, the effort making him groan out loud and clutch his side.

'Great. So they were probably just a couple of traffic cops assigned to a boring guard duty they didn't want to do. They'd have forgotten you in an instant and concentrated on the four blacks instead. Now you've pulled down the entire police establishment on our heads by shooting them. They'll be hunting us down now and they won't let up. *How could you?*' She slammed her hand against the dashboard as her frustration got the better of her. This wasn't how things were supposed to be.

'Hey, I did it for us, Lilou! It's what we do, right – look after each other?' He rubbed his eyes with the heel of his hand. 'God, the pain… it's getting worse. I think I need to see a doctor.'

'*What?*' Lilou stared at him in disbelief. 'You think you can just walk into a hospital and ask to be treated for a gunshot wound? Hey, doc, I've been shot by a cop so can you give me a couple of tablets and fix me up? Don't you think that will cause a few questions to be asked? They'll treat you all right – but it'll be in a prison hospital before they send you to the guillotine. And I'll be right alongside you!'

She threw aside the blood-soaked gauze and took a deep breath, staring through the window into the darkness. She switched off the torch and inside light, allowing her eyes to adjust. Was that someone moving out there or a trick of the light? Probably some animal in the undergrowth. Bloody swamp was probably crawling with them. What kind of idiot would be out here at this time of night, anyway?

She sat back and took a deep breath. Only people like her and Romain – and what did that say about them? Seconds later her manner changed in an instant, the night and her anger and the animal forgotten as if a switch had been thrown. She even smiled when she turned back to Romain and leaned in close, her breathing soft on his face. 'Tell you what, Rom, I know a man in Paris; he's a nurse – one of the best. He owes me a favour. It'll cost us a bit but we'll get you sorted out, what do you think?'

'Really?' He shifted slowly, turning his head to look at her. His breathing sounded shaky. 'Can we do that?'

'Of course. It's only a couple of hours away and we've got plenty of fuel. We can set off right away. He'll do something about that nasty wound. How about that, my love?' She touched his face, then switched on the torch again and wished she hadn't; he looked even worse in the dim light, as if all the life had already been sucked out of his face. 'Sorry for being a bitch just now. I was worried about you, that's all. It got the better of me. Forget all that stuff I said. It's not your fault – you were only trying to help me, I know that.'

He stirred and nodded, his expression dulled by the pain. 'That's right, Lilou. It's always to help you.' He shivered, making his teeth chatter for a moment. 'Always.' Moments later, overcome by shock and the tablets, he was slipping into a shallow, restless sleep.

Lilou clicked off the torch and wondered what to do. Driving to Paris was out of the question, no matter what she'd just said. They were inside any police cordon and anything moving at this time of night would be stopped and checked from top to bottom. But more importantly there was still a job that had to be done, and that wasn't going to go away. Where they were sitting right now was no more than a short drive away from where Rocco lived, which was why she'd driven here as a first stop. All she had to do was bide her time, drive up through the village to check if he was home, and the contract could be fulfilled.

She laid her head back with a dreamy smile and closed her eyes, picturing how they would do it, the two of them. First, though, she'd take a short nap.

When they got going, Rocco wouldn't know what had hit him.

Thirty-seven

By the time Rocco got back to the office to file a preliminary report for Massin, dawn was just an hour or so away. Surprisingly, he felt wide awake, as if he hadn't missed an entire night's sleep, but it left him wondering when the crash would come, as it surely would. He'd spent plenty of similar nights with little sleep or rest, so the feeling wasn't new, merely unwelcome, the price for going too long without a proper break.

He passed Godard and his men and Desmoulins, who were busy checking in the weapons and equipment they'd used from the armoury. The talk among them was muted, but with an undercurrent of tension, and he knew that each man would be running over the night's events in his own way, seeing flashbacks of what they had witnessed. It would take some time for them to relax, but there was no quick way of doing it.

'Hey, Tarzan,' Godard said to Desmoulins, as the young detective ejected the shells from his rifle and handed it to the armourer. 'That was good work you did back there, going through the window. Any time you want to join a proper unit, we'd be glad to have you.' He shot a sly look at Rocco as he said it and fluttered his eyebrows. 'Brains and brawn, a good combination.'

'Hands off, Godard,' Rocco growled, and clapped Desmoulins on the shoulder. 'We need him for when your boys are off playing commando.'

The comments caused a ripple of laughter among the other men, breaking the tension, and Desmoulins ducked his head, flushing at the compliments.

Rocco left them to it and grabbed a quick cup of foul, over-brewed coffee. He was anxious to get his report written up before his face hit the desk. No doubt Monteo would have been quick to notify his masters at the Interior Ministry of the planned rescue, and they would be itching for details of how it had gone, which would put pressure on Massin to provide a detailed briefing.

As he signed it and sent it upstairs, Rizzotti appeared and sat down in front of him.

'You're working late,' said Rocco. 'Or it is early?'

'I got lucky,' the doctor said, barely able to conceal a smile. He waved a piece of paper in the air. 'Good news, I think.'

'I take it you're not talking about your love life.'

'No, I'm talking about the spike-bayonet query. One of my contacts came up with two possible matches. The first was a stabbing in Nice last year. I spoke to their chief pathologist and he confirmed the details. The deceased was a banker who was known to have had dealings in gold bullion through some local businessmen.'

'You mean gangsters.'

'You've got it. The banker had got himself into serious debt and tried a spot of under-the-counter buying and selling to get himself out of trouble using these business associates to move some gold around. Unfortunately he thought he was smarter than they were, but he was mixing with the wrong people. It seems they took exception to him trying to rip them off, and he was found laid out one morning along the Promenade des Anglais with what they thought was an ice-pick wound in his neck. The weapon was never found, though.'

Rocco felt a flutter of excitement at the news. 'And the other?'

Rizzotti checked his sheet of paper. 'An industrialist this time, also stabbed in the neck but earlier this year. The deceased was rumoured to have collaborated with the Nazis during the war, but nothing stuck. More recently, though, he was widely reported to have driven two associates into bankruptcy, causing the wife of one of them to take her own life. They questioned the husband afterwards but couldn't prove he'd had anything to do with the industrialist's death.'

'And the weapon?'

'No weapon was found, but the investigating team did find a scabbard nearby.' He looked up and smiled. 'The scabbard for a number four, mark two spike bayonet.'

Rocco breathed out. So, two good matches, one better than the other, but he wasn't going to argue. True, it only proved the use of a similar weapon, not the user, but it was a decent step forward. And sometimes decent steps were the best one could hope for.

'Where was this second killing?'

'Oh, sorry – I nearly forgot. It was in Geneva, down by the edge of the lake. I don't know if it helps, but there was an additional note against this case, which was that very shortly before his death, the industrialist was seen by an acquaintance in the company of a young blonde woman.'

'No name, I take it?'

'No. She seems to have vanished without trace.' He shrugged. 'It could have been nothing, of course, someone asking directions or a chance encounter. Geneva's a busy place.'

Rocco sat there after Rizzotti had gone, reading and re-reading the note, allowing the facts to slot into place. Two more stabbings with the same kind of weapon, maybe *the* same weapon, and both out in the open. And Caspar had mentioned Geneva. Was this too good to be true or was he over-analysing and making the facts fit to suit his suspicions?

As he put the paper down and felt his head falling forward, he was jerked awake by the phone ringing.

It was Detective Franck Joncquet from Dieppe. 'Lucas. I've been trying to get hold of you since yesterday evening but I gather you've been busy. I thought I'd try one more time.'

'Go ahead, Franck. What is it?'

'I've discovered something else about the morning Raballe was killed. After your visit I got it into my head that someone, even on a quiet road like the one where he was killed, might have seen something. Especially after what Edith Capelle told us about the van. I asked more questions in the area, and finally spoke to the truck driver she mentioned, Emmanuel.'

'Good thinking. What did he say?'

'He admitted it hadn't occurred to him until I mentioned it, but on the morning of Raballe's killing, he'd been driving down the road and saw a young woman taking to an older man with a dog. He'd seen the man before and figured he was local, but not the woman. He didn't think anything of it when the murder was in the news later because he didn't know Raballe by name and hadn't made the connection.'

'Did he give you a description of the woman?'

'Smartly dressed, he said, so he thought she must be a tourist from one of the cities or over from England. She had very short, blonde hair, he said, which he noticed because it was unusual. A bit masculine, in fact, to quote his words. I'll send through a copy of my report.'

Rocco hesitated. The description was familiar, and he thought about the photo from Place Carnot. Was it really this simple or was he simply keen to reach an obvious conclusion? There was one way to find out.

'Could she have been another dog walker?'

'That's just it. I've spoken to others in the area, but nobody remembers seeing a woman walking down there, either before or since. It's pretty much men like Raballe, retired and with plenty of time on their hands. I hope I'm not confusing the picture. I thought it a bit odd, that's all.'

'You were right to call, Franck. It is odd – and thanks for telling me.' Rocco wished him goodbye and put the phone down, his mind in a buzz. Was this merely an odd coincidence, and another woman had been in the area at the time? If not, did it mean the mystery woman from the van hadn't been a lookout but something more? Why would she have risked approaching Raballe, unless it had been to make sure of his identity? Or was there a more damning explanation?

He set out for Les Sables to speak to Bouanga. He needed to get a statement from the former minister about what had happened to him and Excelsiore, so that it could be incorporated in the full report. As he drove, the puzzle Joncquet had just presented him wouldn't go away. It was almost too shocking to contemplate, but the more he thought about it, the stronger the feeling became. Was it possible that, against all expectations, the killer known as Nightingale turned out not to be the man in the team, but the woman?

He arrived at the house to find officers on the gate and others patrolling the grounds, a sudden explosion of personnel that until now had been denied. An example, he thought, of stable doors and horses bolting. But at least it made it more difficult for anybody else to mount an attack.

Claude Lamotte met him at the front door.

'Good timing, Lucas. I was about to leave,' said Claude. 'The others are taking over.'

'Is Bouanga up and about?'

'I'll say. He's been wandering about like a ghost ever since he got back. I don't think he's even tried to get to sleep. Excelsiore, too. She's been asking about Delicat but I haven't been able to tell her anything.' He lowered his voice. 'Between you and me, Lucas, I get the feeling there's something a bit odd going on around here.'

'In what way?'

'I happened to step in the barn out back this morning, just taking a quick snoop. And guess what I found lying on the floor?' He stepped across to the hall table and produced one of the arrows Rocco had last seen in the quiver in the conservatory.

'So?'

'I'm willing to bet my pension, as miserable as it will be, that it wasn't there yesterday. After they took that poor cop away, the floor was clear and I swear there was no arrow anywhere near. Also,' he held up a finger, 'there's a hayloft at the back, and I'd be ready to bet your pension as well that somebody's been sleeping up there. I found a blanket and a jug of water.'

'Who do you think it was?'

'I was wondering if it was Delicat. If he's been here all this time, why hasn't he made himself known now his wife's back?'

It was a question Rocco wasn't able to answer. 'Show me,' he said, and followed Claude to the hayloft. It was reached by a short ladder and measured approximately two metres by four; there was ample space for one person to sleep as long as they didn't mind the risk of rolling off the loft onto the floor below. The area was thick with straw that had been compressed by regular use, and a blanket lay folded up at one end alongside a metal jug of water. The compressed area of straw was small, like the imprint of a boy, and the folded blanket told him everything he needed to know.

Delicat.

He wondered why the little man hadn't gained access to the house instead of sleeping out here. Nobody would have stumbled on him and he'd have been able to hide quite easily. But maybe he'd felt it wasn't his place.

'You're right. It's him.' Rocco went back down the ladder.

'What should we do?' Claude shivered when he joined him at the bottom. 'Makes my shoulders go cold, the thought of him creeping around out there with that bow of his.'

'Don't worry about it. It won't be you he's interested in.'

He left Claude to get on home and went in search of Bouanga. It seemed he now had another mystery: what had Delicat being doing while Bouanga and Excelsiore were being held by the gang? Was he part of the kidnapping, or had he stayed close to the house in the hope that his boss and his wife would be returned? It was the most logical explanation, because what else would he have been able to do, a stranger in a strange country, suddenly separated by force from the two people closest to him and unable to do a thing about it? If, on the other hand, he'd been part of the kidnap gang, why would he have hung around, waiting to be caught? Logic would surely have made him get away from here and keep on running.

Rocco found the former minister in the conservatory, staring out at the open countryside. He looked drawn, his face tinted grey with fatigue and with a definite slump to his shoulders. His suit was dusty and rumpled and his tie askew from a collar grown grubby and creased, yet he seemed not to care.

'I suppose you wish to talk about what happened.' Bouanga didn't turn to greet him.

'I'm afraid I must. I can come back later if you prefer, but it's better if we talk about it sooner, so we can find out who was responsible for what happened to you. The longer we leave it the more chance they have of getting away.'

Bouanga nodded and turned to the sofa, where he sat down with a sigh. 'Of course. I am sorry, I was forgetting that one of your colleagues died in the attack here trying to protect us, and another was wounded. How can I help?'

'First of all, do you know what happened to Delicat? We've seen no trace of him.'

'I'm afraid I do not. He was overwhelmed by the men with guns. He tried to stop them coming for me, but a bow and arrow is no match for a bullet, so I told him to leave us and save himself.'

'And he did that?'

'He obeyed my orders, Inspector. I would not have expected him to do otherwise. I assumed the men would not harm Excelsiore, as they had come after me. I told them she was the cook and they believed me. But they wanted her along anyway, because they had been told to bring her and the child. I told them there was no child here, which they at first did not understand. Then they saw Delicat and thought it was funny, I don't know why. Such people are like children themselves, with simple minds and no feelings.'

'How is Excelsiore? They didn't hurt her physically, did they?'

'She is well. A little frightened, of course, as you would expect after such an experience, but she is a strong person. However, she is especially worried for Delicat.' Bouanga looked away, leaving an unspoken statement in the air like a flag. Finally he said, 'I told you when we first met that she was Delicat's wife, did I not?'

'That's correct.'

'I am afraid I did not tell you the truth, Inspector. For that I must apologise. I said my wife was in Cameroon with our children, which was two lies. It was meant to be a simple ruse to protect her, you see. In that I failed spectacularly.' He took a deep breath, visibly struggling to get out what he wanted to say.

Rocco waited. He was uncertain about where this was going. Having seen the moment of intimacy between the bodyguard and Excelsiore in the kitchen, he wasn't sure what the problem was. They were an odd couple in some ways, and he'd had no reason to question their relationship, but so what?

Then Bouanga put it into words.

'Excelsior is actually my wife, Inspector. Not his.'

So, that explained why they had jumped apart when he'd entered the kitchen; it was guilt, not embarrassment. 'I don't follow.'

'As I said, it was a simple yet stupid ruse. I thought that if my enemies here were aware that I had brought my wife with me, they would gain some leverage to use against me. I could not risk that because I know how these people think. They are utterly ruthless and would not hesitate to harm a woman to get what they want. I'm afraid life is cheap to them.'

'And they wanted what – your capitulation?'

'That, of course, although as I am no longer in the country it would be difficult to assign me any kind of importance at the moment. But that is a matter for the future. However, they would also want to exact revenge for past... misunderstandings. We are a nation in turmoil, you see, still very new in independence terms, like a newborn struggling to find its feet and a new direction. Some... regrettable things have been done – on all sides, I have to say. We have made mistakes and cannot deny that. But much of what was done by me and my colleagues was designed to make the country strong and modern, to be a new force in Africa.' He stopped and raised both hands. 'My apologies, Inspector Rocco – suddenly I sound like a politician seeking re-election. Old habits, I'm afraid.'

'When you said they were ruthless, does that mean they don't usually return kidnap victims?'

'Precisely. People have disappeared in my country, never to be seen again. It is not the same as your country; there are vast areas in Gabon where people do not venture to live. The land is too harsh and unwelcoming and impossible to farm. But if you want somebody to vanish without trace it is ideal.'

Rocco wanted to tell him that there were plenty of places in France where people had been known to disappear, but right now wasn't the time. 'Yet this gang didn't harm her.'

'No, they didn't, for which I thank the Good Lord in Heaven. But I think it was because they had not been told who I am, and neither did they care. They were from the Congo, simple gutter filth with no education and no morals, recruited to take me away and wait for instructions.'

'What do you think was going to happen to you?'

Bouanga shrugged. 'I thought they were in the pay of my enemies and were going to hand me over to them. But since I am still alive and free, thanks to you and your men, I was clearly mistaken.'

'But you must have heard them talking. Didn't they say anything?'

'A little. I heard them talking after they had drunk some cheap brandy and were feeling invincible and very pleased with themselves, which happens easily to people like them. All they were interested in was the payment they had been promised for taking us hostage and keeping us out of sight at a pre-arranged place until they were told what to do.'

'The factory complex where we found you.'

'Exactly so. But they were foolish and did not take us there immediately. Instead they decided to go in search of drink and some drugs. One of them said he had a cousin living in Arras and he could supply them with what they desired.'

'So that's why they were there.'

'Yes. At first they drove us around as if they would not be noticed, never going far but turning back and trying new roads. It was ridiculous; they were acting as if they were on vacation. I offered them money to let us go but they refused and said it would not match what they had been promised. I tried to tell them that there was probably going to be no payment, but they did not believe me and began to utter threats against Excelsiore, so I stopped.'

'That was probably wise.'

'As they were driving us into the town, the car was stopped by a police patrol which must have been searching for us. One of the men panicked and took out a gun and waved it out of the window to make them step back, but the two officers were very brave; they ran forward and dragged him from the car. I think you know the rest.'

Rocco didn't tell him that it had been pure chance. The traffic patrol had been making random checks on vehicles for safety reasons, not searching for the kidnappers and their victims.

'You are probably wondering about my wife and Delicat, are you not?'

'It's not my place to think about it. We all have secrets.'

'Even you, Inspector? I can't imagine such a thing.'

'Even me. But I don't interest myself in the secrets of others... unless they've committed a crime.'

Bouanga smiled. It seemed to take an effort, but he managed. 'You're too polite, Inspector. There are many people who would not be so hesitant.' He rubbed his fingers together reflectively, as if carefully composing his words. 'I told you why I used the ruse about her being my cook, not my wife. What that did was to throw two people together in circumstances that would not have happened otherwise. Excelsiore and I have... not always been harmonious in our marriage. We have not been able to have children, which has been a source of great sadness for us. It has also been difficult for her, with me being a busy member of the government, whereas she is very outward-looking and sociable with many friends back home.'

'I'm sorry.' He realised that if Delicat were hanging around, as Claude had thought, this explained why he wasn't too keen on making his presence known, especially to his boss.

Bouanga waved a hand in acknowledgment. 'Thank you. To be honest, I don't blame her – or him. They are two people who were thrown together in unusual circumstances. It is my fault because I have been too distant for too long.' He sighed and lifted both hands. 'That's life, is it not? It's no good me being... what would you say, masculine about it? What good would it do when I do not feel the way I should about her?'

'What will you do?'

271

'Nothing.' Bouanga's look was direct and free of any guile. 'It has been a situation of convenience for a long time. Now it should stop.'

'And Delicat?'

'I bear him no ill will. It is a great pity to me that he is gone. He has been loyal in his duties, but also a friend and companion. I hope he comes to no harm… for Excelsiore's sake.'

For a man with a questionable reputation, Rocco acknowledged, the former minister had a bigger heart than most men. 'What will you do now?'

'I must return home.'

'Won't that be dangerous?'

'Perhaps. But I cannot stay here forever, and one must face one's future by moving forward. It is the only way.'

Rocco made his excuses and left Bouanga to his reflections. Ironic, he reflected; there was that word again: *masculine.* Bouanga had just used it, and Joncquet said Emmanuel had used it describing the woman he'd seen talking to Raballe.

And before that, Jouanne, who'd used it to describe the woman Rocco had first met in the café in Amiens.

Thirty-eight

Back home, Rocco got his head down and allowed himself to sink gratefully towards a kind of unconsciousness, to forget for an hour or two all about crime and kidnappings and threats to life and liberty, he hoped. He had his gun by his side, and if Nightingale came calling, he'd be ready. All being well, later maybe he'd even go for a run. For now, though, he needed the comfort and luxury of sleep.

Then his telephone rang.

'Lucas?' It was Claude. 'Sorry to disturb you, but it's important. Delsaire just called me. He said his neighbour, François, was out setting rabbit snares during the night and saw a van parked down in the *marais*.'

'So what?' The response came out slurred, his jaw not quite working fully in the half-in-half-out state of slumber. 'It's probably someone canoodling.' And Delsaire, he thought vaguely, local farmer, plumber and allegedly keen but terrible gambler, shouldn't be listening to his poacher-neighbour's gossip.

'It doesn't sound like it. He didn't think anything of it at the time, but it's still there this morning. And he says there's blood all over one of the side windows.'

Rocco snapped awake and swung his feet to the floor, the sudden movement making his head spin. 'A van.'

'A grey one.'

'I'm on my way.' He slipped his feet into his shoes and reached for his gun.

'Do you want me to call the station and get some men out?'

'Good idea. It'll take them a while to get here, but they should set a watch for any grey vans on the roads from Poissons towards Amiens and Paris. If it's Nightingale he might decide to make a run for it once he knows we're on to him.'

'Will do. But why would he come here now? You'd think he'd want to get well away.'

Rocco didn't have to think too hard about that. There was only one reason for Nightingale being here and that was to fulfil the contract. A professional killer's reputation was only as good as their last success; failure could mean the end of their career. And a killer with no work was susceptible to talking – or worse, selling information about past clients. That would be motivation enough to keep on working because some of those past clients might decide to shut the door on any of those secrets coming out.

'No doubt he has his reasons. I'll see you on the road near the entrance to the *marais*. And don't let anyone else in there – if it is Nightingale he's armed and dangerous.'

'Got it.'

He checked again that his gun was fully loaded, then got in his car and drove through the village and on to the road leading past the marshes towards the tiny railway station. It was quiet and serene, with no traffic and only one or two people about on foot, early workers heading out to the farms. Poissons at its very best, in other words, with a spread of warm sunlight filtering through the branches and bringing the promise of a warm day.

He arrived at the first turning to a track off the road, which was one of two leading into the *marais* itself, and saw Claude's car parked up on the verge. Standing next to Claude was the lean figure of Delsaire, dressed in his usual work *bleus* and scratching his head.

'You shouldn't be here,' he told Delsaire as he climbed out. 'If the van is the one I think it is, it's driven by people you don't want to get in the way of.'

'So I heard,' said the plumber, 'but I didn't want anyone blundering in there without knowing where the van is. It's to do with the shooting out at Les Sables, isn't it? Nasty business.'

Rocco didn't deny it. Word would have gone right round the village by now, most of it containing more than a grain of fact. 'It's good of you. Thanks. Where is it parked?'

'A couple of minutes' walk into the *marais* from here, on a bend in the track, where there's a wide pull-in area by a pond.'

'I know the place,' said Claude. 'We won't see it from here but it's close enough to the road to give them warning of any vehicles approaching. If they've done a recce of the *marais*, they'll know they can get out along the other track down there.' He pointed further down the road to where a weathered fish-shaped sign read *Pêche Réservée.*

It was a risk Rocco hadn't foreseen. 'We need to block it off. How long before the others get here?'

'Ten minutes, maybe sooner. They said they were ready to roll the moment they got news.'

It was going to be too tight. If it was Nightingale in there, their presence would already be known and they would be preparing to make a run for it. He couldn't wait. Once out and free, they could go anywhere.

'What exactly did you see?' he asked Delsaire.

'Not much, to be honest. I took a walk down that way because François said it looked as if somebody was sleeping in there. He said he saw some movement and the windows were a bit fogged up, but there was no equipment around to suggest they were fishing. A grey van, it is, with the corrugated sides and a seventy-five registration plate. That's Paris, right?'

'Yes. And you saw blood?'

'That's right. Smeared all over the passenger window. Really creepy, I thought, so I got out of there pretty quick and called Claude. I hope I haven't wasted your time.'

Rocco shook his head. Instinct told him that this was no fool's errand. 'You haven't, don't worry.'

'You're not going in alone, are you?' said Claude. He hefted his shotgun, the up-and-over barrels gleaming. 'I could flush them out with this – and I know the area better than you.'

'I know you do, but I'd rather you go down to the next entrance and let off a couple of rounds. If they know there's a shotgun around they'll steer clear of it and come out this way.'

Claude looked sceptical but nodded. 'Fair enough. But if all you've got is your little pistol, you'd be better taking one of these.'

'This will do me fine. We need to stop them here and now,' he explained. 'If they get away from here they might take hostages, and we know how that will end.' He turned to Delsaire. 'If you see anybody walking down this way, you might like to turn them back until the others officers get here.'

'I hear you.' He walked away up the road ready to play his part.

Behind him he heard the drone of vehicles in the distance, carrying clearly on the morning air. Some way off still, but getting nearer.

Rocco looked at his colleague. There wasn't another person in the area that understood the *marais* as intimately as Claude did, but he also knew that Claude wouldn't stand a chance against Nightingale. He'd hesitate for all the right reasons, which would be fatal. It was better if he could coordinate things from the road.

'Let's start,' he said. 'Give me three minutes and let off a couple of shots. That should set them running.'

Thirty-nine

Romain was dying, Lilou was now certain of it. She had examined his waist again in dismay, and found his shirt was sodden with blood pulsing out with every breath. Everything she'd done to try stemming the flow had failed, and she could see he was growing weaker by the minute.

'Wha– what's happening, Lilou?' he murmured, his voice shaky. He groaned as he tried to move, and stopped as the pain became too intense. 'You have to do something! It's hurting so bad, Lilou!'

Lilou placed a hand on his chest, her fingers now red with blood where she'd been holding the wadding against the wound. She was stunned by the way things had turned out, as if it had all been a bad dream and she'd hoped to wake up and find it had all gone away. But it hadn't. It was all horribly real.

Romain looked at her, his fear showing clearly as the realisation began to sink in that this was serious, that it was no longer the game it had always seemed. 'Lilou?'

'*Bouge pas,* my love. Don't move,' she said softly, rubbing his chest then moving her hand to his face, always her way of displaying affection. 'We'll get you to a doctor and he'll make everything better, you'll see.' A tear sprang from her eye and rolled down her cheek, leaving a path across her skin. She brushed it away impatiently, leaving a reddish smear behind, and smiled at him, then kissed his lips, making small humming sounds deep in her throat like a contented animal consoling its young. 'When you're better we can take that holiday we talked about,' she murmured. 'Remember? You'd like that, wouldn't you – a nice holiday?'

Romain nodded slowly, his eyes never leaving her face. He tried to speak but the words went dry in his throat and came out as a croak.

'Shush, my love,' she whispered. 'Don't say anything. You have to conserve your strength so we can get away from here.' She turned her head as a whistle sounded in the distance, through the trees. It might have been someone calling a dog, a hunter out early after rabbits, perhaps. But deep down she knew it for what it was. They were closing in.

'What's going to happen to us, Lilou?' Romain found his voice at last, like a child, fretful and frightened for what might be about to happen. His head lolled back as if it was too heavy for him to hold and he winced in agony as the movement pulled at his torso and tugged in turn at the flesh around the bullet wound below his lower ribs. 'We can… make a deal… talk to the *flics* and tell them about… Farek, can't we? We know plenty of stuff about him that they'd want to know.' He took a deep breath. 'We could get a lighter sentence, right? Lilou?'

'No.' She shook her head. 'It's too late for that.'

'But why? You could get away,' he breathed. 'If you left now… before they get here. They'd listen to me, Lilou. They'd take me to… hospital and I could say it was all my doing. Everything.' His breathing jumped and held for a moment, then continued, light and fluttering.

'But it wasn't, was it?' Her voice had turned flat, suddenly devoid of emotion. 'It wouldn't be true.'

'They don't know that.' His head dropped forward and he looked for her, his eyes darting to find hers in a frown of concentration. 'I could say it was me... tell them that I'm Nightingale. They'll never know and you'd be away and free. You could start afresh.'

Lilou said nothing. For a long moment she stared at him as if he were a stranger, trying to make a decision other than the one she knew was unavoidable. Then came the sound of two shots, not immediately close by, but loud enough to send up the birds from the surrounding trees. Shotgun, she thought. A threat and a warning.

They were coming.

She made up her mind. She was going to have to let him go. It was best she did this now, she knew that. She couldn't leave him here like this and there was no moving him, not now. She pulled back slightly and moved her free hand, adjusting her position, cementing her resolve. Her expression had changed in an instant, but Romain didn't notice, his eyes moving restlessly as he tried to find a comfortable position away from the pain. Had he been able to see her face he would have noted that she now looked utterly cool, the tears gone as if a portrait had been scrubbed clean and repainted, the mood totally changed.

'Lilou?' he whispered. 'What did you say? I can't hear you. Are we going to move?'

The sound of voices was getting nearer, filtering through the trees from the road. Then came another whistle and in the background, the clatter of a diesel engine and a squeal of brakes. Lilou read the sounds and knew what they meant: a heavy police vehicle. That meant a search team. They would spread out through the marshes and comb every metre of track, every pond and lake. If they took Romain alive that would be the end of everything. She had too much to lose.

Her reputation for one.

She shook her head. 'No.'

'Why not?' He coughed and dribbled blood from his mouth down his chin. 'Why?'

'Because.' She didn't bother wiping his chin, but brought up her other hand, bracing herself against the door. She was holding a dark metal spike, her fingers grasped firmly around the socket end, the point resting against Romain's ribs. 'You're not Nightingale. You never have been. Never will be.'

'No, Lilou…' He froze and she saw everything reflected in his eyes. That whatever softness had been in her face had now gone completely. That the face in front of him was cold and hard and unforgiving, and that he realised what she was about to do.

He shifted in his seat and tried to move away. But there was nowhere to go.

Her eyes flashed and, with a sudden burst of energy, she thrust her hand against him. 'I'm sorry, Romain,' she said, 'but Nightingale is my name, not yours.'

He jerked once, eyes opening wide in shock, as if he couldn't believe what had just taken place, what Lilou had done. Then his body gave up the struggle and he slumped back against the seat, his eyes clouding over and, finally, closing.

Lilou pulled the spike free with a twist of her wrist. She wasn't about to leave it behind; she'd had it too long, used it enough times for it to have become almost a part of her, a part of her legend. A legend she wasn't about to share with anybody. Not even Romain.

She wiped it with a rag off the floor, then slipped it inside her coat pocket. Jumping from the van she ran round to the other side, feet skidding on the damp earth. The noises were closer now, with more engines arriving along the road and men's voices carrying through the trees. She wrenched the door open, stepping back as Romain's body rolled out from the passenger seat and fell to the ground. She didn't even give it a look, but slammed the door and ran back, jumping behind the wheel.

She was gauging her chances against the approaching hunt. If she got going now, she might just be able to get away from here before they mounted a full roadblock round the village. She'd get rid of this vehicle and steal another, and hide up somewhere remote until tonight. Then she'd slip back into the village just when they weren't expecting it and deal with Rocco once and for all. Contract completed.

After that, allowing for a couple of hours in normal traffic to Paris, she could get the rest of her money from Farek and be gone. Give it a week or two to recover and she could start thinking about taking on another contract. She smiled, feeling suddenly lighter. She'd have to find another spotter, of course, but that shouldn't be a problem, not once she put out feelers. Romain would approve, she decided. Well, he'd suggested it, hadn't he? Start afresh, wasn't that what he'd said?

The engine caught at the first touch, and she winced at how loud it sounded, the clatter echoing back off the surrounding trees. She wondered if they could hear it the same way she did. Maybe the sound would be dispersed among trees and foliage, making it hard to judge direction. Too late to worry; she needed to get out of here and on the road, but it had to be *now*.

She stamped on the accelerator and the van lurched forward, the wheels spinning momentarily where they had settled into the soft earth beneath the grass. Then they gripped and the vehicle charged forward as she aimed for the track running further into the marsh. But she wasn't aiming to hide in this damp, muddy swamp, with its lakes and wallows and the overhanging canopy of branches that threatened to shut out all light and life. She was aiming for another track she'd spotted on her brief exploration earlier, this one heading back out to the road away from where the search party was approaching.

She hit a patch of rough ground and the van jumped in the air, then settled with a bang. Bits of equipment in the back crashed around, and she heard the sound of glasses breaking and the thump as something heavy hit the floor. She didn't bother checking but focussed on driving. Whatever was in the back could be replaced and, in any case, the first moment she got she was going to torch the van, erasing any trace that could be used against her.

She found the junction with the other track and hauled on the wheel, pulling the nose round with one eye on the dark water close by. The new track opened up wider, firmer and with a layer of rubble where the locals had tried to make it easier to use. She put her foot down. All she needed was to be out of this stinking mud hole and she could be free and away. Hell, she could even see the double line of trees bordering the road, her route to freedom. A quick tug of the wheel and she'd be out and away.

As the thought entered her head, she saw a small figure to her left, running through the bushes parallel to her, as if eager to make a race of it. A trick of the light, perhaps, or a kid from the village out poaching? She ignored him. She had never countenanced hurting children but if he got in her way, he'd have to take his chances. She wasn't slowing down or stopping for anybody, no matter who they were.

She picked up speed as she developed a feel for the terrain. Low-hanging fronds were whipping at the windscreen and there was the applause-like sound of reeds close to the track slapping against the bodywork, but she could feel the ground beneath the wheels. She smiled as she saw clear sky ahead through the thinning vegetation, and decided that things were going her way at last.

As she rounded a long bend in the track and began to feel a surge of elation at the thought that this would soon be over, she looked up and felt as if somebody had punched her in the stomach. A tall figure in a long, dark coat was walking towards her barely a hundred metres away. Even as she saw him, he came to a stop in the centre of the track. He was holding a pistol in a two-handed grip and it was aimed right at her.

Rocco.

Forty

Rocco heard the vehicle engine start and stopped walking. It was loud against the prevailing silence, but not far off. Behind him the track ended at the road leading into Poissons one way, and into open countryside the other. In front of him lay the silent depths of the marshland, a succession of lakes, ponds, reed beds and muddy stretches of earth where more than one careless walker had lost a boot before retreating to firmer ground. He'd been here a couple of times before, once being hunted by gunmen from Paris, and knew the natural dangers it presented as well as the man-made, but hadn't figured on coming back here again so soon.

He focussed on the sound. Few vehicles came here, save for the occasional weekender from one of the local towns with a licence to fish. Local fishermen either rode in on bicycles or mopeds or relied on walking through the many footpaths from the village to get here. This one, though, carried a familiar rattle, and he quickly discounted the sort of cars used by outsiders.

He tried to track the source of the noise, occasionally muffled and distorted by the trees, signalling movement, and realised he could have done with Claude's intimate knowledge of this place to pinpoint the location. He was guessing it was ahead of him, but was it on this track or another one close by? He continued walking, using his peripheral vision to spot any movement through the foliage hanging down either side of the track. The sound was getting louder, he was sure of it. Then he caught a glimpse of grey among the green, and saw a familiar vehicle cross a gap in the trees, rounding a bend in front of him. It was a hundred metres away and coming towards him, the sunlight through the canopy of trees flickering off the windscreen.

He reached for his gun.

The van was moving fast, skidding and kicking up a splatter of soft earth and rotting debris from the track, the engine whining in protest as the wheels failed to keep a constant grip. It was a risky strategy here, with stretches of water and boggy patches concealed by reed beds on either side, but Rocco figured if he was right, the person behind the wheel was in no position or state of mind to think about safety.

One person in the cab: slight, with short blonde hair, fighting to keep the wheel under control on the uneven ground. A woman. The woman from the Café Schubert.

Nightingale.

He saw her face register surprise, then fury. The vehicle instantly put on more speed, making its back-end shake like a predator preparing itself to launch an attack. She was going to ram him. He didn't need to check the sides of the track to know that it was very narrow here, and that he was suddenly in a vulnerable position. The water was shallow on each side, but below it was likely to be a good couple of metres of soft, glutinous mud.

He held the gun two-handed, trying to decide whether to open fire. It was hopeless trying to stop the vehicle with a few bullets, but he might be able to scare the woman into slamming on the brakes. But what if he didn't?

Eighty metres. He fired twice, aiming dead-centre at the radiator grill. It probably wouldn't do sufficient damage at this distance to bring the van to a halt, but the sound of the rounds slamming into the bodywork might give the driver enough of a shock to make her stop her mad dash.

It didn't. She kept on coming, her face clearly visible through the screen, her expression set and determined.

Fifty metres. He fired again, this time at the windscreen on the passenger side. It dissolved in a shower of fragments, making the women throw up an arm to protect her face.

Twenty metres. He stepped across to the right-hand side of the track, now on the very edge and feeling soft earth beneath his right foot. Half a step and he'd be in the water. She was almost on him when he moved quickly back to his left and dived flat, seeing a flash of lying water too close for comfort.

As he hit the ground, his elbows digging into soft earth and bark chippings, he felt his coat tugged by the front wheel of the van as it roared by. He rolled sideways and turned his head in time to see the vehicle fish-tail dangerously as the woman tried to change direction at the last second. There was a splash and a wave of mud and water sprayed into the air as a rear wheel left the track. But the woman hadn't given up yet. The vehicle miraculously failed to be dragged into the water and ploughed on, regaining the track. The engine roared as the driver tried to negotiate the next turn, but the van hadn't been built for rallying. It skidded sideways, sending up a flurry of debris, and slammed into a large willow, the sound of breaking glass and ruptured metal echoing through the trees. For a second or two the engine kept going, before stuttering and finally cutting out.

Rocco picked himself up as a deathly silence settled over the marsh.

No bird noises, no wind through the trees. Nothing. All he could hear was his harsh breathing and the pulse in his head.

He moved forward, gun ready, approaching the van on the driver's side. For a moment he thought it was over; the woman was lying slumped in her seat. Then she moved and leaned forward, and an instant later had slipped through the empty windscreen like quicksilver and was out over the bonnet and running away down the track towards the road.

He shouted at her to stop, but she didn't even hesitate. He fired a warning shot, aiming at the ground alongside the fleeing figure. It kicked up dirt but if she was aware of it she paid no attention and kept on running. He followed her as fast as he could, feeling clumsy and slow by comparison. Her lighter weight meant she was able to skim over the surface of mud and wood chippings and gradually pull away from him. If she got to the road, she would either run into the police or, at worst, find a hostage to take, and he didn't want to think about that.

At the back of his mind was the certain knowledge that he didn't want to shoot her. But there was pragmatism, too; she'd already tried to kill him and wouldn't stop until she did. If he could take her down without using his gun, it would be a better way to end this.

He reached a bend in the track to find that she had disappeared. He slowed down, his chest heaving at the sudden burst of effort, and looked around, trying to hear anything above the beating of the pulse in his head. There was water on both sides, muddy and still between the reeds, so she hadn't risked going off the track; it would have left too much of a tell-tale ripple. She had to be somewhere up ahead. He studied the ground in front, noting hanging branches, bushes and piled wood where some clearance efforts had been made, anywhere that could offer cover to her. Every few metres around the lakes were small inlets used by fishermen to access the water. Little more than platforms, like small jetties, they were bordered by reeds and tall grass, ideal for privacy and solitude, if that's what you wanted… but also concealment if you were of that frame of mind.

He heard a rustle of foliage up ahead and three shots rang out, clipping the branches of a low hanging willow overhead. He ducked, hesitant about firing back as a volley of shouts erupted not far away. Claude and others, waiting to see what happened, no doubt on tenterhooks. He was facing the road from here, and a careless bullet would go through the foliage and hit anyone standing out there or walking by.

He heard the sound of running footsteps, muffled by the soft surface underneath, but moving away down the track. He stood up and set off in pursuit. Another few hundred metres and she would be close enough to the road to use her gun on anybody unfortunate enough to be out there in the wrong place at the wrong time. They would see a woman running and draw an entirely wrong conclusion. By the time they reacted it would be too late and she would have a hostage, maybe even a vehicle in which to make her escape.

He put on speed, risking losing his footing but spurred on by the knowledge that this had to end, and soon.

Then more shots echoed out, only this time surprisingly close. She must have stopped and doubled back, he realised, and was now waiting for him. He threw himself to the ground as he saw movement up ahead, but not before two more shots came his way, one of them slamming into a tree right next to him. The effect was dramatic. The trunk exploded into splinters, peppering his face with needle-like barbs, prickling his skin and instinctively making him close his eyes for a second. A larger splinter pierced his hand, causing him to drop his gun. It fell to the ground and landed with a soft thump where he couldn't see it.

When he tried to open his eyes, all he could see was a blurred patchwork of light and shifting shadows as the sun played through the trees. The scenery in front of him was now a mixture of disjointed brown and green fragments, all detail gone, like looking into a shattered mirror.

He was on his knees, as good as blind and unable to pick out where she was, what she was about to do. He tried brushing the ground in front of him with his hands, searching for the gun, but it was no good. It could be anywhere. He touched the sides of his eyes and pulled at his eyelids, blinking furiously, trying everything he could to clear them. It was tiny grains of tree dust, he told himself, small enough to have affected his sight without blinding him, yet rendering him temporarily immobile. This close to danger it was a disaster.

He waited, focussing on listening to the sounds around him, for the crackle of brushed undergrowth and the snap of twigs underfoot. If she was coming, she wouldn't be able to do it in total silence. It brought back memories of other places like this, full of foliage and colour, of humidity and heat and the smell of rotting plants, and death. Especially death. And just like then, all the birdsong had ceased.

A branch snapped directly in front of him. Then another. He realised she was probably looking right at him, checking out why he wasn't moving. And closing in for the kill.

Her voice came suddenly, girlish and light, as if she'd won a prize at a fairground. 'Hey – how about that? Looks like I got lucky! And I'm usually so rubbish with guns.'

He blinked in desperation, and his eyes cleared for a second. She was standing in front of him, barely three metres away, outlined against the light. She was holding a revolver, he could see that. Her hands moved and he heard a familiar click as she checked the load, followed by a snort of disgust. 'It's empty! Well, would you believe that?' Her hand moved sideways as she tossed the gun away, and it landed with a plop in the pond nearby.

Rocco breathed with relief. But then her other hand moved and he caught a glimpse of something familiar. A spike bayonet. A cold chill ran through him.

'So, Rocco,' she said softly. 'It's come to this. Just you and me. Do you have any final questions?'

'Sure. Where's your little friend, the pretend cop?' A smear of blood showed on her face, but she didn't look hurt, and he wondered if it belonged to Jouanne.

She shrugged. 'He couldn't keep up. He didn't have the stamina. Pity, really. He was a nice boy, if you know what I mean.' She made a sound that was almost a giggle, light yet with a faint ragged touch that set his nerves on edge. From anybody else it might have been intriguing, attractive even. But not this woman. It made him wonder how close she was to madness.

'He's dead? How?'

'One of the cops at the house managed to shoot back. Lucky shot... but not for Romain.'

'What was that about – a diversion to draw me in?'

'Something like that. It would have worked, too, another time. What is it they say, all the best laid plans need is a lucky idiot?'

'What's your name?' He had to keep her talking, to give himself time to clear his vision and stand a fighting chance when she came in for the kill, as she surely would.

'My name's not important. Romain liked to call me Lilou, but that wasn't it. He thought he was being romantic, so I let him.'

'No name? So you're an enigma, are you? You realise most enigmas remain just that? No names, no faces, just... obscurity. And finally nobody cares. Or were you trying to be France's answer to Bonnie and Clyde?'

'Don't mock me, Rocco.' Her voice turned cold, threatening, a flicker away from anger. She moved closer and Rocco pulled at his eyelids, getting a brief flash of clear vision for a second before it went fuzzy again. This wasn't going to last much longer. He'd already survived longer than Vieira or Raballe.

'I wouldn't dream of it. But Nightingale? You've abandoned your real name in favour of... what – a label? That's a bit dramatic, don't you think?'

'We all have labels. You're a cop. That's a label.'

'True enough.' His right eye was clear, but something gritty was making it swim with tears. He flicked at the left one, still clogged with bark dust.

'Ironic, don't you think?' she mused aloud. 'We have something in common, you and I.'

'Go on, educate me.'

'We both kill people for a living.'

There was no arguing with that. It was an anti-cop sentiment he'd heard before. He'd killed, there was no denying it. You could wrap it up any way you wanted, whether fighting a war or being a cop, but it was a fact. However, there was one difference.

'I don't do it for money,' he said. 'But that bayonet, it's a very personal way of earning your money, isn't it? Quirky. Even twisted, some might say. Does it give you a thrill, sticking that into people? Is that all it is for you – for the kicks? I can't make up my mind.'

Her face went dark at the deliberate taunting, as if she'd been presented with an unpalatable truth. Maybe, he reflected, there was a glimmer of something in there after all. Pride, perhaps? It couldn't be guilt.

'You don't know anything about me,' she snarled.

'I know about as much as I care to. Common rumour has it that you're the spotter for Nightingale, did you know that? Just a spotter… for checking the lay of the land. Whereas the actual killer is a man. That must be galling for you: being awarded only second place on the team.'

'Shut your mouth, Rocco.'

'Of course I know it's not correct. Nightingale is you, isn't it? Jouanne was… what, exactly?'

'He was a nobody.' She said it without emotion, her voice flat. 'He wanted to be like me, and in the end thought he could actually *be* me. Big mistake. He didn't know how. He thought all it took was to carry a gun and be willing to use it.'

Rocco nodded. 'Did he shoot the two cops at Les Sables? Approached them as a colleague and shot them up close? That was unnecessary.'

'That's what I told him. It was stupid. I wouldn't have done it but I wasn't close enough to stop him. He got carried away with himself because he thought it would earn him a reputation – the cold killer. All it did was get you lot on our tail.'

'So tell me some more. We have time – and there's nobody else around. Where are you from? What's your real name? How did you get into the murder business? I mean, it doesn't figure on the study list for a *baccalauréat* as far as I recall.'

'You think I'm stupid, Rocco? You're playing for time. I know your colleagues are close. And you don't get to know anything about me.' She moved forward another step, a faint hint of cologne preceding her and overriding the natural smells around them. She was staring intently at him, he could see that much, and her body was rigid with tension. He guessed she was torn between wanting to get the job done and earn her fee, yet at the same time not wanting to rush, like savouring a glass of St Emilion *grand cru classé* you were reluctant to finish.

Finally she was standing over him. He didn't move. Getting up would merely put himself closer to her as a target, and he had no doubts about how fast she would be able to react. Instead he sat back on his heels. To get to him she was going to have to move closer and lean in, which would throw her off-balance. He listened to her breathing, waiting for the faint catch in her throat and the rustle of fabric that would be the precursor to violent movement. It was going to be a last-ditch effort and the only warning he'd get, but he figured he could do it. It was all down to timing.

'Funny thing is, Rocco,' she said, her voice soft, 'you've been lucky twice, did you know that? The second time was at the house when they took Bouanga and you weren't there. But the first time – yes, there was a first time and I bet you didn't know it – was at that shitty cop bar in Amiens. Remember?' She chuckled, 'If only I'd known that's what it was before I went in there. It would have been so much fun to blow that place clean off the map. It's funny that Romain never said. I think he must have liked the atmosphere a bit, all boys together. But where was I? Oh, yes. You remember when we were talking at the table and you were flirting with me?'

'Don't kid yourself – I wasn't.' The backs of his legs were beginning to tremble under the strain of holding the position, and he got ready to block and move. If he had to he could throw himself off the track and drag her into the water.

'Well, maybe not. Pity, really. We could have been good together. Still, that's your loss. What you didn't know was, I was calculating when to do the nasty on you. Your neck was so close and *so* inviting and… you've got no idea.' She giggled. 'I'd actually got my little friend out under the table ready to do it, do you know that? You were that close, Rocco.' She held up the bayonet in front of him, with her thumb and finger measuring the width of the blade near the point. '*That* close.'

Rocco couldn't help it; the idea that she'd been measuring him like a pig for the slaughter, that he'd come so near to having that thing stuck in his throat without the faintest notion of who she was at the time and no defence, made the hairs move on the back of his neck. That she could talk so easily about it made him wonder again about her sanity. Had she always been mad or had she gradually tipped herself over the edge, driven by the deaths she'd caused? He would probably never know. 'So why didn't you?'

'A bunch of your cop colleagues came in just as I was about to. How about that for poor timing? They blocked the doorway and I knew there was no way I'd ever make it out of the place. I was so annoyed I nearly wet myself. I think Romain did, too, because he didn't even want me going in there.'

She laughed, but there was something in her voice that made him doubt her words.

'Poor Romain. I led him such a merry dance.'

Definitely off her head, thought Rocco, and wondered how to take advantage of it before it was too late. Before she struck.

'You're lying.' Keep her talking, he told himself. Keep her guessing and off-balance.

To his surprise, she replied. 'You're right. I wasn't going to – but I wanted to. I mean, really wanted to. Right there and then, even though I prefer to do it out in the open.'

'So why come anywhere near me? Or is that part of the game for you?'

'You're the big beast, aren't you? The main assignment. And there you were within reach. I wanted to see you up close, to look the mighty Lucas Rocco in the eye and know that one day, maybe not the next or the next, but one day, I was going to get you... and you wouldn't have the faintest idea of what was coming.'

As she finished speaking, Rocco caught a movement in the trees behind her. It wasn't much more than a flicker. Claude or one of the other men, perhaps, coming to help him? If so he hoped they'd do something quick. Or was it a bird, dipping towards the water for a drink or to catch one of the thousands of midges hovering close to the surface, a case of different priorities. In the midst of life, we are in...

'And now I've got you.' Then Nightingale was leaning towards him, her arm drawn back as she prepared to deliver the *coup de grâce*. As Rocco reared instinctively back on his knees away from her, his eyes cleared and he saw a flash of something in the air, followed by a whisper of sound and another noise he couldn't quite place. When he looked up the woman was gasping and tugging at something at the side of her neck, the bayonet fallen from her hand.

The object sticking out of her neck was decorated with an unusual yet familiar design with a small trace of feathers set in the end.

Rocco turned his head and saw Delicat standing by a tree close to the water. The little man looked drawn, his clothes dirty and damp and with a long smear of mud down one thigh. He was staring at the woman, unemotional and still, his bow held down by his side.

Rocco rolled away as Nightingale swayed above him. She was trying to pull the arrow loose, grunting with the effort but unable to shift it. She coughed once, and a splash of red appeared on her lips and dribbled down her chin. Then she went quiet and crumpled to the ground, her eyes wide open and somehow outraged, as if this shouldn't have happened.

Rocco got to his feet and looked towards Delicat, who was standing quite still. 'Thank you.'

Delicat shook his head. 'It is nothing. I should have helped your two colleagues, but I was not able to. And you brought Excelsiore and Minister Bouanga back for me.'

'You know that?'

'I heard the men at the house talking.'

So Claude had been right. Delicat had been back there, sleeping in the barn.

'About Excelsiore,' Rocco said, casting around, his eyes clear enough now for him to spot his gun and pick it up. 'You need to go and see her. She's worried about you.'

The little man shook his head. He seemed uncertain, even lost. 'I cannot. It is impossible for me now.'

'No, it's not. Bouanga knows about you and her.'

Delicat looked shocked. 'How is that possible?'

'Because he's not blind.'

'He will be angry. I have dishonoured him.'

'Actually, he's not. He knows how she feels about you, too.' He stepped around Nightingale's body and started walking down the track towards where he'd parked his car. He could hear voices drawing nearer and Claude calling his name. He had to get them to locate Jouanne, wherever Nightingale had left him, and call this in. 'Come on,' he said to Delicat, 'I'll take you there myself and make sure it's all right. It's the least I can do.'

Forty-one

'It's been a good outcome, Inspector,' said Massin. 'A little unfortunate that we weren't able to hand over a live killer, but I attach no blame to you for that. You did what you had to and the final act was not yours to control. My report shall reflect that fact.'

'Thank you.'

It was two days later, and Rocco had come into the office to see what was happening and make a statement about the events in the *marais*. After a night in hospital having his eyes cleansed and his hand bandaged, he'd been glad to get home again to his own space and the familiar sounds of the fruit rats playing overhead. True, he'd also had to weather being fussed over and fed omelettes and chicken by Mme Denis, secured in exchange for all the gory details, but it had been easily bearable. Now it was time to get back to work.

Massin picked up a message sheet from his desk. 'I have a note here from Inspector Kopa in Neuilly. He wishes you to know that Seb Achay, described as Farek's number two, has turned on his boss in exchange for a reduced sentence. Farek has been taken into custody and formal charges will follow in due course.' He looked up. 'Kopa says you helped with certain details which implicate Farek in the hiring of an international assassin. You must be relieved about that.'

Rocco wasn't so sure. It was the end of a long road and time would tell if the charges stuck and Farek went down. He had no illusions about what a clever lawyer could do, although he doubted even Farek would walk away from this one. At the very least Farek would find himself displaced among the criminal community, water closing over his head. Until that happened, he'd have to continue to watch his back. 'It's a start.'

'Indeed.' Massin picked up a sealed envelope. 'With that in mind I think you'll want to read this.' The outside of the envelope bore the rounded triangular seal of the *Police Nationale*. 'Take a seat.' Then he turned and walked over to the window and stared out at the street scene below.

Rocco opened the envelope and extracted a single sheet of paper. The contents were straightforward and without embellishment. He was being offered a new job in a division of the National Police called *Brigade de Recherche et d'Intervention* or BRI for short. Their sole task was to be focussed on the battle against criminal gangs, of which Paris had more than its fair share. If successful, the idea would be rolled out to other major cities across France in an attempt to interrupt and reverse the recent proliferation of gang activity, involving among other things, drugs, robberies and kidnappings.

Rocco looked up. 'I take it you know what this is?'

'I do.'

'Why me?'

Massin turned, his expression blank. 'Why not? Surely you must know your record speaks for itself. As I understand it, this new division is being set up as we speak. It's a new line in tackling criminal gangs – not too different from what you were doing before you came here only on a more organised basis, with new budgets, new techniques and equipment.' He sat down in his chair. 'You don't need to make a decision here and now, but it's something you should think about carefully. It would represent an important step in your career. If you want it, that is.'

Rocco wasn't sure what to say. It was an initiative that he knew had been talked about for some time, but it always seemed to be one of those proposals that never quite got off the ground. And Massin was right – it would undoubtedly be a great opportunity for him and a return to the kind of work he knew best.

'That's all, Inspector.' Massin pulled his in-tray towards him, a clear sign that he wished to get on with other matters.

Rocco stood up. He wondered what was going on behind Massin's reserved expression, whether this was something the senior officer might have been wishing for or had even engineered. To say they had never been close would be understating the situation. They were colleagues, yes, despite their different ranks, but on the most reserved of terms due to their shared history in Indochina. Massin's attitude towards Rocco on finding they were to work together here in Amiens had been not far short of abrasive. But it had mellowed considerably since then, replaced by a strictly professional atmosphere between them and even a grudging respect.

As Rocco stepped towards the door, Massin said, 'One thing, Rocco.'

'Sir?'

'I would value the courtesy of knowing your intentions, if that were possible? It's not an order, of course. But it would help me prepare the way for your transfer and replacement... should that be your decision.'

'Of course.'

'That said, I hope you choose to stay.'

Rocco held back his surprise, and closed the door behind him. Then he folded the letter into his pocket and walked downstairs.

END

Acknowledgments

My thanks to David Headley, for his continued support as an agent and friend, not just with my other books, but especially in offering to pick up the Lucas Rocco ball and run with it. This is a book I've been wanting to write for a long time, and thanks to David and The Dome Press, I've now been able to do it – and enjoyed it hugely.

Massive thanks also must go to Rebecca Lloyd, my (new) editor, for her sterling – and so gracious – job on *Nightingale*. It must be tough jumping into editing an existing series, with all its history, but Rebecca has done it with aplomb and saved me from making all manner of bloopers. I mean, where *did* all those Citroëns come from?

To Jem Butcher, who came up with the fantastic cover design. Brilliant job!

And, of course, to all the readers who have been asking for another Rocco. Your wish has come true, and I hope you like it.